MORE FROM MARK DAVID GERSON

FICTION

The MoonQuest

The StarQuest

The SunQuest

The Bard of Bryn Doon

The Lost Horse of Bryn Doon (coming soon!)

The Sorcerer of Bryn Doon (coming soon!)

MEMOIR

Acts of Surrender: A Writer's Memoir

Dialogues with the Divine: Encounters with my Wisest Self

Pilgrimage: A Fool's Journey

SELF-HELP & PERSONAL GROWTH

The Way of the Fool: How to Stop Worrying About Life and Start Living It

The Way of the Imperfect Fool: How to Bust the Addiction to Perfection That's Stifling Your Success

The Book of Messages: Writings Inspired by Melchizedek

RESOURCES FOR WRITERS

The Voice of the Muse: Answering the Call to Write

The Voice of the Muse Companion: Guided Meditations for Writers

From Memory to Memoir: Writing the Stories of Your Life

Organic Screenwriting: Writing for Film, Naturally

Birthing Your Book...Even If You Don't Know What It's About

The Heartful Art of Revision: An Intuitive Guide to Editing

Writer's Block Unblocked: Seven Surefire Ways to Free Up Your Writing and Creative Flow

Time to Write

Write with Ease

Free Your Characters, Free Your Story

Write to Heal

Journal from the Heart

After SARA'S YEAR

The Sara Stories

MARK DAVID GERSON

AFTER SARA'S YEAR

This is a work of fiction. Names, characters, businesses, places, events and
incidents are either the products of the author's imagination or used in a
fictitious manner. Any resemblance to actual persons, living or dead, or to
actual events is purely coincidental.

First Edition 2016. Second Edition 2020.

Published by MDG Media International
2370 W. State Route 89a, Suite 11-210
Sedona, AZ 86336
www.mdgmediainternational.com

ISBN: 978-1-950189-23-6

Cover Photograph and Title/Section Pages Sketch:
Ritz-Carlton Hotel, Montreal (cc) Alex Caban
https://commons.wikimedia.org/wiki/File:Ritz_montreal.jpg
*Adapted from the original image and used under Creative Commons License (CC
BY-SA 3.0) https://creativecommons.org/licenses/by-sa/3.0/legalcode*

More information
www.markdavidgerson.com
www.thesarastories.com

*In the depths of winter, I finally learned that within me
there lay an invincible summer.*

ALBERT CAMUS

*Precisely at the moment when our despair
is deepest, fresh winds stir.*

JOSEPH BRODSKY

*There is no heart that does not yearn to be remembered.
There is no heart that does not long to open.*

THE SUNQUEST (THE LEGEND OF Q'NTANA)

For Guinevere

1988

1

Sadie Finkel caressed the roughhewn top of the weather-worn granite marker, avoiding the accumulation of pebbles that documented her decades of graveside visits. The neighboring stones were cracked with age, many unreadable after a half-century of Montreal's harsh winters and blistering summers.

Not Ruth Finkel's. Sadie's mother's stone had aged well, something that Ruth herself had never been given a chance to do, something that Ruth's oldest daughter was not managing at all this August morning. Perspiration greased her boyishly short white hair, glued her teal polyester top to her back and soaked her underarms. Her cream slacks clung to the backs of her thighs. Her forehead glistened and she could taste the salt of sweat on her upper lip.

It would have been a good day for shorts and a sleeveless pullover, but the little vanity Sadie still possessed refused to parade her scrawny arms and legs in public. Better to suffer in the heat than look like a comicstrip stick figure, especially to her mother.

The forecast had called for another day of viscously oppressive midsummer humidity, and Sadie had done her best to avoid the worst of it by getting an early start on her regular crosstown pilgrimage to the cemetery. But life betrayed her, again. First, a savage overnight thunderstorm ripped through the city, cutting power to Sadie's Côte Saint-Luc neighborhood and disabling both her clock radio's alarm and the noisy air conditioner that almost made her one-room basement apartment bearable. When she finally woke up two hours later than planned, she was such a clammy mess that she didn't dare face the world without a shower. From there, she missed each of the two buses and Metro trains it took to get her first to the florist's, then to the cemetery. Well, she didn't exactly miss the second bus. The driver had pulled away from the bus stop and was waiting for the traffic light to turn green. Sadie stepped off the sidewalk and pounded on the door. The driver ignored her.

"Mamzer," she muttered into the empty cemetery, recalling the indifferent glance the young driver had directed toward her before pulling away. "Sorry, Mama," she whispered to the stone, "for my bad language."

"I'm lucky, Mama," she said. "I know I am. To be alive, of course, though I wonder why I am. You're gone. Papa's gone. At my age, that's normal, I know. But Esther, too. And Nate and Manny. They're all gone. Just me, like some sort of Methuselah, going on and on and on…for no reason that I can see.

"Strong as an ox, the doctor says. The new one. The young one. Not 'young' Dr. Callendar. He's dead, too. It's his son, the new Dr. Callendar. Another Dr. Callendar. It's like the family business, all these Dr. Callendars. They also go on and on. At least they have a reason.

"Anyhow, this Dr. Callendar says I'm so healthy I'll outlive him, and he can't be more than forty."

Sadie laid her bouquet of white carnations at the foot of the stone. She liked to think that white carnations had been Ruth's favorite. But it was all so long ago. She couldn't be sure that the one time Papa brought flowers home, they were carnations. For sure they were white, and they couldn't have been expensive, like carnations weren't expensive. Were there carnations at Ruth's funeral, too? There wasn't a lot of money in those days, even for a funeral, so maybe. You couldn't spend much less for flowers than on carnations. Daisies, possibly, but those weren't daisies. Neither time. Daisies she would have remembered. It must have been an extra-special occasion when Max brought the carnations because it never happened again, and cut flowers were a luxury back then. They were still, for her, but Ruth deserved this little extravagance. Not every visit. Once every couple of visits.

Sadie straightened up, ever grateful for her continued flexibility. Apart from a touch of arthritis in her hands, her joints were remarkably responsive for her age. Dr. Callendar's words. But it was true.

Gladys Herzberg was already using a walker, and she was only a year older than Sadie. At seventy-one, Myron Katz could scarcely bend over, which didn't stop him from trying to shtup every widow at the seniors' center, the alte kacker.

Only the good die young, her mother used to say. "Is that why I'm still alive, Mama?" She wasn't sure she wanted an answer. Whether or not it was true for Sadie, it had been for Ruth; so young, barely thirty-six, when she left them. Sadie added a new pebble to her collection and turned to go. "Goodbye, Mama," she whispered. "I'll be back in two weeks, God willing."

When Sadie reached the gravel road that separated where Ruth was buried from the oldest section of the cemetery, she stopped. Here is where she always turned right, toward the graves of her father and brothers. Unlike her time with Ruth, her visits with Max, Nate and Manny were brief and unemotional. Obligations, like income tax. After having spent so many years taking care of all three of them after her mother died, she was damned if she would give them any more time than necessary now that they were dead. She wondered sometimes why she didn't resent her mother, too. Sadie's happiest years ended when Ruth died. It was as though Ruth took Sadie's life with her when she went, leaving the fifteen-year-old to become surrogate wife to an increasingly weak-willed Max and surrogate mother to a pair of whiny boys. As for Esther… Well, the less said the better.

Sadie shook her head free of the past. "A shortcut," she said as she crossed the road and began to weave through the century of stones on the other side, all jumbled together like the shtetl houses many of those buried beneath them had once known. "A shortcut to nowhere," she muttered thirty minutes later, finally conceding that she was lost, as the bells of St. Luc's clanged the three-quarter hour.

Not exactly lost. You couldn't get lost in a cemetery that had a massive church hulking next to it. It was like a giant goyishe vulture, that St. Luc's, waiting to gorge itself on all the dead Jews in its shadow. First the dead Jews, then the living ones. Sadie shuddered and spit three times to ward off the einhoreh, the evil eye. No, you couldn't get lost. How could you when you could see the farkakte thing from anywhere, and hear it, too? You could also hear the rumble of traffic on de la Savane Street from pretty much anywhere. Sadie could hear it from where she stood, now that those godawful bells had stopped their banging. She just didn't know how to get out there from here. All she could see were gravestones and more gravestones, towered over by giant poplars and, on the other side of a stone wall, that butt-insky of a basilica that had no business being there. But roads, paths and gates? Nothing.

Sadie wiped the sweat trickling into her eyes with her sleeve, already moist with perspiration, and stumbled on.

2

Marc-Allan Cameron stared up at his countryman. Robert Burns ignored him, gazing westward from atop his plinth, as he had unchangingly for more than fifty years. The Burns statue was one of the few things that had not been altered since Mac, as everyone called him, had last been here. Dominion Square was now Dorchester Square. Dorchester Boulevard, which bisected the renamed downtown Montreal park, was now Boulevard René-Lévesque. And the Windsor Hotel that Robbie Burns had been watching since the city planted him on the Peel Street side of the square in 1930 and that predated the statue by another half-century was now part-bank tower, part-luxury reno.

Mac half-turned to peer through the trees and across René-Lévesque to the most radical transformation of all, at least for him: The art moderne behemoth on the corner that had been the Laurentian Hotel was gone, replaced by a glass-clad skyscraper, its name the only reminder of its predecessor: La Laurentienne.

He looked back up at Burns. "The best laid schemes o' mice an' men gang aft agley," he heard. They were the poet's words but Esther Freed's voice, a specter from three decades earlier. He sighed. "Maybe you were right, Esther, my queen…my red, red rose. Maybe it's good that our past here has been erased. It was time for a fresh canvas…long past time. It's time for a new painting, for a new present. Maybe even for a new future. If not for me, then for your son…our son."

If Robert Burns could have tilted his bronzed head down in that moment, he would have seen a tall, slender man in black t-shirt and jeans, his wispy white hair disheveled by the light August breeze. The man would glance back one last time at La Laurentienne, smile wistfully as he dabbed bright, hazel eyes with a red handkerchief, then disappear from view as he turned up Peel Street toward Sherbrooke, his step still sprightly six weeks from his seventieth birthday.

Mac had one more ghost to call on.

3

Erik Donnekin pounded on the bathroom door, producing little more than a dull thud against the single plank of solid oak. "Let me in!" he shouted.

"Won't be much longer," a man's voice called back from the other side over the sound of running water.

"I'm cold." Erik stamped his bare feet on the Persian rug. He wore nothing but a pair of color-splotched white boxer shorts with "I'm the Artist Your Mother Warned You About" stamped, stencil-like, across the backside.

"Put some clothes on."

"You sure you want me to?" Erik responded with a suggestive leer. He jiggled the highly buffed brass handle. It was still locked. "C'mon, Bernie. I have to pee."

"There are seven friggin' bathrooms in this suite. Why do you have to use this one?"

"Cuz you're in there." Erik rattled the handle again. "What are you doing in there, anyway?"

"It's a surprise."

"You aren't dying your hair green, are you?"

Bernie snickered. "A few more minutes."

"You didn't say no to the green hair."

"You think I'd look good in green hair?"

"I'll take you in any color hair. Just open the damn door."

"Almost there."

"How about a hint?"

"Patience, young grasshopper."

"I don't have any. You should know that by now." Erik banged once more on the door then padded across the vast suite to the one bathroom he had not yet used. Gold-plated fixtures glinted against the shimmering pinkish-gray porcelain of the sink, bidet and over-sized tub, and a cedar sauna large enough for four sat in a corner. A rosewood medicine cabinet and oak ceiling warmed up the travertine of the floor, walls and shelving.

"So this is what the Queen pees in when she's in town," he had giggled when he, Bernie and Mac first toured the Ritz-Carlton Hotel's opulent royal suite the previous day.

"Which queen?" Bernie had shot back with a smirk.

With its reception room, study, grand salon, two kitchens, two dining rooms, four bedrooms and, yes, seven bathrooms — all done up in a tasteful excess of French and English antiques, sparkling chandeliers, burnished woods and mirror-like marble — Room 810 had left Erik otherwise speechless. He had never encountered anything half as luxurious, not in small-town Nova Scotia where he grew up, not in Halifax where he went to art school and, until now, not in Montreal where he completed his master's degree. Before this, his biggest experience of extravagance had been a weekend at the Lord Nelson Hotel in Halifax, his mother's college-graduation surprise. But the difference between the Lord Nelson and Montreal's Ritz-Carlton was more than a single hotel-ranking star. In Erik's eyes, it was an entire galaxy. Maybe more than one.

Back in their bedroom, Erik pounded on the bathroom door again.

"One more minute. I promise."

"Jesus, Bernie. You're worse than my sister."

"Your sister has a crewcut, wears no makeup and rides a Harley."

Erik laughed. It was true, which was why it was probably just as well that Anders Donnekin died before he could discover that both his kids were crazy artists. Crazy gay artists. How a dour Lutheran teetotaler managed to woo and wed vivacious Britta Tormundsen remained a mystery to him. His mother had a wicked wit that only sharpened after a glass or two of akevitt. Even if she claimed not to understand her son's abstract paintings, she was his biggest cheerleader. After Bernie, of course.

Erik tugged on a pair of clean Levi's, slipped on a charcoal t-shirt, combed his blond tangles with his fingers and patted the light stubble on his cheek. He had offered to shave it off for the special occasion, but Bernie wouldn't let him. "Scruffy artists are hot," Bernie had declared. Erik grinned at the memory as he reached into the walnut Louis XVI armoire for a black leather jacket.

"Not the leather jacket," Bernie called from the bathroom. "I was going to wear that."

"How did you—? Never mind." Erik shook his head and moved his hand to its denim neighbor. "Sandals or sneakers?"

"Sneakers. It's the Ritz."

"I thought that Ritz restaurants would be all preppy and power suit."

"Hey, it's 1988. Anything goes. Speaking of which—" Bernie flung open the door. "Voila!"

Erik spun around and gasped. "It's—it's—"

"Gone?" Bernie reached for Erik's hand and touched it to his newly clean-shaven cheek. "What do you think?"

Erik stroked Bernie's face, free of its reddish-brown beard and mustache for the first time since they met four years earlier. "Who are you and what have you done with my man?" he asked, hand on hip, with mock indignation. "Never mind," he whispered. He removed Bernie's wire-rim glasses and leaned in to kiss him, first on his cheek, then long and deep on the mouth. He pushed him toward the unmade bed that sprawled under a canopy of off-white silk and dominated the largest of the suite's bedrooms. "Let's do this before that no-talent artist of mine gets back."

Bernie jerked free, letting Erik fall back into the rumpled jumble of salmon and silvery-gray linens. "I wish I could, handsome stranger, but we've got places to go and people to see." He threw the leather jacket on over his white t-shirt and picked up a canvas messenger bag from the floor. "Besides, isn't today your fourth anniversary of meeting that no-talent artist of yours?" He grasped Erik's wrist, pulled him to his feet and kissed him again.

"Yesterday, actually. That no-goodnik always gets it wrong." He took Bernie's hand and scanned the bedroom. "Are you sure you have everything?"

"I'm sure, Random Artist Guy. We can come back up after lunch if I've forgotten anything. Let's go or we'll be late." He hustled Erik out of the bedroom and into the palatial grand salon.

"This place is so over the top," Erik said, twirling Bernie around the room's groupings of armchairs, settees and side tables. "This grand saloon alone is three times as big as my old place on Greene Avenue. Hell, each of these royal bathrooms is bigger than that whole apartment." He dropped onto a sofa and slapped the seat. "This piece could pay our rent for a year."

"If we were paying rent."

"We need to talk about that." Erik's tone turned serious. "We can't live off your celebrity father forever."

"If we're lucky, today will buy us fortune as well as fame, and none of that will matter anymore. "

"You're right, but—"

"C'mon, handsome. Our limo's waiting."

"Are you sure you shouldn't call Sarah? There's no reason to think she'll show up this year. After all—"

"I thought I was supposed to be the worrier."

Erik hugged Bernie. "I just want everything to be perfect for you today. Especially today."

"It's always perfect if you're with me." Bernie squeezed back. "Always." He paused. "Especially today."

"I love you, Bernie Freed."

"I love you, Erik Donnekin."

"What about Sarah?"

"Oh, she'll be there."

4

Sarah Swartz leaned back and closed her eyes, letting the surf-like whoosh of traffic outside the Diamond taxi wash over her. Was this trip to the cemetery going to be another waste of a morning, another letdown? After so many disappointments, why wouldn't it be? She and Bernie had made a *Same Time, Next Year*-like pact four years earlier, after the death of his mother, her best friend for almost her whole life: Bernie would pursue his newly discovered passion for art and she would reclaim her long-ago, long-lost dream of being a writer. They would go their separate ways and meet up again after twelve months at Esther's grave to share their accomplishments.

Only Bernie had not shown up. Not the first year, nor the year after that. If he made it to the cemetery the third year, she didn't know. She was in a Royal Victoria Hospital room recovering from pneumonia. Pneumonia in August. How crazy was that? They had said no contact except for emergencies, she and Bernie. Well, this had been an emergency, hadn't it? So she tried calling him from the hospital, but he had disappeared: There was no Bernie Freed anywhere in the 514 area code.

So why was she bothering to shlep out to the cemetery today? Sarah felt for her oversize handbag, retrieved a book from it and opened her eyes to a flattering black-and-white photograph of herself on the cover.

All these months later, she was still trying to figure out how they made her look so good for the picture. Most days her hair would make an old Brillo Pad look like haute coiffure. And makeup? She was sixty-five and she still hadn't gotten the hang of it. Her mother had not believed in makeup, of course. According to Gertie

Schumacher, you went out into the world with what God gave you. It wasn't for you to meddle with His work, even if, like a much younger Sarah, you were convinced that He had badly cheated you in the looks department.

How Esther had grown into such a beauty expert with no mother and that old prune Sadie for a big sister, she never knew. Yet she had. Lucky Esther had never had to work at it. She was like a model from day one, she was that gorgeous: dark hair, dark eyes, fair skin and full lips, all put together in a way that never failed to turn heads. Even in the hospital, all skin and bones and with practically no hair from the cancer, she was pretty.

Back when they were teenagers, Esther tried to teach Sarah how to make the best of her "natural assets." That's what Esther had called Sarah's round, flabby face and steel-wool hair. Unnatural liabilities: That's what they had always been to her. Sammy Kaplan hadn't minded. Better that he should have, the schmuck, and never married her. Jack Swartz never minded, either. For that she was grateful. Sarah smiled as she always did when she thought about her second husband. *Mind you, my Jack was no Cary Grant himself. More like a W.C. Fields. Me? I'm Shelley Winters. Not the sexy Shelley Winters from* A Double Life *or* Night of the Hunter. *That's more like Esther. No, me, I'm the blob Shelley Winters from* The Poseidon Adventure.

Sarah studied her picture on the dust jacket. Somehow, those two magicians barely out of their teens — a boy for her hair and girl for her makeup — had made her seem almost glamorous. *Maybe I can cut out the picture and glue it to my face because I will never look this good again. Or maybe I can get those kids to move in with me, so they can "do" me every day. More like three times a day.*

She touched her hair. Gertie had not believed in hairdressers and for much of her life, neither had Sarah. It was Jack who had encouraged her to pamper herself like that. Other ways, too. Sammy sure never did. *I should have gone to the hairdresser yesterday instead of last week. Then I could have looked more like this movie star on the cover.* Yesterday, however, Sarah had not been planning a ride out to the cemetery. It was only today when she woke up to another August 10 anniversary that she decided to try this final time. "If he doesn't show this year," she had stated to Jack's photograph on her mantelpiece, "that's it. No more." She swore, too, that she wouldn't fuss, given the probability of a fourth no-show, but she did, with a rare pair of pantyhose, her favorite summer dress and a pair of low heels that she was already regretting.

As her taxi roared down the access ramp to the sunken Décarie Expressway, Sarah stroked the title emblazoned across the book jacket, right under what would normally be her double chin, and her name below it. Not either of her married names and not quite her maiden name. Her writer's-dream name.

"*Sara's Year* by Sara-without-an-h Schumacher," she said softly. "That's why I'm going to the cemetery," she continued under her breath. "Bernie or no Bernie, I have to show Esther. I have to tell her that I'm finally that Jewish Canadian author I wanted so bad to be. Not the first. It's years too late for that. And not the best. I'm sure of that." Sarah closed her eyes again and conjured up the two teenage girls who had dreamed such big dreams all those decades ago on the streetcar ride home from the Westmount Library: Esther of being the first great Jewish Canadian woman artist and Sarah of being the first great Jewish Canadian woman author.

"I did it, Esther," she whispered. "Thanks to you, I did it."

5

Bernie and Erik stood outside Galérie Walter Klinkhoff, half a block east of the Ritz, while a white Mercedes-Benz limousine idled at the curb behind them. Erik gazed up at the narrow, nineteenth-century row house and put his arm around Bernie's waist. "It looks terrific," he said. "Better than terrific." He gestured toward the painting that filled most of the five-story graystone's main-floor bay window: a textured, brilliantly colored acrylic that depicted two teenage girls, one wearing *Wizard of Oz*-like ruby slippers and both seated at a 1930s lunch counter. The notation under the framed canvas read "*Chez Stella / At Stella's*. Bernard Marc Freed. 1985." A banner across the top of the window proclaimed in bold red type: "Bernard Marc Freed: Reflections."

"I am so excited for you, love. Your own show. And at the Klinkhoff. They don't show every Tom, Dick and Bernie, you know. Just my Bernie."

"You're sweet."

"It's true."

"Mac keeps telling me much the same thing. I don't think this could have happened without him. I know it couldn't. Not here, anyhow. He and Walter go way back."

"Don't sell yourself short. Who does Klinkhoff handle? Canadian classics like Arthur Lismer and A.Y. Jackson. And Anne Savage, for God's sake. Some of the biggest names in Canadian twentieth-century art. And not only the old-timers, either. Great contemporary artists, too, like…Bernard Marc Freed."

Bernie forced a grin.

"If your stuff wasn't good," Erik continued, "it wouldn't be here. It couldn't be here. You know that, right?"

Bernie said nothing.

"Even my mother likes it, and you know she's a great connoisseur. 'Why can't you make nice paintings like that handsome boyfriend of yours?' she keeps asking." He mimicked his mother's heavy Scandinavian inflection.

"I like your mother. It's too bad she couldn't be here today."

"Yeah. She'll come after Labor Day, she said, with Sven."

"Sven?"

"I didn't tell you about Sven?"

"Another new boyfriend?"

"With the accent on 'boy.' I sure hope they never get married. I'd hate to have to call him Dad when he's only three years older than me." Erik sniggered.

Bernie stared up at the painting, at the ruby-slippered teenager. "I wish my mother…" His voice trailed off.

"Your mother would have been proud, Bernie, just like Mac is. Super-proud. I know she would. Sarah, too, when she sees it. She'll— What's that word you use? Kuh-something?"

Bernie chuckled. "Kvell. I hope so. She'd better. She started all this." He turned to Erik. "Us, too, in a way. If she hadn't plunked herself down on that bench in front of Galérie Cinq Arts that day…"

"And if you hadn't come in later that afternoon by yourself…"

"And if you hadn't tried to pick me up…"

"And totally freaked you out…"

They both laughed.

"You did, you know," Bernie said.

"I kinda freaked myself out, too. Not because I chatted you up. I'll chat anyone up, especially about art."

"What, then?"

"I never said?"

"Uh-uh."

"I'll tell you on the way." Erik opened the limo door, pushed Bernie in and crawled in after him. The Mercedes pulled away from the curb and turned south on Stanley Street. Instead of making his way to the Ville-Marie Expressway, the quickest route, the driver circled the block back to Sherbrooke and, at Bernie's request, headed west so they could drive through Westmount.

"I freaked out because I gave you my card," Erik said ten minutes later as they passed the stark, modern makeover of a Victorian townhouse that was Galérie Cinq Arts. "Believe it or not, I'd never done anything like that before. I was afraid you would think I was some kind of slut."

"You mean you weren't?" Bernie asked teasingly.

"I never thought you'd call."

"I almost didn't. I ripped up your card and threw it away. Twice. We have a lot to thank Sarah for."

Erik took Bernie's hand. "And your mother. She's the one who really started all this."

Bernie nodded. "All of it."

6

You started it, Annie. All of it. Mac stared at the emerald swirls, chocolate furrows, undulating hills and slender, lenticular cloud suspended UFO-like in the center of a green and lavender sky. Together, they formed a compelling backdrop for the giant plough in the painting's foreground. "*La Charrue / The Plough. Anne Savage. 1931-33. Don de / Gift of Arthur Gill,*" the card next to it read.

Art…Canada…Esther…Bernie. Even Halifax and Anna, in a strange sort of way. Without you, Annie, I would not be standing here. I couldn't be standing here. I would be totting up figures three thousand miles away in a gloomy, dark-paneled Cameron-MacCready office overlooking Sauchiehall Street or tromping up and down the haberdashery aisles like some latter-day Harry Gordon Selfridge. Can you see me as a retail magnate? No? Me, neither.

Mac had always wanted to tell Anne Savage how much he owed her, how much she had changed his life. He wanted to tell her that first time they met, in 1956 at her one-woman show at the YWCA, but he was too in awe of her. She was a celebrity in those days. Everyone in Montreal knew Anne Savage, if not for her art then for her teaching. Generations of young Montrealers had passed through her Baron Byng High School art room. Few had failed to be transformed by the experience.

That August afternoon the Y's exhibition space was jammed with art lovers and former students, all eager to speak to her, and Mac was merely another anonymous admirer. No one had heard of Marc-Allan Cameron yet. That they would soon after was thanks in some measure to Annie's influence.

When she saw his work a few months later — Mac had persuaded his dean to bring Annie down to Halifax to give a talk at the art college — she became an instant champion, securing for him his first show outside Nova Scotia. Within a year, his work was in demand all over Canada, and it didn't take long for his renown to explode beyond his adopted country's borders. His and Annie's paths rarely crossed after that.

But even had he not been tongue-tied by Anne Savage's fame and hurried along by the snaking queue pressing up behind him back at the Y, he had been too emotional to be entirely coherent. Not because of Annie. Because of Esther. Because of what had taken place less than an hour earlier a few blocks away in Room 1612 of the Laurentian Hotel. Because of what had nearly kept him from showing up to the art opening at all.

Besides, the biggest change in his life, the most revolutionary transformation of all, had yet to occur. It wouldn't for another twenty-eight years.

Four improbably short years ago, Annie.

But the initial shift, the one that ignited all the others, began with this painting, with *The Plough.*

Mac stared into the painting's distant hills, allowing himself to be pulled out of the Montreal Museum of Fine Arts and back to a time long before he had heard of Anne Savage, back to a time when Canada was little more than a distant colony across a vast sea and art the vaguest of interests. It was as if Annie's plough was slicing not only through the loamy Quebec soil of her painting but deep into the furrows of his memory…

It's October 1938. As a treat for his twentieth birthday, Mac's parents have bundled him onto the crimson-and-gold *Coronation Scot* train for ten days in London with his mother's sister, Emmeline. They will join him at the tail end of the visit, but by then the damage will have been done: Marc-Allen, as he still is in those days, will not continue his training to ultimately take over the reins at Cameron-MacCready, the family business. Marc-Allen will be an artist.

Mac couldn't know anything about that when the streamlined locomotive of the London, Midland and Scottish Railway swept into Euston Station six and half hours later. He couldn't know it as he tramped the half-mile through drizzly fog to the slightly shabby

Fitzrovia townhouse of his more than slightly disreputable aunt. He would not know it for four more days — until the afternoon of his birthday, when Emmeline insisted that he accompany her to an exhibition of colonial art at the Tate Gallery.

"Why would I want to spend my birthday looking at art?" he groused. "Canadian art, at that."

"If 'A Century of Canadian Art' is good enough for the King and Queen," Emmeline huffed, "it's good enough for you." George VI and Elizabeth had toured the exhibition a few days earlier.

Mac grumbled, but Emmeline could never be dissuaded from any scheme she set her mind to, and she had set her mind to ensuring that her nephew would not be chained to a Glasgow department store for the rest of his life. It was her invitation that had brought Mac down to London for his birthday, and the Tate was the first thrust in her offensive. "You won't be sorry," she added enigmatically when he finally relented.

Mac, though, was certain he would regret it. He only agreed when Emmeline promised him a pub dinner around the corner at the Morpeth Arms, said to be haunted by prisoners and guards from the dreaded Millbank Penitentiary that had once stood on the Tate site. If he could get down to the original holding cells deep in the pub's cellar, like some of his friends had done, he might even catch a spectral glimpse of the convict said to have died there during an escape attempt. It would almost be worth suffering through an hour at the Tate for that.

By the time Mac and Emmeline got to the Morpeth Arms, however, chased out by museum staff at closing, Mac had forgotten about grisly tales of prison life and could talk only about Emily Carr, Tom Thomson, Arthur Lismer, A.Y. Jackson and a forty-two-year-old artist-teacher from Montreal named Anne Savage. It wasn't the "century" of Canadian art that transfixed him. It was the contemporary artists who captured his imagination with their bold strokes, vivid colors and simple, yet dynamic expressions of a country he only knew from textbooks and British Empire maps.

The exhibition filled five rooms at the Tate, two hundred and sixty-three pieces in all. But it took only one painting to forever alter the course of his life. Anne Savage's *The Plough* wasn't the most famous of the modern pieces. It wasn't even the best. Yet it was the one that spoke the most eloquently to him. If on this day at the Montreal Museum of Fine Arts, *The Plough* sliced into his memory, on October 28, 1938, it sliced into his soul to reveal the artist he never knew he was…the artist he never expected to want to be. Even as he and Emmeline wandered through the Tate's labyrinthine galleries, he kept returning to *The Plough*, to those hills that beckoned to him from thousands of miles away and to the distant soil from which he somehow knew his own art would one day emerge.

His parents would be disappointed, especially his father. What could they expect, leaving him alone with Aunt Emmeline for a week? A rail-thin spinster with a sharp nose, pointy chin and horsey teeth, Emmeline Mandeville was Elise Cameron's oldest sister and the scourge of a family that took pride in its longstanding Tory conformity. Emmeline had no use for either Tories or conformity. To the outrage of her father, she started voting Labour in 1922, but only after her beloved British Socialist Party was annexed by the Labour Party, "those crypto-Communist pirates and criminals," as she described them. Labour's "milquetoast" policies, politics and politicians, she opined, were barely better than the Conservatives, but she was damned (her word) if she would forfeit her hard-won vote by staying home on polling day. After all, she had marched with that other Emmeline, the notorious suffragette Emmeline Pankhurst, and she still regretted that she had never managed to get arrested for the cause.

To her mother's shame Emmeline was unmarried by choice: "This ugly duckling has turned down more offers in the past six months," she once boasted, "than most Gibson Girls get in a lifetime." That didn't mean she lived by herself. Sometimes a man, generally younger, shared her bed; sometimes it was a woman, generally older. Not only did Emmeline Mandeville rarely sleep alone, her townhouse off Fitzroy Square was rarely empty. A gaggle of fellow eccentrics and bohemians was nearly always in residence, and every Sunday morning, when respectable Londoners were installing themselves in their church pews, Emmeline was hosting one of Fitzrovia's most popular salons, attracting everyone from a young Dylan Thomas to such established literary luminaries as George Bernard Shaw and Virginia Woolf.

No one shared her bedroom this week, though, and the house had been cleared of all transients. Nothing would divert Emmeline from her plan of action for her nephew, nor would she give Mac any opportunity to be daunted by the more outrageous of her artist friends.

"Another pub ghost tomorrow?" Emmeline asked, her mouth stuffed with cottage pie. "I know one in The Strand where you might see a Cavalier. The George. The building is new, but its cellars go all the way back to the Civil War."

Mac regarded her strangely.

"It's but a short walk to St. Martin's Place," Emmeline continued.

"St. Martin's Place?"

Emmeline's eyes twinkled mischievously. "The National Portrait Gallery, in case you might want to take that in, too…while we're in the area, you know."

"I'd like that," Mac replied. "Oh, and the gallery, too." He smirked and chugged down the last of his pint. "I've never been."

"I'm sure we can make some time for it," Emmeline said. "After the ghost, of course."

"Of course." Mac paused. "I might like to paint people," he added thoughtfully.

It would take more than Mac's dozens of visits to St. Martin's Place over the next decades to squeeze even one portrait out of him. It would take Bernie. It would take his son.

7

Sadie steadied herself on "Rosalie Friedman, Died 5th Aug. 1915 Aged 72 yrs.," who stood upright and more solid than she felt after weaving through the jumbled jungle of gravestones for nearly forty-five minutes. Rather, she felt like Rosalie looked: cracked, dulled and faded after three-quarters of a century in this farkakte maze of a farkakte cemetery. At least Rosalie didn't have to worry about puddles. Sadie's right sneaker was spattered with mud from the one she had tripped into. She wiped the perspiration from her neck and forehead, glared at Rosalie and stumbled on and past "Gerald Rotenburg," "Sylvia & Isidore Finkelstein" and a dozen more stones too worn to read. "The good news," she muttered to "Chaim Sternberg, Dear Husband, Brother, Father & Son, 1893-1917," stopping to scowl at him, "is that if I die, they can bury me right where they find me." She strained to see past the dense wall of poplars that marked some sort of boundary up ahead. *If they find me.*

She reached the poplars as St. Luc's began its eleven o'clock toll and leaned into the dense, trunk-hugging foliage, yearning, not for the first time, to disappear inside a tree.

When she was growing up, a mature elm stood in the lane behind Clark Street. It probably wasn't as tall and majestic as she remembered it, but it soared high enough to reach the Finkels' third-story flat. Sadie could see it from the window of the bedroom she had to share with Esther, and she treasured it: It was the only tree on their grim, gray block and she spent hours dancing around it. It wasn't really dancing, not like Les Grands Ballets Canadiens danced these days. It was more like running, jumping, skipping and flinging herself around the wizened trunk. Sometimes, Ruth joined her and they would make up strange songs to go with their questionable dances.

Then, Ruth died and the dancing stopped. Instead, a fifteen-year-old Sadie would sneak out back after dark, after she had fed and cleaned up after Max, Manny, Nate and Esther, after most of the lights in the neighboring buildings had been extinguished, and would wrap herself around the elm, hugging it until her arms ached, hoping it would absorb her within it, wishing she never had to go back inside.

A few months later, she came home from school to find a city truck lumbering out of the lane, hacked hunks of tree hanging off its sides. A fresh stump sat in a bed of wood chips and sawdust where her elm had stood, surrounded by a scattering of leaves and twigs. Sadie stared at the desecration, paralyzed. As much as she longed to run to what was left of her tree, embrace it and weep, she couldn't. She climbed three floors up the back stairs to the Finkel flat without once looking back.

Until that moment she had still harbored dreams of becoming a dancer. She knew she would never be good enough for the real ballet, but there was this strange, exotic woman called Isadora Duncan who had passed through Montreal in 1922. She didn't do "the ballette," as Ruth called it. Instead, the eccentric dancer ran, skipped, jumped and flung herself across the Monument National stage, like Sadie did around her elm. Had done. There was no more elm. There were no more dreams. Even Isadora Duncan was dead, strangled by her own scarf in a freak accident in France the year before.

Nor were there any more tears. Sadie never cried again. Not when Nate died at Dieppe during World War II. Not when Max died, finally, still grief-stricken over the death of his beloved Ruth. Not when Esther died, the nafkeh. Not when Manny died, the putz.

Not until now. Sadie touched her cheek. It was wet. She had not thought about that elm tree in forever, or the dancing. "Sentimental fool," she muttered, wiping her eyes on her sleeve and disentangling herself from the poplar.

Ahead, just beyond the narrow gravel road that led to the main gate, de la Savane Street and the Metro, the newest part of the cemetery stretched for hundreds of yards in a checkerboard grid, as neat and ordered as the tangled old section behind her was not. Sadie stepped onto the road then immediately scrambled back into the concealment of the poplar boughs. Was that Bernie across the way? The beard was gone and he was wearing a leather jacket like some Hells Angels biker, but she was sure it was him. She peered out from her hiding place to scrutinize her surroundings. Yes, she was across the road from Esther's grave.

How the hell had she found herself here, at the one place in this zoo of a cemetery that she had purposely avoided for three years? She hadn't been since the unveiling ceremony for her sister's stone. And who was that goyishe boy sitting on a bench down the way? What's a blond Aryan like that doing sitting by himself in a Jewish cemetery? A neo-Nazi probably, waiting with his spray can until Bernie's gone. *I should maybe warn Bernie? Nah. He'll get what's coming to him. Unless they're in the same gang?*

Sadie sensed a slight movement to the left and turned her head as the church bell clanged for the eleventh time. *Sarah? Sarah Swartz? What's that nosy, chaleria doing here?*

If Bernie was practically unrecognizable in his leather jacket and jeans, so was Sarah. Her hair was a steel-wool tangle like always, but she was dressed nice. Sarah never dressed nice. No, that wasn't it. Sarah always looked like she *tried* to dress nice. Even as a teenager, even before, there was something not right about the way she looked. Things didn't fit the way they should. Things didn't look the way they should. Shoes were all wrong. And makeup? Best to say nothing about Sarah and makeup. Sadie was no fashion plate. But Sarah? Sarah was a fashion balagan. A disaster. Not today. Today, you could almost call Sarah stylish in her red-and-black summer print and low heels. Almost. For once, her purse wasn't one of those suitcases she insisted on hauling around. Yes, it was huge, like Sarah had always been. Yet it was — dare she say it? — fashionable, like it came from Ogilvy's not Kresge's.

I must be dreaming. This whole thing: Bernie, Sarah, tramping through the cemetery. Any minute, I'm going to wake up. If I'm lucky, I won't remember any of this. She closed her eyes and imagined herself back in her lumpy single bed in her Kildare Road apartment. She opened them again when St. Luc's bonged the quarter hour. Nothing had changed: Sadie was hiding in the poplar tree in the cemetery, and Sarah and Bernie were across the road at Esther's grave. They were talking but Sadie was too far away to hear. She watched as Sarah pulled something from her purse. A book. She passed it to Bernie. Now, he retrieved something from his messenger bag. A piece of paper? A card? He passed it to Sarah. *What are they doing? Some sort of drug deal? I wouldn't put it past that Sarah. Bernie, either.*

A few minutes later, Bernie waved to the Nazi, who grinned, got up from his bench and started toward them. *No paint-sprayer. A concealed knife? Or a gun? They are part of the same gang. Maybe Bernie's having Sarah killed? She should maybe scream? No. Why should she get killed, too?* Bernie and Sarah strolled arm-in-arm toward Blondie. Suddenly, Sarah pulled free. Was she going to try to make a run for it? Not in those shoes, she wasn't. No, she was going back to Esther.

I'll throw up. I know I will. Bernie and the Nazi. They're kissing. I knew he was a little faygele, that Bernie. "Chaloshes," she muttered. *In public, yet. It's revolting. More revolting than revolting.* She looked away in disgust, back at Sarah, who was bent over, leaning something against Esther's stone.

Sadie didn't budge from her hidey-hole until Sarah and her two pansy boys had disappeared from view and St. Luc's had set off its racket again. She crossed the road to Esther's grave and frowned at the inscription: "Esther Finkel Freed. 1923-1984. Beloved mother, wife and friend." More disrespect. That's all Esther and her son were ever about. "You forgot you were married to Harold Coopersmith?" she snapped. "He loved you like no one else, and you threw him out. It killed him, that's what it did. You didn't know he died, of a broken heart, probably. How could you with him up there—" She turned her eyes heavenward, then dropped them to the ground. "And you down there."

That's when Sadie noticed the two oversized postcards that Sarah had left. One was a new-book announcement. Something called *Sara's Year.* The picture on the cover, it was Sarah…an almost flattering photo. Almost. "By Sara Schumacher," it said under the title. *A book, she wrote?* "Candid. Literate. Full of heart," was spelled out in big, bold letters across the top. Across the bottom: "Available August 1." *Your maiden name, okay. But where's your h, you pretentious little shit…?*

Sadie reached for the second card. For an art show, it looked like, with a bright, brassy, strange sort of painting on the front. *I know what I like and this isn't it.* She examined it more closely. "Got in himmel!" she shrieked, quickly checking to make sure no one had heard. "You," she whispered at the granite slab. "It's you." The picture was of Esther and Sarah as teenagers — fifteen, she'd guess — perched on stools at the counter of that dumpy Westmount diner that were always sneaking off to, thinking she didn't know. What was it? Stella's. Stella's Lunch. Well, she did know. And a lot more besides. She traced Esther's figure with her finger. "What kind of narishkeit is this?" Esther was wearing glittering red pumps on her feet, like those ruby slippers in *The Wizard of Oz*. Sadie turned the card over: "Reflections," it read. "Bernard Marc Freed." *Bernie?* "Your son's an artist?" she breathed at the stone. "Like…like…"

"Like I wanted to be?" Esther's voice.

Sadie spun around. No one was there.

"Like you didn't want me to be?"

I'm going crazy. This really is a dream. It has to be.

"Like you wouldn't let me be?" Esther's voice as clear as if she were alive, standing right there instead of rotting six feet down, under Sadie's feet. "Good Jewish girls don't. Isn't that what you said? Isn't that what you made Papa say?"

Sadie leapt back in terror, certain that a demon arm would lurch up from the grave, grab her leg and haul her into the ground to join her dead sister.

Only when she had fled the cemetery and was standing on the Metro platform waiting for her train did she realize that she was holding the two postcards. She peeked again at Bernie's. "Vernissage: 10 août / Aug. 10," was written under her nephew's name. "17h-20h / 5-8 p.m."

Today?

Today.

8

Mac checked his watch. *Shit.* How long had he been staring at *The Plough*? He had planned to take in the Paul-Émile Borduas retrospective while he was here. Now, there wouldn't be time, not even for a quick peek.

If Anne Savage had started him on his artist's path, Borduas had shaped his approach. Mac could still picture the lanky, slightly rumpled artist the first time he saw him, shrouded in a bluish haze of cigarette smoke, surrounded by students in one of the lounges at the Nova Scotia College of Art, his jarringly vibrant *Abstraction verte* on an easel next to him. "The important thing is to be able to create," Borduas had proclaimed with a fiery zeal that would, two years later, get him fired from his teaching post in Montreal.

Mac couldn't argue, thanks to Aunt Emmeline and those Canadian artists. Unfortunately, the war interrupted his dreams. But as soon as he could, Mac made his way to Halifax and enrolled in the college that Anna Leonowens, the real-life Anna of *Anna and the King of Siam*, had founded and that Arthur Lismer of the Tate exhibition had once presided over as president.

As predicted, his parents balked at both his plans and his choice of venue from which to pursue them. There had been weeks of explosive arguments — between him and his father, between his father and his mother and between Emmeline and both his parents. In the end, Mac and Emmeline prevailed and his father grudgingly agreed to pay his first year's tuition and to make a modest contribution to his living expenses.

Mac had never seen anything like *Abstraction verte*. He found its bold jumble of green, white and red strokes on a sea of black both confusing and compelling.

Never shy, he asked Borduas what it was.

"I don't understand any more than you do," the artist replied. "Whatever it is you are searching for in the painting, I'm searching for it, too."

"Then how do you know what to paint?" another student asked, a baffled expression on her face.

"I have no preconceived idea," he confessed to his rapt audience. "I obey whatever impulse comes first."

That became Mac's creed, too. He would scan the blank canvas in a meditative sort of way and, when the inclination struck, begin to paint. The result, what critics and academics now called "an idiosyncratic brand of abstract expressionism" but which Mac refused to categorize or label, had propelled him to artistic superstardom. Only once had he disregarded his intuitive practice, and that had not turned out well.

Mac saluted *The Plough* then hurried past both the neighboring gallery, where his *Eighteen by Twenty* took up most of a wall as part of the museum's permanent collection, and the gallery after that, which held the Borduas exhibition, catching a glimpse of *Abstraction verte* on the way. He would try to get back to the MMFA for a visit with Paul-Émile before leaving town, but he didn't dare stop now. Although it was only two blocks back along Sherbrooke Street to the Ritz, he needed to shower and change before meeting Bernie, Erik and, with luck, Sarah Swartz for lunch at the hotel's Café de Paris.

For months Sarah had been the unidentified "mystery guest," with both Bernie and Erik refusing to reveal who they hoped would be joining them for their pre-vernissage celebration. All Bernie would reply to Mac's grilling was, "Mumm's on the table and mum on the surprise." That and in an echo of the enigmatic Emmeline, "You won't be sorry."

What a schemer that Bernie was. He must have inherited it somehow from Aunt Emmeline, not from his mother. Esther never struck him as a schemer. A planner, yes. Too much of a planner, perhaps. Not at all like Mac's seat-of-the-pants way of doing art and pretty much everything else. But Emmeline…

It wasn't until Emmeline sailed out to Halifax for his first show, at the Leonowens-Fyshe Gallery back in 1947 that she confessed: His giving up retail for the life of an artist had not been his idea at all; it had been hers all along.

Mac smiled at the memory. *I miss you, Aunt Emmeline. I wish I had told you about me and Esther. I know you would have had some brilliant advice. Or a battle plan. You always had a battle plan.*

9

Sadie watched the Metro's concrete tunnel whoosh by through the window, doing her best to ignore the old woman staring back at her. The old woman would not be ignored.

"Look at me," she spat. "Look at what you did to me. Maybe I was never pretty like Esther, but I was never ugly. You made me ugly."

"Shut up," Sadie hissed.

"You made me a witch, a venomous, vindictive bitch of a witch. You did it. You. Only you."

"It wasn't me. It was Papa and Manny and Nate and Esther. They did it, not me. It was them."

"You. You and Ruth. You and your mother."

"No," Sadie cried softly.

"Yes, you did, Hadassah."

"Don't call me that," Sadie snapped. "Don't ever call me that."

"I shouldn't call you by your own name? Sadie Hadassah Finkel. That's you, isn't it? Or am in the wrong Metro car?"

Sadie closed her eyes but the reflection in the window was burned into her: coarse, crudely cut white hair framing a bony face dominated by a beaklike nose that could have belonged to Margaret Hamilton in *The Wizard of Oz*. She felt for the postcards in her purse. *What was he thinking, that Bernie, sticking Judy Garland's ruby slippers on Esther in his picture?* She touched her lips. The lips were the worst of all: thin lips that had not seen lipstick in years. Decades. Cruel lips. Lips that rarely turned up in a smile. They weren't smiling now.

Hadassah. When was the last time anyone called me Hadassah?

"No." The nine-year-old girl's usually pleasing face twisted into a pursed-lipped pout as she pointed an accusing finger at the gurgling infant. "If you're going to call her Esther, you can't call me Hadassah."

"What's wrong, bubeleh? It's a pretty name. Why shouldn't you like it all of a sudden? What does it have to do with the baby?" Ruth put her arm around her daughter. Her daughter shrugged it off and stalked across the kitchen.

"I won't answer to it. I won't."

"Zeeskyte…"

"No."

"Don't answer back to your mother, Hadassah," Max chided her gently. "Good Jewish girls don't talk like that. You're a good Jewish girl, aren't you?"

The girl turned her back on her parents. Her shoulders trembled.

Max raised his bushy eyebrows at his wife. Ruth rose from the table and stood behind her daughter. Her face was drawn and pale from thirty-two hours of labor, and she was still unsteady enough on her feet that she gripped the back of a kitchen chair with one calloused hand for support. As worn out as she was from the ordeal of recent childbirth, all those hours of labor were nothing next to more than a decade of six-day weeks at Yitzak Kaufman's sweaty, noxious schmatta factory. She reached out to touch the girl's shoulder but pulled her hand back, kneeling instead. Yes, her Hadassah could be willful sometimes, but not without reason. She was a good girl, mostly.

"You can tell me. Whatever it is, you know you can tell me. You can always tell me."

The girl hiccuped, swallowed tears she refused to show and half-turned to her mother. "Mrs. Tobias told me that Hadassah was Queen Esther's other name. It says so in the Megillah. Esther and Hadassah: They're both the same person. I don't want to be her. I don't want her to be me. How can I be me if she's me?"

Max groaned. How clever they thought they had been. Esther and Hadassah. Two sides of the same coin. The names would make up for the difference in the girls' ages. It would erase those nine years. It would make them inseparable. Now, they would be enemies? He covered his face with his hands.

"No one can ever be you," Ruth murmured soothingly. "Only you can be you. Esther is Esther and Hadassah is Hadassah. Always, Right?"

"I can't," she said. "I won't." She wiped her nose with the back of her hand.

Max pulled a giant white handkerchief from his pocket and passed it to his daughter. She took it without looking at him and blew her noise loudly.

"We could call you Harriet," Ruth offered. "That's what some of the teachers call you in school, isn't it?"

The girl nodded then shook her head. "That name…" She would not speak it, not ever again. "It's really my middle name, isn't it?"

Ruth nodded.

"Really, my name is Sadie, right? I mean, it's my first name, right?"

Ruth nodded again.

"Can I be Sadie from now on, Mama? Please?" She turned to Max. "If it's my first name, it's really my real name. Isn't it?"

Theirs may have been an arranged marriage, but it must have been one arranged not only in a Russian shtetl but in heaven, because the instant Ruth and Max set eyes on each other, weeks before their wedding, they fell head over heels. More than that, they quickly discovered that they could exchange whole libraries of words and feelings with a single glance. They did that now. Max knew he should put his foot down, be tough like his father had been. He knew, too, it wouldn't work. His daughter was strong, stronger than his Ruth, and she was the real Esther, a queen of queens. An empress, like that Victoria had been.

"Papa?" the girl pleaded.

"Yes, princess," Max said. "You can be Sadie. We'll tell Nate and Manny when they come home. Tomorrow, your Mama will write a note to Mrs. Tobias at the school, and all of us we'll try to remember."

Sadie, as she now was, rushed to her father, threw herself into his lap and buried her face in his chest. "Thank you, Papa. Thank you. Thank you. Thank you."

"If we forget sometimes and call you Hadassah, you won't be mad?"

"If you forget, I'll remind you."

"Nicely?"

Sadie nodded.

#   #   #   #   #

No one ever called her Hadassah after that, not even in school. No one dared. Until now.

Dou dou dou. The familiar three-note chime signaling the train's start woke Sadie from her reverie. "Damn!" The train was leaving Villa-Maria. Her station. For a moment, she thought about getting off at the next stop and crossing over to catch a northbound train back to Villa-Maria. Only for a moment. She hated being on the train when it stopped at Place-Saint-Henri, never mind leaving it to stand on the platform. She would be mugged for sure, or worse. No. She would wait an extra stop. It's not that she considered the working-class neighborhood around Lionel-Groux to be a whole lot better, but the Metro's orange and green lines met there, so it was busier than Place-Saint-Henri. Much busier. She would be safe there. Well, safer.

Yet when Sadie crossed to the blue-and-white train idling on the other side of the tiled platform, she found herself not returning north on the orange line but heading east on the green line, toward downtown...toward Galérie Walter Klinkhoff.

10

Mac stepped off the elevator into the rich blacks, ambers, russets and golds of the Ritz-Carlton lobby.

We'll meet again

Don't know where, don't know when

That song. Was someone on the grand piano in the Palm Court? Was it in his head? It didn't matter. It had to stop.

But I know we'll meet again some sunny day

It didn't stop. He had to get out of the hotel, or at least out of earshot of that song. But his feet refused to obey his brain's command to move, and he stood motionless on the white marble floor as gleaming brass doors whispered shut behind him.

Keep smiling through

Just like you always do

His pulse quickened. He felt himself gasping for breath. This was crazy. Mishigas, Esther would have called it. Narishkeit.

Till the blue skies drive the dark clouds far away

He stumbled onto the brocade chesterfield tucked under the sweeping staircase to the mezzanine. He inhaled deeply, then again. This was worse than when Bernie told him that Esther was dead. How could it be worse than that?

We'll meet again

Don't know where, don't know when

He closed his eyes. He had never had an anxiety attack. Not ever. Not even when flying for the RAF during the war. Not even when he was shot down, and that was crazy, heart-stopping mishigas. He would not have an anxiety attack now.

But I know we'll meet again some sunny day

He would not.

11

Slowly, too slowly, Mac's heart stilled its pounding and his breathing returned to something resembling normal. "We'll Meet Again" had played itself out and segued into a series of more contemporary melodies. How many, he didn't know. From where, he also didn't know. He rose to his feet, but his feet again declined to cooperate. He collapsed back onto the sofa, shut his eyes and let the soft susurrus of the lobby wash over him, praying for it to erase all memory of that song.

Get a grip, Cameron. You would think you were back bombing Berlin.

"I was trained to fly a bomber," he muttered. "No one ever trained me for this."

Between finally completing Esther's portrait a few weeks earlier and his visits that morning to Dorchester Square and the museum, Mac had been certain that he'd silenced the final ghosts of his past. It was turning out not to be true.

In a strange way, the Ritz's royal suite was one of those ghosts. Although much more opulent, it reminded him of his first afternoon of lovemaking with Esther, in the suite he had booked for them at the Lord Nelson Hotel in Halifax. Then, the Lord Nelson was one of the most elegant hotels in the city, like the Ritz always had been in Montreal. That was the real reason he had wanted to make the Ritz the pied-à-terre for this visit. How could he know that that blasted song from all those years ago would haunt him here?

Still, the Lord Nelson connection was a silly reason, so silly that he had felt foolish sharing it with Bernie and Erik when they wondered about his hotel choice.

"Wouldn't you rather stay at the Four Seasons again or the Château

Champlain? Or the Queen Elizabeth?" Bernie asked "They're more, well...I don't know..."

"Modern?" Erik inserted.

Bernie nodded. He and Erik were curled up together in the Victorian love seat in Mac's rural Nova Scotia studio, watching him fuss with his latest painting, one that would likely join Bernie's debut exhibition the following month in Montreal. Mac was reluctant to include the piece, fearing that it would upstage Bernie's work. But Bernie had insisted, and Walter Klinkhoff was not going to turn away a new Cameron, even if it was unlike anything Mac had ever shown and even if Mac wasn't sure he was prepared to sell it.

Erik poked Bernie. "Just because Pops here makes art that's starker than stark and bleaker than bleak doesn't mean he doesn't secretly get off on mega marble, gilded ceilings, gaudy chandeliers and overstuffed, antimacassared sofas." He stroked the arm of the love seat and winked at Mac.

Bernie pushed Erik's arm away and jumped on him, tickling him mercilessly. "I think you're confusing my father with my boyfriend," he teased.

Erik squirmed, unable to get out from under Bernie. "Stop!" he squealed, giggling uncontrollably.

Mac was barely aware of the horseplay. His focus on the painting in front of him was absolute. He had been this way as long as he had been making art. You could set him up with canvas, easel and paints in the middle of Spring Garden Road at Christmastime and he would be oblivious to the Halifax traffic, crowds or cold. He was even more obsessive about this piece, more determined than ever to get it as close to perfect as he could manage. After one more daub of umber and an intentional smudge with his finger, he set his brush down and stepped back, wiping his hands on a paint-splattered rag.

"I don't know," he said slowly, half-turning to Bernie. "This may not be finished in time."

Bernie pecked Erik on the cheek and shoved him off his lap. "You always say that and it always is."

"This one's different."

"You always say that, too."

"Not like this one." He returned his full attention to the canvas.

"Can I see?" Bernie stood.

"Not yet."

"Please? You haven't let me see any of it. You always let me watch your progress."

"I was teaching you then. You don't need me to teach you anything anymore."

"That isn't true."

"It is. You're your own artist now." Mac had no doubt that the show in Montreal would prove it.

"If I lie and say I believe you, will you let me see it?"

"When it's finished." Mac picked up a brush, dabbed it in the flesh-tone base he had blended onto his pallet and moved his hand toward the canvas. His hand stopped when it was less than an inch away. Shaking his head, he wiped the brush clean. "Like I said, this one's different."

"You're right, I guess. For me, too." Bernie dropped back onto the love seat. "About the Ritz. Are you sure?"

Four years earlier when the Montreal Museum of Fine Arts acquired his *Eighteen by Twenty*, Mac had angled to be put up at the Ritz. Instead, the museum installed him at the Four Seasons a few blocks east. The curator of contemporary Canadian art likely assumed that the austere concrete high-rise better suited the modernist flavor of Mac's work than did the late-Edwardian elegance of the legendary Grande Dame of Sherbrooke Street, and Mac wasn't prepared to reveal his real reason for wanting to stay there.

As it turned out, the dazzling, celebrity-studded reception held at the museum in honor of the acquisition took place only hours after Esther's funeral. While Mac was drinking champagne and accepting congratulatory handshakes, a mile and a half away Sarah was telling Bernie about him and Esther. If he had only known — about Esther, about Sarah, about Bernie. But all he could know was what the phone book and the 411 operator told him that afternoon: There was no Esther or Morris Freed in the metropolitan area.

"You don't want to stay at the Ritz?" Mac asked. "The Ritz-Carlton was good enough for the Rolling Stones and for Elizabeth Taylor's wedding, for the first one to Richard Burton. Not to mention royalty. It isn't good enough for you?"

Bernie laughed. "You sounded almost like Sarah then."

"I'm looking forward to meeting your Sarah…now that you broke down and confessed that she's your mystery guest."

"That was the longest my man's ever kept a secret." Erik hugged Bernie.

"I had to tell. If I hadn't you would have exploded. You are worse with secrets than I am."

"What a liar," Erik countered. "If it hadn't been for me, you would have spilled about Sarah ages ago."

"Says you."

"Damn right, says me."

Bernie grinned. "You're probably right. Anyhow, it doesn't matter now. You're both going to love her. I know you will."

"If it wasn't for Sarah, I wouldn't be here. You, either. So, yeah, I know I'm gonna love her. Lots." He squeezed Bernie's hand.

"I hope I haven't screwed things up with her," Bernie said. "I mean I hope she's okay. I keep thinking I should have called after she didn't show up for our cemetery meeting last year."

"You didn't show up the first two years," Erik reminded him.

"I know. It felt like the right thing to do, like trusting that she'll show up this year feels right, even though that wasn't part of our deal. I've been trying to trust those feelings. It hasn't been easy."

"For any of us," Mac said. "But an artist has to trust his gut, his heart—"

"His intuition," Erik and Bernie completed the familiar invocation in unison.

Mac chuckled. "Yes, his intuition." He made a final, tilted-head inspection of his canvas and headed for the door. "No peeking."

"If you're finished for the day, can I turn off the CD player?" Erik implored. *The King and I* movie soundtrack had been playing softly on auto-repeat all afternoon. "I'm as gay as the next guy when it comes to Broadway musicals and I know how important this show is to you guys, but if I hear 'Getting to Know You' one more time, I'm going to have to think about getting to un-know both of you."

"*Movie* musicals, mister," Bernie corrected. "If you can't get important stuff like that right, they're going to take away your gay card. Anyhow, without Yul Brynner and Deborah Kerr—"

"And Marnie Nixon singing for Deborah Kerr," Erik interjected. "That should get me my gay card back."

"We'll discuss that later." Bernie smirked. "In private." He pressed the stop button on the Philips player. "But without this show, you'd be talking to dead air right now, cuz there'd be no Bernie."

"I know, I know." He wrapped his arms around Bernie. "And I will never, ever say a mean word about Rogers and Hammerstein, Walter Lang, Irene Sharaff, Yul Brynner, Deborah Kerr, Marnie Nixon or all those Siamese children. I just need a break from them."

"And have one, you shall," Mac said. "How about we regroup in the kitchen for a *King and I*-free pot of tea and some of Rita Ferguson's oatcakes?"

"Yes to kitchen and tea," Erik replied. "Mega-no to oatcakes. I love Rita, but I love my teeth even more. If Rita's ancestors had stockpiled those oatcakes in their armories, my great-great-great-great-grand-Vikings would never have conquered Scotland. You guys might have invented curling earlier, too. As snacks, those oatcakes make great curling stones." He followed Mac and Bernie out of the studio.

"That's how my auntie made them," Mac said. "Mind you," he quipped, "she also catered the local curling team."

"Emmeline made oatcakes?" Bernie asked incredulously.

"Never. That would be my father's sister, Agnes. I never told you about her. She died when I was nine but it would be impossible to forget her oatcakes. She was the one who was my 'auntie.' For all her leftie eccentricities, Emmeline was very proper. She would never let herself be called auntie. Only aunt." He pronounced it with an exaggerated English upper-class accent. "Aunt Emmeline could barely boil water for tea, let alone make toast. You boys are lucky it isn't genetic."

"Maybe it is." Erik tilted his head at Bernie.

"No more Bernie Freed Specials for you," Bernie retorted in a mock huff.

"You owe us at least one more of your, um, omelets," Mac said. "Don't forget you're on KP tonight." He ran cold water into the kettle. "Tea for you, too, Bernie?"

"You British and your tea," Bernie said.

Mac set the kettle on the stove and switched on the gas. "You know," he said softly, "you sounded almost like your mother then."

"What is it with the British and their tea?" Esther asked. Her tone may have been jocular but her dark eyes betrayed her panic as they darted from painting to painting to painting and from skylight to window to door, picking out everything in the gallery except Mac, who stood less than a foot away from her.

With only two weeks remaining until its grand, New Year's Day reopening, the Leonowens-Fyshe Gallery was almost ready for its first art show since before the war. Most of the canvases had already been hung on freshly painted walls, but a handful remained propped against anything that would hold them up in the stark, ultramodern, two-story space that was unlike anything Esther had ever seen and that belied the building's squat, frumpy Prince Street exterior.

It was a small news item in the Halifax *Herald* that had brought her here, attracted by the Leonowens name. In Nova Scotia, Leonowens meant Anna Leonowens, who had made her way to Halifax after her retirement from the royal court of Siam, only to become a vocal advocate for art education and women's suffrage. The newspaper article had failed to mention that the gallery's inaugural exhibit would feature the abstract slashes and whorls of one Marc-Allan Cameron, a student at the Nova Scotia College of Art and the one person in all of Halifax that Esther was trying to avoid…for fear of what she might do were she to see him again.

And here he was, staring at her with those puppy-dog eyes that reflected back at her everything that she felt for him and shouldn't — she, a married woman and trying to be the good Jewish girl she had been brought up to be.

Mac remembered that moment with a mix of sadness and joy as he pried open the tin of oatcakes and spooned Irish Breakfast tea into the Brown Betty teapot before filling it with boiling water from the kettle. Of course, it had been foolish of him to offer Esther tea all those years ago at the gallery, but that's what you did in those days when someone was in shock. And Esther had been in shock. Her face had still not regained its color after washing out to a ghostlike pallor when it was he who opened the gallery door to her tentative knock. Mac could tell that she longed to flee and he was grateful for the paralysis that kept her rooted impotently in place.

Tea: That was the cure-all back home. Here in the postwar New

World, however, it was more likely to be alcohol, which was why a few minutes later Mac pushed Esther out the gallery door and around the corner to the Carleton Hotel, where liquor was available as long as you ordered a plate of inedible food to go with it.

When he and Esther next met, they really did have tea. It was a planned meeting this time: the following afternoon at Murray's restaurant in the Lord Nelson. Mac hadn't been sure that Esther would show up. She had only half-promised when she left him outside the Carleton the previous day. Thank God she was there when he rushed in, even if her face was pinched with anxiety. He didn't know how long she had been waiting, but she had been at the table long enough for the pot of tea she had ordered to get cold. Mac sent it back for fresh, more for Esther than for him. He would have chugged down a sink full of cold dishwater to be with her.

That was the day they made love for the first time. He had booked a suite for them, complete with champagne and a trio of vases each filled with a dozen red roses, praying that he would get to share it all with Esther but not daring to believe it would happen. After their Murray's tea and a wintry walk through nearby Victoria Park, it had. If that one wish of his was fulfilled, in a frenzy of passion almost desperate in its intensity, his next was not: As they lay naked in each other's arms, the Dinning Sisters' "We'll Meet Again" crackling in from the Viking console in the sitting room, Mac asked her to leave her husband, to not return to Montreal, to stay in Halifax with him. To be his Queen Esther for all time.

Her silence was all the answer he needed. It would be ten years before he would see her again.

We'll meet again
Don't know where, don't know when
But I know we'll meet again some sunny day

Forty-two years later, he still could not bear to hear to that song.

12

Émile Pelletier ran a finger down the handwritten list of names in his reservations book. The leather-bound volume lay open atop a buffed-walnut lectern a few steps inside the elegant, blue-and-ocher luxe of the Café de Paris. The mâitre d', tuxedo-clad even at lunchtime, scanned first inside the restaurant then through the french doors to the tables outside in the Ritz Garden. "Non, M. Cameron. Your party is not here. Would you care to wait? With a glass of wine, perhaps? Or a cocktail? I can have it brought to you outside in the garden or over in the Palm Court, if you would rather wait there."

The elegant dining room was nearly full, a mix of Holt Renfrew shoppers resting up before crossing Rue de la Montagne for their next lap around the luxury department store and Armani-suited executives lingering over their latest deal. One table for two was conspicuously unoccupied.

"I can seat you at M. Trudeau's table again, if you prefer," Émile offered.

"He doesn't lunch here?" Mac asked, still a bit shaky after his panicked reaction to hearing "We'll Meet Again" ten minutes earlier in the lobby. The restaurant was mercifully music-free.

"Non, monsieur. Breakfast only. He's very regular, our M. Trudeau. He comes in every weekday at seven thirty and orders the same breakfast you had with him today."

"A glass of milk, dry toast and a soft-boiled egg."

"Précisement."

"Boiled no more than four and half minutes, he told me."

"C'est vrai," Émile confirmed. "Quatre minutes et demi. Pas une seconde de plus. That is the rule for M. Trudeau, yes. Just a few seconds more and he can tell the différence."

Mac gazed across the room to the empty table. "He is still quite the man."

"Oui, monsieur. Quite the man, as you say."

The former prime minister of Canada had been tapping on his four-and-a-half-minute egg when Mac ambled into the Café de Paris for breakfast. The boys weren't up, not that he would have heard them if they were. Two bedrooms and twice as many bathrooms separated their royal bedroom from his royal guest room.

Mac could have taken the more palatially appointed vice-royal bedroom next door, but the three of them had been crammed into Mac's farmhouse-cum-studio for nearly four years now and the boys deserved some real relationship space. Boys? Bernie was thirty-one and Erik twenty-seven, yet Mac couldn't help but think of them as boys — like the twenty-eight-year-old "boy" he had been when he first met Bernie's mother.

Esther was one of the other reasons he was up and out early. Mac had a few ghosts to exorcise and old friends to call on before he would be ready for lunch with Sarah and for Bernie's art opening. When the previous evening Mac had outlined his plans for the morning, Bernie and Erik offered to join him. He could sense Bernie's disappointment when he declined. But this piece of Esther belonged to Mac, not to their son, and this series of visits was best made solo.

"Mac!"

A cultured voice familiar to all Canadians pulled him out of his musings. He searched out its source as Pierre Elliot Trudeau rose and motioned for Mac to join him. Mac had met Trudeau a handful of times over the years at one cultural event or another and it still surprised him that a man with such stature and so commanding a presence stood only five-foot eight.

"Mr. Trudeau."

"I'm not Prime Minister anymore, you know. Call me Pierre."

Mac couldn't imagine calling him Pierre.

"Sit."

Mac did, uncertainly. He wasn't feeling chatty. Nor did he want to linger over breakfast. But this was Pierre Elliott Trudeau. How could he refuse?

"Alfred," Trudeau called out to a passing waiter.

"M. Trudeau?"

Trudeau turned to Mac. "What will you have?"

"Uh, a pot of black tea and a croissant."

"Thé, croissant," the young waiter repeated and started toward the kitchen.

"Attends," Trudeau ordered.

Alfred stopped.

"Do you know who this man is, Alfred?"

The waiter stammered an unintelligible reply.

"This man is Canada's greatest living artist. That's who he is."

"Monsieur?"

"Alfred Lajeunesse, meet Marc-Allan Cameron."

Alfred bobbed his head.

Wishing he had skipped breakfast, Mac forced a smile.

"When you get off work, Alfred," Trudeau continued, "you must stop at the Musée des beaux-arts. It's a crime that they have only one Cameron, but it is a magnificent one. Will you do that?"

"Bien sur, M. Trudeau. Oui, M. Trudeau." To Mac, Alfred repeated the only safe words he could think of. "Thé, croissant?"

"Non, non," Trudeau interjected. "Canada's greatest living artist needs more sustenance than tea and a croissant. Wouldn't you agree, Alfred?"

Alfred fidgeted with his jacket sleeve.

"Bring M. Cameron what I'm having."

"Bien sur, M. Trudeau." Alfred backed away as quickly as decorum would allow.

"Smart boy," Trudeau continued to Mac. "He won't be a waiter for long. He got the job because his mother has been one of the house-keepers here for years. It's paying for his business studies at HEC, the École des hautes études commerciales. He'll go far. Maybe even Prime Minister one day." He took a sip of milk. "You don't mind that I ordered for you?"

Mac tried to mask his distaste. Toast with neither butter nor marmalade accompanied by a barely cooked egg sounded, well, gross. That was an Erik word and it perfectly suited the occasion. Once again, he regretted stopping in the Café de Paris for breakfast. "Of course not, Mr. Trudeau."

"I'm not Prime Minister, remember? It's Pierre."

"Sir."

"Not sir, either," Trudeau scolded. "If you insist on calling me sir, you will give me no choice. I will have to start calling you Mr. Cameron."

"Pierre, then," Mac conceded.

"We're practically intimate, you know."

What am I supposed to say to that?

"I look at your work every day," Trudeau continued. "Your *Anna L.* hangs in my study at home and I have your *Expressions* in my office at Heenan Blaikie, which—" He glanced at his watch. "Damn! I have a meeting."

Moments later, Pierre Elliott Trudeau was gone, but not before insisting that Mac come to Cormier House, his historic Pine Avenue residence, for dinner before returning to Nova Scotia. "I want Justin, Sacha and Michel to meet you," he said, shaking Mac's hand. "Oh, and bring your boy and his friend," he called over his shoulder as every pair of eyes in the restaurant followed him out the door.

"Could I have that pot of tea and croissant after all?" Mac asked when Alfred appeared soon after bearing the prime ministerially mandated milk, egg and toast.

"Oui, M. Cameron. Of course. Shall I leave these for you as well?"

"Lord, no."

"Yes," Mac repeated, returning his gaze to the mâitre d'. "Quite the man."

13

After asking Émile to hold a table for him overlooking the Ritz Garden and promising to return in twenty minutes, Mac wandered back through the hotel lobby and out to the street. *No white limo yet.* He crossed Drummond to the Klinkhoff Gallery and smiled up at the bay window and Bernie's painting. It would move inside and be replaced by a poster before the gallery doors opened for the vernissage at five. In the meantime it was attracting admiring gazes from just about everyone who passed by.

"You would be proud of him, Esther," Mac whispered. "Of me, too, I hope." He squinted westward along Sherbrooke. No sign of Bernie's limo. He hesitated for an instant then turned to face the old Berkeley Hotel, ten-story centerpiece of the Maison Alcan, an office and retail complex that had saved a group of heritage buildings from the wrecking ball a few years earlier. With the Klinkhoff and its next-door Victorian twin, the Maison Alcan completed a historic streetscape typical of downtown Montreal's Golden Square Mile, the affluent neighborhood that was home to the city's English-speaking tycoons from the mid-eighteenth century until shortly before World War II. Mac had nearly stayed at the Berkeley back in 1956, but the streamlined art moderne look of the newer Laurentian had seduced him. That wasn't the only thing that seduced him on that trip.

No longer a hotel, the Berkeley still sported its triple-arched entry, which now served a twofold purpose. On the west side and spilling out onto the pavement with a scattering of tables was Café des Artistes, its name a tribute to the prestigious art galleries along the city's most elegant thoroughfare and its 1920s decor an art-deco reimagining of the original Berkeley dining room. Through the center and eastern openings, the Alcan's main doors led into a jewel-like lobby, where a modernized version of the hotel's original brass-doored elevators rose to pricey office suites. Two doors down, in the onetime mansion that anchored the far side of the Alcan compound at Stanley Street was a bookstore specializing in Canadiana: Librairie Atholstan, named for the nineteenth-century newspaper magnate who built it in 1894.

Mac scanned Sherbrooke for Bernie's limousine one last time, then slipped into the bookstore, which occupied most of the building's main floor, its connected rooms having been restored to their Beaux Arts splendor, with high corniced ceilings, carved-marble fireplace-surrounds and reproduction period furniture. Mahogany bookcases set off the store's Wedgwood blue walls and its register sat incongruously atop an ornate, giltwood-style table inset with verde antico marble. The joyful intensity of Glenn Gould's classic recording of Bach's *Goldberg Variations* offered a spirit-lifting backdrop to the somewhat staid setting.

As Mac passed into the front room, which featured new releases and bestsellers and a bin of LPs and CDs, he collided with a tall, spindly woman with angular features. In her mid-seventies, she was dressed in dirt-smudged cream summer slacks, a dusty teal top and a pair of white-and-magenta Adidas, the right one mottled with splotches of dried mud. What looked to be a permanent frown was pasted on her face.

"Excuse me," Mac offered apologetically.

Sadie harrumphed at the man in the light-tan linen suit and white, open-necked cotton shirt. He seemed vaguely familiar, she thought. Probably some gonif of a politician she had seen on the front page of *The Gazette* or being harangued by Barbara Frum on the CBC. *I bet he's just come from the Ritz, where he's been shtupping his mistress and eating and drinking away my tax money.* She harrumphed again, and again when he appeared to be following her toward a series of low-rise displays by the window.

Mac had popped in for a quick browse, mostly to see if the new Margaret Atwood was available. *Cat's Eye.* It was supposed to be about an artist, so of course Mac was curious.

"Next month," the clerk told him.

Then Mac noticed the display for a book called *Sara's Year.* Mac had an artist's memory for detail and he was certain that he had seen the face on the cover before, though not recently. However, the author's name, Sara Schumacher, meant nothing to him.

Next to him, the ill-tempered woman was comparing the store editions of *Sara's Year* to a postcard she had pulled from her purse announcing the book's publication. As one, they reached for the identical copy. The woman glowered at Mac and grabbed it. Mac ignored her and pulled another from the shelf.

Each for individual reasons, Sadie and Mac opened to the first page of *Sara's Year* and began to read.

"Autumn was already dying into winter when Sarah Schumacher and Esther Finkel strode up to Paul Epstein and announced, 'We've come to play.' The thirteen-year-old boy could not believe his ears. 'No way,' he exclaimed and turned his back on them, but not before he sneered, 'Good Jewish girls don't play street hockey.'"

"Oh, my God!" Mac studied the cover more closely. *Sara Schumacher is Esther's Sarah.* Sarah Kaplan. Where had he seen her? He was more certain than ever that he had, somewhere. Where? He continued reading.

"Shit," Sadie muttered, oblivious to the man standing next her. She continued reading.

"That's the story I would have made into a book had I done it fifty years ago like I planned. That book — *Good Jewish Girls Don't*, it would have been called — starts and ends on St. Urbain Street, on what in those days was the heart of Jewish Montreal, and it has a happy ending for everyone, except maybe for Paul Epstein. In that story, good Jewish girls do.

"The story I am about to tell you is a different story, a true story. It starts and ends in a cemetery, and the happiness of the ending isn't so clear. I probably still could have called it *Good Jewish Girls Don't* because in a way that's what it's about — for the real Sarah and the real Esther. So, maybe they are the same story after all. You'll have to decide."

"Shit," Mac said, looking at his watch.

"Got in himmel," Sadie exclaimed, slamming the book shut.

14

Sadie collapsed onto a window seat in the Café des Artistes. In an hour the cafe and sidewalk tables would fill with afternoon shoppers. They would fill up again two hours after that with the nine-to-five crowd stopping in for an after-work cocktail or cappuccino. Now, with its sparse lunch offerings, the restaurant was nearly empty. Only three other tables were occupied: one by a goateed McGill professor scowling over a mountain of summer-term papers, a second by an elderly tourist couple quietly arguing over some arcane local attraction Sadie had never heard of, and a third by two young men in their mid-twenties focused only on each other.

"Faygelech," Sadie grumbled. "Everywhere, faygelech."

The brunt of her contempt, though, was reserved for the twin androgynous Goths, with their spiky black hair, black nail polish and eyeliner, black leather vests over black t-shirts, tight black Levis and black Dr. Martens. "Freaks," Sadie muttered, just loud enough for them to hear her as they reached the door. They gave her the finger before leaving.

At Atholstan's, Sadie had pushed her way in front of the politician, thrown money onto the counter for her copy of *Sara's Year* and fled. Her plan was to walk a block down to the Peel Metro station and get herself home as quickly as possible. Yet the minute she stepped out of the bookstore, it was all she could do to stumble next door into the cafe. Had she ever been this tired? Maybe in those final months before she retired from Morgan's. She still refused to call it The Bay, even though the Hudson's Bay Company had owned it since 1960 and had forced the venerable department store to adopt its name a dozen years later. She certainly would never call it La Baie, and no language law could make her.

Twenty-eight years she had sold ladies coats and dresses at Morgan's; another twenty years before that at Reitman's, starting at the chain's first store on St. Lawrence Boulevard and later helping to open their new store in Snowdon. No surprise that she should find herself in the schmatta business like her parents. Only she worked at the other end of the trade: the selling, not the making. Not that any coats and dresses were made on Park Avenue anymore, like it was when Mama and Papa worked there. Now, it was all cheap chazerai, thrown together in Taiwan or Korea or some other godforsaken place.

Those last years before she retired were the toughest. First, she was forced out of Morgan's tiny Queen Mary Road outlet when those anglo Hudson's Bay bastards closed it. Queen Mary Road was easy for her to get to from home; the main downtown store, not so much. But that's where she had to go or lose her job. She was fifty-nine when that happened. Who else was going to hire her? So, of course she went. Then those crazy Quebec separatists took over the provincial government and her manager told her she would have to learn French if she was going to stay on the sales floor, a sales floor that already exhausted her at twice the size of her old one on Queen Mary Road. Sadie went to the French classes the store made her take, but she could never manage more than a few rudimentary phrases. Suddenly, before she knew it, she was sixty-five and it was all over. Just as well, or they probably would have fired her.

No. As drained as she once felt from her commute, from trying to learn French and from being on her feet all day, this was worse. So much worse. She was more than physically worn out from dragging herself through the cemetery, only to then be dragged downtown. She felt hollowed out, as though there was nothing left inside her.

She glared at *Sara's Year*. She hadn't bothered to wait for a bag, she had been in such a rush to escape the store and that man. Who was he that he was so interested in Sarah Schumacher's story. Why was he buying the book? For that matter, why did she buy it? Had she ever bought a hardcover? If she had, it would have been a long time ago. Lifetimes ago. With Jimmy, it must have been. *Jimmy Harcourt. Whatever happened to Jimmy Harcourt?* She jerked her head sharply, as if to shout, *"No!"* No to Jimmy and no to memories. She didn't want to think about him or about the past. Why, then, had she bought the damned book? Her meager pensions from Morgan's and the government sure didn't cover books she didn't need, books that cost $21.95. Yet how could she not buy it? Esther was in it. No doubt she was, too, and it was full of lies. How dare that Sarah Schumacher poke her big nose into Sadie's family's business. The book was drek. It had to be. *I should bring it back and get my money. Would they take it, I wonder?* She knew they would, and she knew she wouldn't.

The book stared up her from the round, chrome-framed Bakelite table, daring her to open it. Sarah stared up at her from the cover, daring her to read what she had written. *Damn you, Sarah Schumacher. Damn you, Esther. Damn the lot of you.* She shoved the book onto the empty bentwood bistro chair next to her.

"Madame?"

Sadie glanced up, but not far up. The pixie-like server stood barely five feet. Her red hair was cut in a Louise Brooks bob to match the cafe's 1920s theme; her white-aproned, below-the-knee black waitress dress, likewise. Her name tag said Sylvie.

"A coffee," Sadie said more brusquely than she intended. "None of those silly cappuccino things. A plain coffee. You have plain coffee?"

"Of course. I'm just brewing some fresh. Cream and sugar?"

"No. Yes. Milk, no sugar. You have two percent?"

"I don't think so. I'll check." Sylvie started toward the kitchen, then turned to look back. The woman was staring out the window. Her lips were moving, but Sylvie was too far away to hear what she was saying or if she was saying anything at all. The woman didn't look crazy, but you never knew. You got all kinds coming into a downtown cafe, even on Sherbrooke Street.

Sylvie returned five minutes later with a mug of black coffee and two matching creamers. Sadie continued to stare out to the street.

"Ma'am?"

Sadie turned slowly to face a startled Sylvie. The woman's face was lined and haggard. If it was possible to age ten years in a few minutes, this woman had done it. Although her right hand was pressed onto to her left, Sylvie could detect the slight tremor she was attempting to mask.

Sylvie placed the mug in front of Sadie. "I couldn't find any two percent," she said, "but I did find some skim." She placed the creamers on the table. "So I brought you one of each: a skim and a whole milk, in case you want to mix your own sort-of two percent."

Sadie said nothing.

"Ma'am? Are you all right?"

Sadie opened her mouth to deliver her customary sharp retort, then shut it. Instead, she nodded and attempted to offer a smile to the friendly waitress. What emerged instead was a pained grimace.

"If you need anything else…" Sylvie retreated.

What I need, you can't give me. No one can give it to me.

Sadie returned her gaze to the window. She didn't notice the man from the bookstore hurry past, nor did she see a white Mercedes-Benz limousine pull up to the curb a few minutes later. All she saw, again, was her own reflection.

15

Sylvie watched the old woman through the circular window in the swinging kitchen doors. After a few minutes she turned away, passing through the empty kitchen and into a tiny room in the back of the cafe. Stacks of bills, menus, catalogs, order sheets and other papers leaned perilously against each other, Pisa-tower-like, atop a cluttered oak desk pushed into the corner. Pinned above it was a series of rough charcoal sketches, artists' renderings of a proposed expansion, upward to the Berkeley's second floor.

A glass étagère, as sleekly ordered as the desk was not, rose up to the ceiling against the opposite wall, its bank of silvery Pioneer stereo components emitting the only light in the burrow of an office. LPs packed the bottom two shelves. The shelving above the receiver, turntable, cassette deck and CD player was jammed with tapes and compact discs. A pair of thigh-high Acoustic Research speakers flanked the bookcase, and a tangle of wires snaked out of the room, linking the system to four remote speakers in the dining room, all tucked discreetly out of view so as not to dilute the 1920s feel of the space. Little of the music was authentic to the 1920s and 1930s. Instead, it was dominated by retreads: contemporary recordings of period music, along with soundtracks and original cast recordings of shows like *The Boyfriend, Thoroughly Modern Millie, Dames at Sea* and *No, No, Nanette.*

Sylvie thumbed through the compact discs. She was saving up to get a player of her own; they had been around for only a few years and were still too expensive for her student budget. But CDs didn't need to be flipped like LPs did, which made them perfect for a restaurant. It had taken some persuading on Sylvie's part to get owner

Greg Archambault to add a CD player to his sound system. He was addicted to vinyl and had only reluctantly added an auto-reverse cassette deck the previous year because it meant that music could play continuously. Now, though, he was hooked on CDs, and spent all his spare time — and cash — over at Sam the Record Man, buying up his favorites as they were rereleased on disc.

Sylvie picked out a Helen Forrest recording — right era for the song, wrong era for the singer — popped open the CD drawer and dropped the disc in.

I'm mad about the boy

I know it's stupid to be mad about the boy

She returned to the kitchen door and peered out into the restaurant. No one looked like they needed help, except for the old woman, and Sylvie was sure that no waitress could offer the kind of help she needed.

If only she could read lips.

16

"You are a coward," the face in the window said.

"You don't know what you're talking about," Sadie snapped.

"I'm talking about lots of things. So many things, I wouldn't know where to begin."

"Then don't," Sadie snarled.

"I'll start with one, an easy one."

"I'm not listening."

"Of course, you are. Pick up the book, Sarah's book."

Sadie shook her head.

"How hard is it to pick up a book?"

"I'm not talking to you. You're not real."

"What are you afraid of?"

"Lies. People are always telling lies about me." Hadn't the boys told lies about her in school? That she was easy. They called her easy because she wasn't. Because she wasn't pretty like the other girls, like her sister, they assumed things. When she told them they assumed wrong, they called her a nafkeh, a slut. Not to her face, of course. But one boy told another boy told another boy told his girl-friend who told her best friend and on and on. It didn't take long before all of Baron Byng believed it. The few who didn't, that was almost worse. They didn't think anyone would ever want to go with her, so it couldn't be possible. And Esther? She never knew what Esther believed. But why wouldn't she believe it?

"Not Jimmy. He never believed the lies."

Sadie didn't want to talk about Jimmy.

"Why should it matter so much now? Baron Byng was a long time ago."

"It didn't stop there," Sadie said. Hadn't the other salesgirls told lies about her at Reitman's? That's why she left. She was a good seller. The best. She could sell a bikini to an Eskimo, everyone used to say.

"They don't call them Eskimos anymore," the face reproached.

"They don't call it Morgan's anymore," Sadie retorted. "And now it's not even Reitman's, its Reitmans." She pronounced it Reetmans. "No apostrophe because of those separatists, and saying it wrong because of the goyim. That doesn't change anything. That doesn't change the lies." She paused. "Because I was so good, because I was better than any of the other girls, they made it so the manager thought I was stealing. Like I would steal. From Reitman's? I may be lots of things, but I'm no thief. Not then. Not now. But that Mrs. Gutkind, she believed the girls. 'Her special girls,' she called them."

"What happened?"

"You know what happened. I wasn't so special. Gutkind said that if I quit, she wouldn't fire me and she would say nothing. She would write me a reference. So I quit. What else was I going to do? That's how I ended up around the corner at Morgan's." She sipped her coffee. It was good coffee, even black. She had forgotten to mix the creamers that Sylvie brought. That wasn't true. She hadn't so much forgotten as she wasn't thinking coffee and creamers. Coffee and creamers was Café des Artistes in August 1988. But it wasn't August 1988 for her and that wasn't Sherbrooke Street through the window. It was the sales floor at Morgan's on Queen Mary Road, the ladies' coats and dress department, and it was September 1950.

"I was smarter at Morgan's," she continued. "There, I made sure the other girls were better sellers than me." She slammed her mug down. Coffee slopped onto the table.

Sylvie started over with a rag, saw the look of fury on Sadie's face and decided that there was an emergency in the kitchen. She disappeared back through the swinging doors.

"That's when I decided," Sadie declared.

"Decided? Decided what?"

"That I would never do my best again, that I would never stand out again, that I would never make anyone jealous enough of me to lie about me. Not ever again."

"Did it work?"

"Of course it didn't work." Sadie snatched *Sara's Year* from the chair and pushed it against the window, into her reflection. "More lies."

"You don't know that."

"I know." Sadie let the book slide down to the table. "I know," she whispered.

17

With the engine idling, the driver's door of the Mercedes limousine opened and a liveried chauffeur emerged. He dodged the rushing river of Sherbrooke Street traffic and darted around the front of the car to open the rear door, reaching in to help Sarah. Erik clambered out after her and they both turned to face Galérie Walter Klinkhoff. Bernie climbed out last. He pressed a few bills into the driver's hand and joined Erik and Sarah as the limo drove off.

"I needed to come here first," Sarah said, contemplating her fifteen-year-old self in the gallery window. "Before the Ritz. You don't mind?"

"How could I mind after I stood you up both those years?" Bernie put his arm around Sarah. "I'm sorry about that. I'm sorry I didn't keep my part of the bargain."

"What's that?" Sarah pointed to the painting. "Of course you kept your part of the bargain."

Bernie tried to steer Sarah away from the gallery and toward the Ritz. "Mac will be waiting for us."

Sarah resisted, her eyes glued to the painting in front of her. "Your Mac has waited almost a half a century to meet me. A few minutes more shouldn't matter. Anyhow, he's already seen me. He just doesn't know it yet. You think he'll recognize me after thirty-two years?"

"I bet you haven't changed a bit," Erik said, grinning.

"A few more pounds." Sarah patted her ample stomach. "Plus a lot more wrinkles and no more red in my hair. Other than that I'm exactly the same. Like you are after thirty-two years."

"How about after twenty-eight? I haven't been around thirty-two years."

"You're only a baby!" Sarah exclaimed, and to Bernie: "You cradle-robber, you."

Bernie laughed. "If you're going to make Mac wait, do you want to go in? I've told Mr. Klinkhoff all about you. I know he would give you a private tour."

"For that, I can wait." She stepped closer to the building, her eyes still on Bernie's painting. "Look at you," she said, her voice tinged with awe. "Look at me."

"Like I said—" Erik pivoted from painting to Sarah and back. "You haven't changed a bit."

Sarah chuckled. "You caught yourself a good one," she said to Bernie. "He's a lying flatterer, but he's cute." She pinched Erik's cheek.

"I know I did." Bernie pinched Erik's butt.

Erik slapped his hand then grabbed it.

"So, how did you and this random artist boy, you know…?"

"Get into each other's pants?" Erik asked.

"Erik!"

"That part, I don't need to know details."

"Now you've embarrassed her," Bernie scolded.

"Embarrassed? Me? Not a chance. Just because I don't need details doesn't mean I don't want to know what's going on. In general terms, you know. More or less."

"From what Bernie's told me, it's because of you we're together. So, thank you."

"I'm glad. It's because I'm a nag. Once a Jewish mother, always a Jewish mother."

"Not only Jewish mothers, you know. Norwegian mothers are just as bad. I should know."

"So?" Sarah asked. "What happened? Inquiring minds want to know."

"He seduced me." Erik giggled.

"I did not."

"Who walked into whose gallery?"

"Yes, but—"

"And who called me the next day all stuttery and nervous?"

Bernie pulled a business card from his wallet. Strikingly colored scarlet, teal and yellow, it bore Erik's name, along with his old Westmount phone number and post office box. It had been ripped into eight pieces and taped back together again. "I keep this with me all the time," he said, "to remind me what I almost lost."

"You're sweet." Erik kissed him on the cheek.

"I know." Bernie kissed him back. "Besides, I came by him honestly," he said to Sarah. "'Montreal Jew swept off feet by Nova Scotia artist.' Sound familiar?"

"You got to keep yours. I'm glad." Sarah smiled sadly at the teenaged Esther in the painting. "Not like your mother."

"No," Bernie said. "Not like my mother. But without Mom, none of us would be standing here, would we?"

Sarah, Bernie and Erik fell into a reflective silence, each pulled into thoughts of the woman who, in dying when she did, so dramatically transformed their lives.

"So, Ms. Schumacher," Bernie continued after the angry blare of a car horn pulled them back into the present moment, "what were you doing all those years, when you weren't shlepping out to the cemetery for no reason?"

"And when I wasn't worrying about what happened to you?"

"That, too."

"I was doing what I promised to do. I was doing that." She rapped the copy of Sara's Year in Erik's hand. "And you? You must have been studying art to make such a picture...so good a picture. At Concordia University, maybe, like Sylvie Ryan? You remember Sylvie from Dominique's?"

"Sure. Dominique's daughter. You wouldn't let her have my first sketch. You said I would need it to paint that." He pointed to *At Stella's.* "I didn't believe you."

"I know you didn't. There were lots of things you didn't believe that day."

"I ended up believing them. All of them."

"Sylvie should know about this, don't you think?"

"She does. We ran into her in Café des Artistes yesterday." He jerked his head toward the restaurant. "She works there part-time. She'll be at the opening later, when she gets off. Dominique, too, if she can make it."

"Everyone knew about this painting except for me?" Sarah asked.

"Pretty much." Bernie grinned.

"And if I hadn't shown up at the cemetery?"

"I would have sent that hunky limo driver to kidnap you. I saw how he was ogling you."

Sarah smacked him with her purse. "So, you didn't answer my question about school. I couldn't ask Freda Kimmel whether you were at Concordia. She died. She was in the hospital same time I was. I was lucky. I got out alive."

"Does that mean they took her awful painting down from next to Anne Savage's at the Westmount Library?"

"If Evelyn Waugh had her way, it would be long gone," Sarah said. "Instead, she is. Evelyn retired from the library last year. The new librarian there is younger than your boyfriend here. Heather something. I don't even know if she has a last name. She's too young, maybe, to have a last name. She's so young, she probably likes what Freda painted."

"I doubt it. Nobody could like it. What was it called? *Silly Shards*? No, *Silver Shards*." He turned to Erik. "You remember it, hon?"

"Remember it? I have nightmares about it. About Freda, too. I took a class with her once. She was one crazy lady."

"She was a crazy teenager, too, back when we were at Baron Byng together. I could tell you stories," Sarah said, "but not now. Never mind Freda Kimmel. Answer my question, already. Did you study at Concordia or at that Halifax art college, like your Erik here, to get so good? Or in Toronto, at the art school there?"

"None of those places."

"Where, then?"

"Private tutoring," Bernie replied, "from a master in the rural wilderness of Nova Scotia."

"Don't let him fool you," Erik said. "I had to bust my ass for years at both NSCAD and Concordia, but this boy wonder here is a natural. Ask Mac. Sure, he guided him a bit. Bernie did the rest by himself, though. He's amazing. And now he's in the Klinkhoff."

"Anne Savage's gallery," they chanted in unison and burst out laughing, as they headed back toward the Ritz, never noticing the doleful woman sitting in the window of the cafe next door, gazing blankly out the window and seeing nothing but her own face staring back at her.

1984

18

Mac scowled at the blank canvas resting on the easel in front of him. It scowled back, as it had every day for nearly forty years. Not this same canvas, of course, and not from this same spot. Mac had replaced it dozens of times — sometimes hoping a different size would free him; other times, praying that shifting the easel a few yards back or to the left or right would somehow make a difference. He even attempted different media: One week he would set out charcoal, another week it would be watercolors or chalk pastels. For two months two years earlier, he had reached back in time to the oils he started out with in his twenties, before abandoning them and returning to acrylics, his medium of choice for more than a decade.

Music, too, failed to inspire him. He scoured used record shops for the songs he and Esther had shared: "Rumors are Flying" and "To Each His Own" from their first time together, in Halifax in 1946, and *The King and I* movie soundtrack from their second and final time, in Montreal ten years later. "We'll Meet Again" was an exception. That was the one piece of music that he could not bring himself to hear again.

Only recently he had come across Bernard Hermann's score for *Anna and the King of Siam* in a dollar bin outside a Wolfville thrift shop. The LP was worn and scratched, barely playable, much like he felt about himself these days. It didn't draw the painting out of him, either.

Anna and the King of Siam. That's where he and Esther met, in Halifax at the premiere screening of the Irene Dunne/Rex Harrison film at the old Capitol Theatre on Barrington Street. Neither was out looking for love that day in the drizzly November gloom: Esther was married to Morris Freed; Mac was married to his art. Yet they both found it, at first sight, as corny as it still sounded all these years later.

The Capitol was gone now, for just over a decade. Mac had stood across the street that Saturday, as close as the demolition crew would let him, and watched the wrecking ball smash into the old building again and again, feeling each thunderous blow as though he not the landmark theater were its target. And as each piece of wall crumbled and crumpled in a billow of choking dust, a piece of him crumbled and crumpled with it. He stayed the full three hours, his face streaked with tears, until a mountain of rubble was all that remained of the old movie palace. That and a fragment of the marquee, proclaiming the final double bill from six weeks earlier: *Son of Flubber* and *Superdad.*

Mac sat through both screenings at the Capitol that final week. The theater was no longer the elegant showpiece it had been in November 1946. The carpets and seats were worn. Paint and plaster were cracked and peeling. Some of the baronial-style fixtures had already been ripped out and sold. Mac had hoped to sit in the front row of the mezzanine, where he and Esther sat, where he first knew that there could be no life for him without this woman he had just met. But the mezzanine had closed years before, according to the gum-cracking teenager selling overpriced popcorn and candy bars. Instead, Mac sat in the back row, the auditorium empty except for a scattering of other middle-aged Haligonians, like him less interested in the flickering Disney offerings onscreen than in the memory-steeped walls of the now-tatty theater.

When one final swing of the wrecking ball pulverized the marquee, Mac stumbled up Spring Garden Road to the Public Gardens. Even as its trees sprouted luminous green buds and its flowerbeds were vibrant with newly planted color this May afternoon, to Mac it was infinitely more dead-feeling than it had been that wintry day all those years earlier, when the trees were bare and flowerbeds had been stripped…but Esther walked at his side.

The following week, he packed up his Dartmouth home and studio and moved back across Halifax Harbour into the city. Maybe being back in Halifax would somehow return Esther to him.

Like every other time he moved his studio, Mac put his Celtic superstitions to work on the elusive portrait: He burned the current blank canvas before leaving the old studio and stretched a fresh one as his first act in the new space.

Mac had moved his studio often over the years. His first, after he arrived in Canada from Scotland and enrolled in the Nova Scotia College of Art, was in downtown Halifax. It was a stereotypical garret that blazed stiflingly in the summer, forcing him to paint in his underwear. In winter, as gale winds off the Atlantic thrust through the widening gaps in the shingle siding, he wore fingerless gloves and as many shirts, sweaters, jackets and scarves as he could and retain some semblance of mobility.

In the years after graduation, Mac moved all over Halifax, Dartmouth and Bedford as his stature in the Canadian art world grew, landing finally in a bright, spacious home on affluent Bloomingdale Terrace. From there, it was a brisk, thirty-minute walk across town to his office and studio back at the art college.

Now, decades after that drafty attic, he had traded city life, with its teaching responsibilities and social obligations, for the solitude of rural Kings County and a rambling farmhouse in the agricultural foothills of North Mountain seventy miles away. And still this painting, the only one that had truly ever mattered, eluded him.

Mac draped a cloth over the canvas to avoid its accusing stare and dropped to the worn love seat by the window. He turned his back on his studio, with its wall of framed honors and awards and its racks of paints, brushes and other supplies, and gazed out on maples aflame with fall colors and apple orchards heavy with ripe fruit. His creative output was no less abundant. Finished abstracts, darkening in tone and hue with each passing year, lay scattered around the room. More, many more, had found homes in galleries and art museums across Canada and around the world. One even hung in the White House, a rare contemporary piece by a non-American, a gift a few years earlier from Prime Minister Pierre Trudeau to President Jimmy Carter.

All the success and acclaim paled next to this singular failure.

"Esther," he sighed. "Where are you?"

Mac stared at the door of Room 1612. Its final click echoed noisily in his skull, along with Esther's final, trembling words: "You will never know all the gifts you have given me. You will never know how grateful I am…how grateful I will always be." She wouldn't let him respond. She touched her fingers to his lips when he tried, then she stroked his cheek, rose and, without looking back, walked out of the room and out of his life, again.

Mac let his head drop back to the hotel pillow, only to be enveloped in the flowery fragrance of Esther's Plaisir perfume and the musky scent of their recent lovemaking. He closed his eyes and replayed the day's extraordinary events. What could he have said differently that would have altered this outcome? What could he have done differently that would have kept Esther by his side, that would have kept her next to him, forever?

It had all seemed so magical, coincidence piled on top of pleasing coincidence, from the moment he heard that Anne Savage would be opening a rare one-woman show to discovering, once he had made his travel plans, that *The King and I* would be opening in Montreal on that same day. This day.

Anne Savage and Anna Leonowens: two of his greatest idols. While his standing in the art world now eclipsed hers, Mac had been an Anne Savage fan since that exhibition at the Tate before the war. That Savage had been Esther's high school art teacher at about the same time and had remained a powerful influence in her life in the years that followed only added to the appeal.

The same was true with Anna Leonowens. His mother introduced him to Margaret Langdon's fictionalized biography during the war, while he was home on leave, and he was instantly drawn to Anna's irrepressible spirit. When he later learned that Leonowens had established what was now the Nova Scotia College of Art, he knew that that was where he had to pursue his dreams of becoming an artist. His first show and the first glimmerings of his eventual fame were also tied up with Anna: at the Leonowens-Fyshe Gallery.

Esther, he would later learn, was just as crazy about Anna. That's why they had found themselves, and each other, at the Capitol the day *Anna and the King of Siam* opened in Halifax. That's why, a decade later, Anna would throw them back together here in Montreal for the opening of *The King and I*.

He glanced at the bedside clock radio. It was nearly four. If he was going to get to the YWCA by five for the Anne Savage vernissage, he would have to get up, shower and get dressed. The Y was barely a ten-minute walk from the Laurentian Hotel, but he was a mess. He didn't move. Instead, he switched on the clock radio on the nightstand. The Platters assaulted him with their latest hit, "My Prayer."

My prayer is to linger with you
At the end of the day in a dream that's divine
My prayer and the answer you give
May they still be the same for as long as we live
That you'll always be there at the end of my prayer

He turned his face into the pillow, inhaled Esther's scent and wept.

A rooster's raucous crow catapulted Mac back to the present. He had inherited Rocky with the house, the only rooster he had ever met that couldn't tell time. Rocky cock-a-doodle-do'd as easily at midnight as at noon, never made a sound at dawn and rarely crowed at the same time two days running. He also hated the barn and spent his days flouncing back and forth in front of the kitchen door. The instant Mac opened it, Rocky would storm through, wings flapping maniacally, and make a beeline for the living room and his preferred roost, which also happened to be Mac's favorite armchair. Only a swinging broom would budge him. Sometimes.

Mac reached for his easel. Should he unveil the canvas for another try? No. What was the point? He pulled his hand back and left the studio, trading it for the living room and Rocky's conveniently if uncharacteristically vacant chair. He lit a fire and picked up the morning's *Chronicle-Herald* crossword, abandoned earlier when he got stuck on an eleven-letter word for "Dixie dilettante."

"Alabamateur," Mac said aloud and inked in the clue. The next clue was "artists' pads." He tapped the five blank squares with his Parker Jotter. "Lofts," he said. He held the pen over the newspaper, writing nothing. After a minute he dropped the paper, pocketed his ballpoint and reached for the poker. He stabbed at the hardwood log until sparks raced up the chimney, tossed the newspaper with its unfinished crossword on top of it, watched it ignite, then collapsed back into his chair.

Mac was not a sentimental man. Once his mother died, he never returned to Glasgow; Nova Scotia was Scotland enough for him. Even his Scottish burr, never pronounced, had flattened through his years in Canada, and his accent was now an untraceable blend of old country and new. He also had no attachment to his completed paintings; once they left his studio, he didn't care if he ever saw them again. Some he preferred never to see again.

But Esther? Mac reached into a side-table drawer and pulled out his two *Anna* ticket stubs, faded and cottony soft from having been so often rubbed between his fingers. Esther was different. All these years later, he still couldn't get her out of his system. He was sixty-six and he felt like the twenty-eight-year-old who had first opened his umbrella for her in front of the Capitol.

He warmed at the memory and half-smiled. Esther had thought he was a soldier or sailor trying to pick her up. He had been an airman during the war, an RAF pilot. And he wasn't trying to pick her up…at least not until she spun around, furious at his cheek, and her fury melted at the sight of him. That was when he knew he couldn't live without her.

Yet he had. Alone.

Of course, he dated once in a while. Friends were always trying to fix him up. He even got close to marriage once. He and Adele Cartwright, one of his colleagues at NSCAD, went together for five years and everyone expected them to marry. When Mac finally asked, Adele turned him down. "I can't compete," was all she said. She left for Toronto soon after, for a job at the Ontario College of Art. Last Mac heard she was married and was a curator at the Vancouver Art Gallery.

After his experience with Adele, Mac realized that Esther's ghost would never stop inserting itself between him and other women. He rarely dated after that.

If Mac had exorcised other of his demons by painting them, that particular form of therapy didn't work with Esther. She refused to be painted.

19

Bernie shut his eyes and leaned back into the driver's seat. It was so quiet here, almost too quiet for the city boy he had always been. Almost too quiet, but not quite. He needed stillness right now, needed to be free of distraction so he could collect his thoughts before starting up the car and turning into the next drive.

So many thoughts to collect. Was it possible that these were his first peaceful moments since he walked out on his mother's funeral two months earlier? It sure felt like it. From that instant until this one, chaotic upheaval had been the norm, a relentless rollercoaster of heart-stopping inner and outer revolution.

The morning of the funeral, he had woken up a conservative, somewhat dull tax accountant for Revenue Canada, a faceless back-office bureaucrat who may not have loved his job, but didn't think he hated it. He had never been much of a playboy with the women, nor had he been a monk. Although he dated occasionally, he was equally happy with a good book or an old movie on the VCR. Then, there were his parents. No one really knows his parents, and Bernie knew less than most, at least about his father, a civil service lawyer who died when Bernie was six. As for his mother, she always seemed to be struggling — first as a single parent, then through two unfortunate marriages until, in the end, cancer took her.

Within days of her death, most of the "facts" of his life turned out not to be facts at all. They disintegrated like some ancient parchment, along with much of his identity. He quit a government job that he realized he detested and set out to explore artistic gifts he never knew he possessed. His heterosexuality was suddenly in doubt when a disturbingly intriguing artist named Erik Donnekin began flirting with him. And his parents? His mother, he learned, had secret passions he could never have suspected. As for his father…

Bernie opened his eyes. Hubbard Mountain Road was idyllic on this autumn afternoon. On one side of the gravel, stands of fiery oak and maple encircled a sprawling clapboard farmhouse painted a cheery yellow and white; on the other, ripe, red McIntosh apples freckled a densely planted orchard. Fifty yards ahead, the dirt road disappeared into the spruce-lined drive that hid his destination.

What would he say to the man who lived at the end of that drive, the man who was his father, the man who didn't know he was his father? Bernie had been asking himself the same question since the afternoon of his mother's funeral, since the shocking moment when Sarah Swartz revealed that Morris Freed was not his father at all. It had taken Bernie most of those two months to track down the elusive and now-reclusive Marc-Allan Cameron, the man who had been one half of his mother's secret, abandoned passion. Artistic ambition had been the other half.

Three-thirty, according to the clock in the dashboard. Bernie didn't even know if Mac was home. If he wasn't, Bernie would wait. It had taken all his courage to come this far. If he drove back to his Wolfville B&B, he might never return. He reached for the key, still in the ignition. *No. Not yet.* He let his hand drop to the coffee-table book that sat next to him on the passenger seat. *MAC: A Cameron Retrospective.* Once upon a time, Bernie would have stared at the incandescent abstracts in confused frustration. Once upon a time, all this would have been disturbingly alien.

Once upon a time, that would have mattered.

Bernie still didn't understand most of what he was seeing in this book that he had thumbed through countless times over the past two months. Erik had helped him to be okay with not understanding. Erik had helped him to be okay with many things…more things than any twenty-seven-year-old should need help with.

"Abstract expressionism, sort of." That's how Erik described Mac's work…Bernie's father's work.

As for Mac, he refused to be labeled, encouraging all artists to take the same stance. "Labels are for critics and theorists. Artists paint what they paint." Bernie read those words for the umpteenth time in Mac's essay at the front of the book. They were the same words Erik quoted back at him, from the days when Mac was Erik's professor at NSCAD.

Bernie smiled at the thought of Erik, walking home to his tiny Westmount apartment from Concordia right now. His boyfriend. Whoever would have thought that Bernie Freed would be describing anyone as his "boyfriend," let alone an artist from Nova Scotia, let alone one who grew up fifteen miles from where Bernie was sitting.

My lover is an artist from Nova Scotia. My mother's lover, my father, was an artist from Nova Scotia.

Bernie found it difficult to believe all the coincidences — Jung would have called them synchronicities — that had brought him to rural Nova Scotia on this autumn afternoon. Ironies, too. So many, he could fill a book with them all. If he was a writer, he could. *Let Sarah do it. She's the writer. I'm the artist.*

"I'm the artist." He spoke the words aloud, as he had so often recently, still not fully believing them.

"Believe it." Erik's voice. It would be Sarah's, too, only he wouldn't be seeing her again for nearly a year.

Bernie set the book down and stepped out of the car, his mother's burgundy Toyota Corolla. He could have flown out, but he had needed to slow down after the whirlwind that was Erik…the whirlwind that had been his life since the funeral. Besides, he hadn't known what to expect and couldn't know how long he might need to be away. The two-day drive had been something of a meditation, what felt like the first time he could breathe and still be in motion. And the three-hour ferry ride across the Bay of Fundy from New Brunswick to Nova Scotia had been his first opportunity to try out his traveling art kit: the pencils and pastels he had picked up at Le Boulevard des Arts to fill out the artist's starter kit from Sarah that launched it all. He had sketched all over the Princess of Acadia, braving the icy winds on deck to draw bits and pieces of the fittings: benches, railings and lifeboats, not to mention parts of the boat he had no names for. He even quick-sketched some of the crew. "Art practice," one of his books called it.

The air was much warmer here in the Annapolis Valley, yet it was still cool in October. Bernie tilted his face up to the sky, closed his eyes and let the sun's heat wash over him. Although he had not yet met Mac and had not seen much of Nova Scotia, it felt good to be here. It felt right. It was almost as if some ineffable something about this place touched his heart in a way that Montreal never had, as if this tiny slice of a tiny province eight hundred miles away from what he had always known to be home felt like home in a way that his hometown never had.

Bernie opened his eyes, his gaze settling on the nearest row of apple trees, just a few steps away. Macs. *Perfect.* He glanced around to make sure no one was watching and quickly plucked an apple. Juice squirted into his beard and onto his glasses as he took a bite. Another first: He had never picked an apple, had never knowingly tasted any fruit fresh from the tree. Apart from summer camp, which he had despised, he had barely spent any time out of the city. McIntosh apples were what his mother bought when he was growing up, but he didn't remember any Mac having been as sweet as this one.

When he was finished, he flung the core into the orchard, wiped his face and hands on a handkerchief, stepped back into the Corolla and turned the key.

20

A colonnade of mature maples formed a scarlet canopy over Eden Road on this gilded October afternoon, autumn's final gift of warmth and color before the gray, gloomy chill of November would plunge Montreal into its first bitter taste of winter. Bicycles raced up and down the street, weaving carelessly around the passel of hockey stick-wielding boys who chased each other and a dirty tennis ball noisily across the cracked pavement.

Thwack!

Sadie winced as stick met ball. Her shoulders tensed and she jerked around reflexively, ready to leap to safety if necessary. But boys, sticks and ball were turning down Marlboro Road behind her, headed away from her destination at the end of the street.

I should never have come. What kind of masochist am I that I came?

Sadie couldn't see the house yet. A few weeks from now, the leaves would be off the trees and the view would be clearer. A few weeks from now, the SOLD sign would be down and someone would have moved into the house. Her house it should have been, not some stranger's. Like Gerry Rosenbaum should have been her husband, not Esther's. Harold Coopersmith, too.

Maybe Gerry was a little bit of a crook, but I could have protected him. I could have found a way to fix things, to fix him, to keep him out of jail. Then I would have found a way to keep him honest, to make him good. Not like Esther did. Esther abandoned him, walked away from him when he needed her most.

Four houses. Three houses. Two houses…

Sadie stood in front of 2158 Eden Road. The modest brick-and-fieldstone bungalow looked much the same as it had the last time she saw it, the day she moved out. The day she was pushed out. Well, not exactly the same. That August day, the maple was thick with leaves, sweet alyssum carpeted the rock garden in white and purple, and the forsythia bordering the front walk was neatly trimmed. Today, the flowers were dead, the shrubbery was overgrown and the lawn was flecked with dandelions. Who had made sure the lawn was mowed and the garden tended? She had.

Six months she had lived here, taking care of that ingrate of a sister of hers…washing her, feeding her, cleaning up after her, making sure she made it to her doctors' appointments, her radiation appointments, her chemotherapy appointments. Watching the house while she was in the hospital. It was more than that tenant Mona would ever have done for Esther. Much more. That's why Mona had to go, so Sadie could move in to take care of her sister.

So, what did her sister do? She left this house and everything else — *everything* — to that faygele son of hers. And what did he do? Throw her out on her tuches before shiva was barely over.

Why did I come? Because the thought of going home to her dark, dank basement apartment was more than she could bear. Because even with Esther dead, this empty house felt more alive than her apartment ever had, that one-room hole in the ground that felt more like a grave than any kind of place for the living.

Harold had suggested she move, but where else could she go on her miserly pension? It wasn't like he offered to pay anything to help, and he had all that money from when he left the university. Still, he was a good man. He was. *Now that Esther's gone, he can come back to me. After a suitable time, of course.*

Sadie glared at the house, spit on the lawn and walked on, the sound of boys and street hockey fading into the distance behind her.

He won't come back. They never come back. None of them. Not Harold. Not Gerry. She turned down Johnson Avenue, ignoring the temptation to look back.

And not Jimmy. Especially not Jimmy.

21

Mac shoved the ticket stubs back into the drawer and pulled his copy of *Anne Savage: Portrait of a Canadian Artist* down from the shelf next to the fireplace. He opened it to page sixty, its corner nearly as well-thumbed as the *Anna* tickets, and as he had done dozens of times over the years, squinted at a grainy photo of Anne Savage's Baron Byng High School art room to see if he could recognize a teenage Esther among the students. Was she one of the girls at their desks hunched over drawing paper? Was she one of the ones focused on the costumed model posing atop a long wooden table? Was she the model? Or was she there at all? Anne Savage, overseeing the scene from the back of her classroom, would know. But Anne Savage was dead.

Mac had flown back to Montreal for her funeral thirteen years earlier. Of course, he had wanted to pay tribute to Annie. He owed her a lot. But if he was honest, his real reason for being at the service was in the hope that he might catch a glimpse of Esther. No luck. If she was there, he missed her.

As he had also done more often over the years than he cared to admit, Mac picked up the phone and dialed long-distance directory assistance, first for Montreal, then for Halifax. Just in case, he also tried Ottawa, Winnipeg and Vancouver. This time, he added Calgary, Edmonton and Victoria. No Morris Freed. No Esther Freed.

He set the phone down and switched on the stereo.

I just called to say I love you
I just called to say how much I care
I just called to say I love you
And I mean it from the bottom of my heart

"Perfect," Mac muttered. He punched the power button on the Sony receiver to silence Stevie Wonder.

Maybe I should never have retired from NSCAD. Maybe I should never have given up teaching. Maybe I should never have left Halifax. All I do now is rattle around this house, and all I paint is everything but the one painting I really want to paint.

Rocky's squawking interrupted his increasingly frequent descent into self-pity. *Who needs a guard dog when I have a killer rooster?* He heard a vehicle pull into the drive, a door slam shut and a rap on the kitchen window. No one used front doors here. *It must be Ian Ferguson with the apples.*

"It's open," Mac called. "You can leave them inside the door."

No reply. He wasn't surprised. Ian Ferguson was a taciturn sort. His Rita was the chatty one. Rita would undoubtedly level a nonstop volley of neighborhood gossip at him when he dropped by later for coffee. As usual he would offer to pay for the apples. As usual they would refuse.

"Macs for our Mac," Ian would say and not much else as Rita thrust a mammoth slice of her oven-fresh homemade apple pie at him as soon as he sat down in the Fergusons' never-renovated 1950s kitchen. Rita would make him take the rest of the pie home, along with a tin of her melt-in-your-mouth shortbread or hard-as-rock oatcakes. She always did.

The kitchen's yellow-swirl Formica table, unfailingly scrubbed to a mirror-like sheen, and matching vinyl chairs, nearly as shiny, would carry a hefty price tag in one of the vintage stores on Toronto's Queen Street West. But along with the rest of the farmhouse's original furniture, fixtures and appliances, they belonged in their natural habitat, just as Ian and Rita did.

Mac was grateful to the elderly couple. In a community only superficially welcoming to outsiders, the Fergusons had adopted him almost immediately; to replace their only son, he suspected, killed in World War II.

Mac was the lucky one, if surviving a war that claimed most of your friends could be considered a lucky thing. First, he was lucky to have survived the Battle of Britain. Then when he was shot down south of Calais a year later, luck was with him again: He managed to parachute to safety, and although he broke his right leg on impact, he was found by a sympathetic French farmer whose brother-in-law was, luckily, a sympathetic doctor. Mac sat out the next year a few miles outside Le Touquet, masquerading as the farmer's mute brother. He was smuggled back across the English Channel in 1943, just in time to get suited up for the Battle of Berlin, which, luckily, he made it through without injury. Luck was with him again when the war ended: Mac was among the first British servicemen to be demobilized in a process that, for some, dragged on for eighteen months. He was home by July 1945 and, in one final stroke of luck, managed to snag a seat a few months later on an American Overseas Airlines DC-4. The airline had recently launched regularly scheduled trans-atlantic service between London and New York. Mac got off the *Flagship Copenhagen* at Gander, made his way across Newfoundland to the ferry docks at Port aux Basques, crossed over to Nova Scotia on the *SS Burgeo* and was in Halifax by Christmas.

According to Aunt Emmeline his wartime good fortune was nothing less than Destiny, with a capital D. "How could you die when you were fated to create Great Art?" she asked again and again.

"I don't know about the great part," he replied once. "I do know that every time I was shot at, which was often, and all through that tedious, treacherous time in Le Touquet, art kept me going. It was the only thing that kept me going. I would remember those paintings at the Tate, especially Anne Savage's *The Plough*, and I would remember how it felt to paint my own, once you got me going, that is. I would imagine that I was holding a brush and letting it guide my hand across the canvas. I could almost believe that what I was painting in my head was real, was right in front of me. In those moments, I swore that I would live through whatever happened, however terrible it might be, so that I could come back and paint, so that I could get to Canada to paint."

Four decades later, despite his wartime experiences, Mac had his doubts about Emmeline's version of destiny, especially after it teased him with Esther, not once but twice…only to steal her from him in the end.

22

"It's open," a man's voice called out. "You can leave them inside the door."

Someone was home. Was it Mac? Whoever it was was expecting a visitor. Whoever it was was not expecting him. Bernie nudged the door open and stepped into the small mudroom. Hanging on wooden pegs above a pair of Kodiaks and another of rubber boots, both caked with dried clay, were a navy pea jacket, an olive parka from Mountain Equipment Co-op and a red Gore-Tex slicker. He wiped his feet and continued into the kitchen. Flames danced feverishly in the coal-black Newmac stove, giving the room a cozy feel, despite the sleek, almost antiseptic look of the starkly white cabinets, appliances, table and chairs.

He followed the sound of Mac's voice along a gallery-like hallway lit with track lighting and hung with an eclectic mix of modern and portrait art. Thanks to Erik, he recognized a few of the signatures: Christopher and Mary Pratt, Toni Onley, Paul-Émile Borduas and Guido Molinari. Other names were new to him: Daniel Taylor, Catherine Everett and Léonel Jules. There was even a Freda Kimmel, a much less obnoxious representation of his mother's schoolfriend's work than the garish oil hanging next to Anne Savage's *Quebec Farm* in the Westmount Library.

He stopped at the end of the hall and peered into the living room. Mac sat with his back to him, staring into the fire. There was little Bernie could discern from a head of longish, thinning gray hair, the collar and single elbow of a red-and-black plaid flannel shirt and one tan moccasin slipper. Instead, he scanned the room. Shelves crammed with books occupied the wall on either side of the fieldstone fireplace. More art, most of it modern, filled much of the remaining wall space, all of it spotlit with more track lighting, aided by a large skylight punched into the ceiling. The furniture was an eclectic mix of 1960s Mies van der Rohe and timeless comfort that managed miraculously not to clash: a pair of Barcelona chairs and an overstuffed sofa and armchair, along with a set of antiquey end tables that would not have looked out of place in his mother's house. Mac sat in the armchair, the sole surface not crammed with books, magazines and papers.

"Excuse me?" Bernie tried to say. Nothing came out. He rapped lightly on the doorframe and coughed softly.

"Ian?" Mac turned. "Oh, I thought you were— Never mind. Who are you?"

"Marc-Allan Cameron?

"You aren't selling anything are you?" Door-to-door vending was rare in a rural area with houses spread so far apart, but it was not unheard of. Mac was not in the mood to engage with a salesman. Or anyone, really. "Because I'm not buying."

"No, I'm— I'm sorry to bother you…but…"

"Do I know you? You aren't one of my students, are you?" He studied Bernie. There was something about him, something he couldn't place. "No, that's not it. I do know you, though. Don't I?"

Bernie fidgeted with the zipper on his windbreaker.

Mac's expression shifted from uncertainty to incredulity. "Wait." He picked up *Anne Savage*, still open at page sixty, and stared at the photograph. It was one of the girls in the back. How had he missed her? She was the only one staring into the camera, as if she somehow knew that someone would be looking for her in this picture one day. He raised his eyes back up to Bernie, his face screwed up in confusion. "I…" he began. He didn't know what to think. He didn't know what to say.

"I know I should have called," Bernie said clumsily, "but…but I couldn't find a phone number for you. I almost couldn't find you. It's just that… It's just that I— This is kind of awkward. More than kind of. Would it be okay if…well…if I came in?"

Mac stumbled to his feet. "Of course. I'm the one who's sorry. So rude of me." He studied Bernie's face again. "Who are you?" he whispered.

23

Sarah stood at the corner, waiting for the traffic signal to change. Like a true Montrealer, she had crossed against every red light on the ten-block walk from her Kensington Avenue apartment. This intersection was different. Across the road, laying claim to the northwest corner of Sherbrooke and Claremont as it had nearly nonstop for more than half a century, was the restaurant that had been part of Sarah's life for almost as long. Sure, it had only been Café Bistro Chez Dominique for fifteen years or so. But it had been Stella's Lunch for decades before that and Stella was Dominique's aunt, so it was pretty much the same thing.

The light changed and still Sarah did not cross. Instead, she surveyed The Richelieu, with its dark, pollution-stained brick rising five stories above a concrete-paneled ground floor streaked with sixty years of soot. Opening out to the intersection was Dominique's candy-stripe awning, a recent bright addition to the building's somber facade. A late-fall straggler occupied the sole sidewalk table, her face turned skyward to catch the last of October's warmth. The table must be new, thought Sarah. Dominique swore that she would never apply to the city for a patio license. Knowing Dominique, she hadn't. Sarah chuckled.

"I wonder if anything else has changed," she said softly, "like it has for me." Normally, Sarah would be one of the first to know whether Dominique had any plans for her cafe. But ten weeks was a long time. Not counting the war years she had spent in Halifax and her travels with Jack, it was the longest Sarah had ever stayed away from this place that held within it so much of her personal history.

Long before adulthood destroyed their teenage dreams and as

often as they could get away with it, Sarah and Esther had traded the multilingual tumult of their densely packed immigrant neighborhood for the genteel, treelined tranquility of what was then WASPy Westmount — for its stately public library, its jewel-like conservatory and this cafe. It was barely four miles from Clark Street and home. It might as well have been another planet.

This was where she and Esther always stopped after their secret visits to the Westmount Library on Elaina Drew's library card, until Sadie found out and not only barred them from returning but did her best to get the Baron Byng librarian fired for encouraging the illicit outings. This was where, still teenagers, they plotted their escape to Paris to seek inspiration from their role models: Gertrude Stein for Sarah and Marc Chagall for Esther.

This was where too few years later, their dreams still alive if crippled, each revealed her marriage plans to the other, neither prepared to divulge her misgivings about her friend's choice. It was not until long after they had all returned to Montreal from Halifax that Sarah would confess that she had always found Morris more than a little boring and Esther would convey her longstanding concern about Sammy's bursts of uncontrolled anger. Esther hadn't argued: Morris was dull, but she loved him as much as she could love any man, or so she thought at the time. Besides, he had rescued her from Sadie. As for Sammy, Sarah knew that no one else was likely to propose to her, a short, chubby twenty-two-year-old that no other man ever paid attention to. Good Jewish girls were supposed to get married, so when Sammy asked, how could she say no, temper or no temper?

This, too, was where Esther declared that she was carrying Mac's child, and this was the first place Sarah and Esther met after first Morris's death, then Sammy's. It was also where Esther told Sarah that she had cancer and where, days before she was hospitalized that final time, she continued to minimize its severity.

And this is where, the day of her own funeral, Esther managed to bring her son and her oldest friend together to make sure they did not repeat her regrets.

"So far, so good, Esther," Sarah whispered.

Sarah's eyes traveled up to the second floor, to the window directly above Dominique's entrance. Apartment 52. How could she and Esther have come to this building week after week, year after year, without knowing that Hal Ross Perrigard was eating, sleeping and painting directly above them? Hal Ross Perrigard: a contemporary of Anne Savage who had not only exhibited with her but had been taught by some of her same teachers.

"I bet we saw him in there dozens of times, when he was alive and it was Stella's," Sarah said, tilting her head toward Dominique's. "For that matter, you probably walked right by his mural in the Laurentian Hotel when you and Mac…you know."

She patted the oversized book she carried under her arm: *Canada: The Foundations of its Future.* "It's all in here, Esther. Well, some of it. That old coot, Hugh Vickers, told me the rest when he sold me this book on my way over here. I know it's a history book and you know I don't care much about history, but it's by Stephen Leacock, so maybe it's funny like Stephen Leacock is always funny with his stories. But Stephen Leacock isn't why I got it, either. I got it because Perrigard did some of the pictures. So I got it for you, Esther. I know I can't give it to you, so I'll give it to Bernie when I see him next year. He'll appreciate it, I think. The synchronicity, for sure."

This time, when the light turned red, Sarah stepped off the curb. "Maybe if we had known about Apartment 52, maybe if we had met this Hal Ross Perrigard in Stella's, maybe if you'd had him as well as Miss Savage nagging at you, maybe you would have let yourself be that artist after all. Maybe." Sarah shook her head as she dodged the traffic on Claremont. "No, probably not."

24

Mac inspected the young man sitting across from him at the kitchen table. Whoever he was, he had to be related to Esther. He had her eyes. Not the color. Esther's were chocolate and this boy's were greenish, almost hazel. But there was a certain transcendent something about those eyes, a spark that he invariably recalled when he thought of Esther. This boy's hands, too. One of the first things Mac had noticed about Esther were her long, slender fingers. He remembered thinking that she might be a musician, wishing she might be an artist like him. She was, even if in the end she wasn't.

Could this be Esther's son? No, that was too bizarre. How would Esther's son know about him? The woman he remembered would never have revealed her infidelities. Not to her son. Especially not to her son.

Bernie stared back, as unaware that he was being scrutinized as Mac was. Was this man truly his father? Did Sarah really know what she was taking about? Was he about to make a bigger fool of himself than he already had just by showing up here? Bernie had seen pictures of Mac, of course. He had spent the previous two months collecting every book and article he could find about "Canada's Jackson Pollock." His neighbor, a librarian at *The Gazette*, was a willing accomplice, delivering stacks of photocopies to him every few days. In exchange Bernie had to promise to disclose the reasons for his obsession the minute he returned from Nova Scotia. It was different to be sitting across from the man. Bernie's research had revealed something of Marc-Allan Cameron the celebrity artist. They had revealed little about Marc-Allan Cameron the private man. They had revealed nothing about the Marc-Allan Cameron his mother had loved…the only man his mother had loved, if Sarah was to be believed. He tried to see what his mother had seen in the face across the table. He couldn't, of course. He then tried to see his own face in Mac's. Sarah insisted that there was a subtle family resemblance. Bernie was never able to see it in the photos. He couldn't see it now.

A log crashed noisily against the stove's door, jarring both men out of their respective trances. Yet neither knew how to break the silence.

"I was about to make some tea," Mac said at last. "Would you like some?"

Bernie nodded. "Please."

Mac rose, opened one of the kitchen cabinets and pulled out a hand-thrown pottery teapot, two matching mugs and the trademark teal, white and coral of a Fortnum & Mason tea canister. Fortnum's Royal Blend was one of his few remaining indulgences from the old country. He filled a cast iron kettle with cold water and set it on the Newmac. After staring at it for a few minutes, willing it to boil, he sighed and turned back to Bernie.

"Biscuits?" he asked. "They're shortbread. Do you like shortbread?"

Bernie nodded again. "Sure."

Mac retrieved two plates and a tin of Rita Ferguson's homemade cookies from another cabinet. He sat back down, perching at the edge of his seat. "You know who I am," he said. "I think it's time you told me who you are and why you're here."

"My name is… I'm… I think…" Bernie swallowed hard. "I think you knew my mother," he said softly.

"Esther."

"Yes." Bernie paused. "How did you know?"

Mac said nothing.

"I'm Bernie. Bernie Freed. Bernard Marc Freed."

"It's good to meet you, Bernie. Does your mother know you're—Bernard *Marc* Freed?"

Bernie nodded. "My mother…" *If what Sarah says is true, this might be a bigger shock to him than I am.* "She's dead," he said. The words caught in his throat, even after two months of repeating them. "She died in August."

Mac's heart stopped. At least that's how it felt. He clutched his chest. "Esther's dead?" he croaked, barely breathing.

Bernie leapt to his feet. "Are you all right, Mr. Ca— Mac?" He filled one the mugs with water from the tap and thrust it at Mac.

Mac gulped a deep breath. Another. He could feel his heart beating again, even if that space in his chest still felt hollow. He gripped the mug in two trembling hands and sipped. "Thank you," he whispered. "I'm okay." He set the mug down. "Go on. Please."

Bernie nibbled on a cookie, not sure how to continue. *How do you tell a man who has almost had a heart attack in front of you that he's your father?* "I wanted to come sooner, but it took me a long time to find you. I had to… Well, it doesn't matter now. I thought you were in Halifax. At NSCAD."

"I was. I retired."

"No one there would tell me where you were or how to find you," Bernie said, feeling awkward all over again, this time for intruding on Mac's privacy.

"No," Mac said. He stared past Bernie and out the window. The sun had dipped below the tops of the trees, casting a golden aura above the orchard. For reasons he could not articulate, it made him sad. "I told them not to." He returned his gaze to Bernie. "But who… why…?"

"Because…because…" Bernie looked into Mac's eyes, wet with tears. He turned away, embarrassed for Mac and frightened for himself. "Because you're my father," he blurted.

25

Erik rummaged through the paint-splattered canvas backpack resting on his lap. He pulled out a dog-eared sketchpad, a scuffed Walkman, a pair of headphones and a handful of jazz cassettes, piling them next to him on the wood-slat bench. He then reached to the bottom of the knapsack for a lined yellow notepad, a can of Canada Dry ginger ale and a leather case bulging with drawing pencils: Staedtler graphites in sixteen degrees of hardness mingled with Derwent watercolors and oil pastels in every conceivable hue. After setting pad and pencil case on the other side of the bench, he yanked on the soda can's pull-tab and leaned into the opening to suck up the frothy overflow before it spilled onto his Levi's.

He chugged down half the ginger ale then leaned back and shut his eyes, letting his jangled thoughts dissolve into the gentle burbling of the water that spilled out of the stone cherub in the center of the shallow, green-tiled pool. The Victorian-style Westmount conservatory with its tinkling fountain and exotic plants was one of Bernie's favorite spots, so it had become one of Erik's, especially with Bernie chasing all over Nova Scotia searching for Mac.

In a way, the jewel-like greenhouse was as responsible for him and Bernie getting together as was that woman Bernie had told him about, Sarah Swartz. It was to the turreted, red-sandstone Westmount Library and its attached conservatory that Bernie had fled the morning of his mother's funeral. It was there that Sarah found him, hunched over the *Oz* books of his childhood. And it was from there that, soon after, Bernie and Sarah just happened to stop in front of the Sherbrooke Street gallery that just happened to be exhibiting one of Erik's paintings.

Erik opened his eyes. "If I didn't believe in synchronicity before then," he said to the cherub, "that sure would have done it." He slurped down more of his soda. "I mean what are the odds of any of that? For that matter, what are the odds that the father Bernie never knew about would turn out to be my favorite art prof at NSCAD?" He finished the ginger ale, lobbed the can into the nearest trash bin, picked up the notepad and plucked a carmine-red Derwent from the pencil case.

"Dear Mum," he began, "I—" He stopped and let the pencil hover over the page as he stared beyond fountain, cherub and potted palms and out the glass wall to the stately oaks and maples of Westmount Park blazing with fall colors. He was only writing a letter because he couldn't get his mother on the phone. Why the hell did she never erase the messages on her answering machine to clear space for new ones, not that it would matter. She never listened to any of her messages. What was the point of her having a telephone, let alone an answering machine? Smoke signals would be just as effective, and less expensive. Erik had even tried calling Britta's latest boyfriend; she spent most of her time with him these days. He was never home, either, and he didn't have an answering machine. *Those two are as hard to track down as Mac is, now that he's left the art college. I hope Bernie has some news for me tonight when he calls…if he calls.*

Erik had been eager to join Bernie on his Nova Scotia odyssey. It would have been good to get home for a bit, especially now that Bernie was in Wolfville, possibly a few blocks from Erik's mother's house, the house Erik grew up in. Erik dropped his eyes to the notepad and pressed the tip of his pencil to the page, but he wrote nothing. If he were in Wolfville, he could tell his mother all his news instead of having to write it in a letter. He ripped the page free, crumpled it into a ball and dispatched it to join the soda can. "I am not a writer," he said to the blank page. "That's why I'm in art school. Can't I just send a picture?"

"Dear Mum," he began again, this time in burnt umber. Maybe a different pencil would get his thoughts down more easily. "Clear your damn answering machine so I don't have to write this damn letter! I have so much to tell you and you know how much I hate letter-writing." He did have a lot to share. About Bernie, of course. He had told Britta a little, a week after he and Bernie met in August.

But Erik was superstitious: He had not wanted to reveal too much until he was sure this one would stick. He'd had too many false-start relationships, and when they broke up, his mother was inevitably more disappointed than he was. But Bernie? By now Erik was almost sure that this one was a keeper. Almost. He stared at the notepad but still wrote nothing. Over the phone, his mother unfailingly knew what to ask to draw him out. On paper, he never knew how to say what he wanted to say.

Bernie would not be Erik's sole news. Britta was always hungry to hear about Montreal. After fleeing Norway for Canada in 1940, barely three weeks before the German occupation and days after their wedding, she and Anders traveled outside the province only once: for a delayed honeymoon to Parlee Beach near Shediac in neighboring New Brunswick. Over the years, the more Britta heard about Canada's metropolis, the more she longed to visit. It reminded her of the Europe she had been forced to leave behind, especially of the Paris she had visited once with her parents. Yet whenever she would raise the possibility of a holiday in Montreal, Anders would mutter something about "Satan's lair" and "extravagance" before changing the subject, usually to something related to the rural Norway he yearned for.

Then Anders died, in the silliest way possible: He tripped while strolling along the dike that overlooked the mudflats just outside Wolfville, tumbling down the side of the levee and drowning in the shallow water. Suddenly, Britta was a single mother with only a modest insurance settlement to support her, her son and her daughter. A Montreal trip — any trip — was beyond her means.

So she was thrilled when Erik was accepted into the MFA program at Concordia — for her son, of course, but also because she hoped it would get her to Montreal. It hadn't yet, which made her all the more eager for firsthand stories about it.

Erik knew that his mother would also be keen for an update on his thesis, now nearing completion, and even keener to know whether he had agreed to take the job teaching art at Dawson College that had been offered to him. Even if Britta hadn't tried to influence him, Erik was certain that she was hoping he would accept: With her son settled in Montreal, Britta might at last get to fulfill her dream. It didn't matter to her that Montreal had forfeit its title as Canada's largest city to Toronto a decade earlier. It was still the closest to Europe she was likely to get.

Erik dropped the pencil onto his lap. *That fucking thesis.* That's why he was in Montreal and not in Nova Scotia with Bernie. Easygoing Bernie, who hardly ever said no to anything Erik asked, had refused to let him go with him. It was their first real quarrel and it lasted for days.

"You've worked too long and too hard to give it all up," Bernie had argued for the umpteenth time. "What about Dawson? It's a terrific opportunity, and you'll lose it if you don't have your degree. You won't have a degree if you don't finish that thesis."

"Fuck the thesis," Erik grumbled. He dropped onto Bernie's bed, narrowly missing the half-packed suitcase. "I'd rather be with you," he said softly.

Bernie stuffed a half-dozen socks into the black Samsonite case.

"I could help you find him. Mac, I mean. You've never been down east but I know the area. Mac, too. I know people who know him. At NSCAD and…" Erik's voice trailed off. Bernie wasn't listening. He was staring into the bedroom closet, focused on its unsatisfactory contents.

Bernie plucked a white Arrow dress shirt from its wooden hanger and draped it over his arm. He added a second, this one pale blue, and glared at the unstylish shirts, pants, suits and ties arrayed before him, all relics from his time as a government accountant. He flung the two shirts into the corner with the other clothes destined for the charity shop and pulled down a pair of black jeans instead, folding them into the suitcase.

"So that's where those jeans went to," Erik said. "I was wondering what happened to them." He grabbed them from the suitcase, clutched them to his chest and ogled Bernie. "If you're going to get into my jeans, I'd rather be wearing them at the time. You know they're mine, right?"

"Uh-huh." Bernie snatched them back and tossed them into the case. "But they look better on me and off you." He dove onto the bed, on top of Erik. The suitcase clattered to the floor. "Like these." He unfastened Erik's jeans.

Two hours of lovemaking later, Erik gave in. He hated that Bernie was right, but he was: It would be stupid to abandon his thesis and put his December graduation and the Dawson job at risk. He spent the night at Bernie's and tearfully watched him drive away the next morning.

"Dear Mum," Erik scrawled onto a fresh page, this time in steel gray. "I miss Bernie." As he stared at the page, his eyes welled up with tears. He wiped his face with the back of his hand, threw the pad onto the bench and returned the pencil to its case.

If only Bernie would ask, Erik would walk away from his thesis and the teaching gig, hop in a rental car and drive out to be with him in Nova Scotia. Bernie would never ask. Erik loved him for that and didn't, all at the same time.

"How did I ever fall for this guy?" he asked the cherub. The cherub did not reply. "You're an angel. You're supposed to know stuff." The cherub remained inscrutable. Whatever wisdom it possessed, it wasn't prepared to reveal. At least not yet. Erik sighed.

After Jeremy and Bruce, his first real boyfriends, dumped him, Erik swore that he would never again get involved with a guy who was barely out of the closet. He had met Jeremy Mitchell during his first year at school in Halifax, at The Alternate Book Shop on Barrington, a few blocks up the street from where Mac first met Bernie's mom back in the 1940s. Erik struck up a conversation over a copy of Armistead Maupin's *Tales of the City*, they discovered that they were both art students — Jeremy was a year ahead of Erik at NSCAD — and the rest was history. If six months could be called history. Once Erik had helped guide Jeremy past his initial discomfort with his sexual orientation and had shepherded him through Halifax's tiny gay scene, Jeremy broke it off, tearily arguing that he needed more experience before could be ready to settle down. Bruce Paterson's story was not much different, except that Erik met him in one of Mac's classes and Bruce called it quits for the same reason after four months.

Now, here he was with Bernie. Not only had Bernie not poked even a single tentative toe out of the closet when they met, but it was Erik who dragged him all the way out...something else he had vowed he would never do again. He had tried that once before, with Calvin Hutcheson. What a disaster that had been.

It was just that Erik's coming out had been so uncharacteristically effortless and angst-free that he didn't see why he shouldn't make it that easy for others. Calvin did not end up seeing it that way.

Erik was a senior at Horton High in Wolfville when, not yet eighteen, he snuck into an R-rated screening of *La Cage aux Folles* at Acadia University. As he headed home two hours later, it struck him that he was probably gay, and he realized just as immediately that that was why he had always felt different from every guy he had ever known. Unlike most of the gay men he would ultimately meet, he felt no shame, no anxiety and no confusion. Only relief and a rare sense of belonging — not to the drag culture of southern France but for the first time in his life to something. Anything.

Now, six years later, he still could not believe that Acadia's film society had picked a movie about gay people to show. As a college town Wolfville may have been slightly more progressive than were its neighboring communities. But it was still a small town, one that had remained largely untouched by Stonewall's ripples of gay-lib revolution. Back then, he knew it would be smart to say nothing about his newly discovered identity, not even to his best friends or to the couple of Horton kids he was sure were also gay.

Until Calvin.

Calvin was Horton's top athlete and football star. Calvin was an A student who had already been accepted into Toronto's York University with an eye toward its august Osgoode Hall Law School. Calvin was popular with the guys. Calvin was more popular still with the girls. Yet some intuitive something within Erik insisted that it was all a facade, at least the part about the girlfriends. Today, he would call it his gaydar. Then, he just knew that something about Calvin was off, and he knew he was right. Still, he said nothing, not even when Calvin started cruising him. Cruising? There was no other way to describe what was happening. Wherever Erik went, Calvin seemed not only to be there but to be eying him intensely.

Then one day after class and toward the end of the school year, Calvin cornered Erik in the Horton cafeteria. Calvin may have been head of the debating team and a lawyer wannabe, but that afternoon he was anything but eloquent. He fumbled and mumbled and stuttered and asked meaningless questions about a problem in math class. Meaningless, because Calvin consistently aced math while Erik was lucky to squeak by with a C. Finally, Calvin glanced nervously around the room to make sure that no one was within earshot or watching them and leaned in as close to Erik as he dared.

"Are you—" His eyes traveled in every direction but Erik's before he continued, mumbling so softly that Erik could barely hear him, "A homo?" Calvin shook his head. "No, no, that isn't right. I mean..." He almost swallowed the word as he squeaked it out: "Gay?" Before a dumbstruck Erik could reply, Calvin continued, scarcely audibly and in a single, unpunctuated breath as his face grew redder and redder. "You don't have to answer really you don't and I should never have asked I don't really know why I asked so I'm sorry but if you say you are I'll never say anything it's just that if you are it's just that—" At that point, Calvin ran out of air or courage or both. He covered his face with his hands and his shoulders began to tremble.

Erik wished he could reach out and take his hand or hug him but he didn't dare, for his safety as much as for Calvin's. After all, this may have been 1978, but it was Horton High School in Wolfville, Nova Scotia, not some bar in the Castro in San Francisco. He watched Calvin helplessly for a few minutes then whispered. "It's just that you're gay?"

Calvin's shoulders quaked then stilled. His face covered, he nodded. "I-I think so," he gasped. "Maybe."

For three weeks Erik met Calvin nearly every day at the edge of town, on the same dike path that had killed Anders Donnekin. Calvin was terrified those first meetings — that they would be seen, that everyone would know, that he would be shunned or, worse, ridiculed, that he would be dumped from the football team, that he would be thrown out of school, that York would take back its scholarship, that York would withdraw its acceptance, that his conservative parents would find out. But the more they walked and talked and the more Erik explained how it was to be gay in San Francisco and New York and Montreal and Toronto, at least from what he had read, the more Calvin relaxed. By the end of the third week, Erik had fallen for Calvin, hard, and Calvin said he felt the same about Erik. They agreed to skip school the next morning and meet back at Erik's after his mother had left for work. It was time to find out what it meant to be gay, in the bedroom.

Erik took extra care the following morning, spending so long in the bathroom that Britta pounded on the door, warning him that he would be late. Once Britta had pushed him out of the house and he had made it down to Greenwich Road, he slipped into the grounds of the Old Orchard Inn next to the school, waited until nine-thirty, then returned home, where he spent a further half hour fussing in the bathroom. Calvin was due at ten.

Calvin never showed up.

Erik returned to school that afternoon, worried that something had happened to his friend. Had some of Calvin's worst fears been realized? Had his teammates found out? Had his "friends" beaten him up? Yet when Erik tracked him down to the football field after school, Calvin was acting like his old, pre-gay self — horsing around with his athlete cronies and surrounded by a bevy of giggling cheerleader-types. For twenty unendurable minutes Erik observed it all, unnoticed, from his perch high up in the bleachers. Then he skulked away.

Calvin never spoke another word to him. When they passed in the school corridor or on the street in town, Calvin acted as if Erik wasn't there, as if he didn't exist.

Erik saw him for the last time a few weeks later, two days after graduation. Calvin was in the front passenger seat of the family Lincoln, his father behind the wheel, as the car headed west along Main Street. The Hutchesons' car slowed behind a Volkswagen that was waiting to turn onto Central Avenue just as Erik emerged from the Bank of Montreal on the corner. Erik could tell that Calvin was trying to act like he hadn't noticed him, but it was different this time. This time, Calvin met his glance, only to immediately drop his eyes.

It was a fluke that Erik found himself in the gallery the August afternoon Bernie wandered in. The owners had called him a few hours earlier to talk about staging a solo exhibition of Erik's work. Although Jeffrey Hudson and Pierre Marquette had been buying and selling art in Montreal for nearly forty years, Galérie Cinq Arts was their first venture focused solely on emerging artists and Erik Donnekin was one of their earliest discoveries, which was why his *Untitled* occupied a prominent place on their wall. If the striking abstract had yet to sell, Jeffrey and Pierre were convinced that it was only a matter of time. The painting — a rough, thunderbolt-like streak of scarlet slicing through a blue-green oval, with a precisely drawn upside-down triangle in brilliant yellow in the upper left-hand corner — had attracted favorable notice from *The Gazette*'s art critic and had already been scoped out by several local collectors. A full show was the next logical step.

By dinnertime the basic details had been ironed out: Erik would start painting as soon as he finished his thesis and the show would open six to eight months later — in spring or summer 1985. Now, Erik, Jeffrey and Pierre were in the tiny conference room at the back of the gallery, celebrating their creative partnership with the coq au vin and French Bordeaux that Pierre had brought from home. When they heard the front door open and peeked into the gallery to see who had strolled in, they agreed that the handsome young man in the dark suit was not a serious customer. So Erik left the two men to their dinner and went out front to attend to the browser.

As usual, Erik talked too much. This time it was a combination of nerves and excitement at the cute guy sitting in front of *his* painting who also happened to be clutching books on Marc Chagall and Anne Savage, two of his favorite artists. Erik couldn't know that Bernie's mother had just died (hence, the dark suit), that Bernie was about to become an artist himself (even Bernie didn't know that yet) and that Marc-Allan Cameron was Bernie's father. All he knew as he thrust his business card at Bernie was that he had acted like an idiot and would probably never see the guy again.

How wrong he was.

Bernie called the next evening, they met again the following day…and the day after that and the day after that and the day after that. Erik and Bernie had seen each other nearly every day since, and most nights, until Bernie left for Nova Scotia without him.

Part of Erik was scared that the Bernie thing was going to end badly, like it had with Calvin, Jeremy and Bruce. Deep down he knew that Bernie was different, that he was nothing like Calvin, Jeremy or Bruce or any of the other guys he had dated…that not only was Bernie a keeper but that he, Erik, was finally one, too. Still, his confidence had been shaken the previous night when Bernie failed to call.

Every night since leaving Montreal, the instant long-distance rates dropped at eleven, Bernie had telephoned from wherever he was. Until the night before. That night, Erik forced himself to stay awake until after one, waiting for the phone call that never came.

Would Bernie call tonight? Or was this the beginning of another ending? Erik didn't want to think about it, but he couldn't stop himself, and the cherub was not helping.

Finally, he stuffed his pads, pencil case, Walkman and headphones back into his knapsack, threw the bag over his shoulder and left the conservatory.

"He will call tonight," he repeated, mantra-like, through the twenty-minute walk home. *He has to.*

26

The glass doors whooshed open and Sadie stepped into the over-air-conditioned chill and blinding fluorescence of the Provigo supermarket. Banners in brilliant reds, greens, oranges and yellows hung from the high ceiling, each screaming the chain's "si vite, si bon!" slogan and showcasing larger-than-life groupings of flawless fruits and vegetables: apples, grapes, peaches and plums, and tomatoes, lettuce, carrots and cucumbers — all glistening with condensation.

"They should look so good in the bins," Sadie muttered as she stood motionless on the street side of the turnstile, unsure whether to continue into the store.

This was her first visit back to Provigo since Bernie threw her out of Esther's house. Normally now, she shopped at the Steinberg's in Cavendish Mall. But she was here, and she had already tortured herself with a visit to the house — her house — a few blocks away. Why not continue the torment? Besides, it would be shorter to carry her few groceries from Provigo to the bus stop and from the bus stop to her apartment than to shlep her shopping bags all the way through Cavendish Mall and then clear across its endless football field of a parking lot.

Sadie let her eyes drift from one aisle to the next. How often had she walked those aisles for Esther? How often had she fussed over what her sister might be able to eat and keep down after all those radiation and chemotherapy treatments? It wasn't easy to know what to buy when whatever Esther managed to eat one week she puked up the next. Yet Sadie never complained. Not once. It didn't matter what she thought of Esther; she was the big sister and it was her duty to help. Even if Esther hadn't thrown Harold out, he would never have been able to cope. Harold was a mensch but he couldn't boil an egg, let alone play nurse to a dying woman. So who else was going to take care of Esther if not Sadie?

She pushed through the turnstile, freed a cart from the corral and made her way to aisle four. Not once in those six months had Sadie walked up the aisle where Provigo stocked the Kraft Dinner and Hamburger Helper. In her regular Steinberg's, she could find her way to those shelves with her eyes closed. That's because Kraft Dinner and Hamburger Helper is mostly what she ate at home, day after day, week after week, month after month — for six years, since her retirement. Not once while she was at Esther's had she had to buy that chazerai. For the first time since leaving Morgan's, she had been able to eat regular food instead of crap. Thank God for Esther's grocery budget, though not for a whole hell of a lot else in her life. Whoever had praised retirement as some sort of golden age had no idea what he was talking about.

Of course it was a he. A she would know better, would know what it was really like to pinch pennies on my joke of a pension.

Sadie tossed three boxes of Kraft Dinner and two of Hamburger Helper into the cart, added a quarter kilo of the cheapest ground beef from the meat counter and a liter of skim milk from the dairy cooler, then made her way to the front of the store. As she stood in line, she fantasized about abandoning both cart and Provigo and walking up to the far end of the shopping center to Murray's for a bowl of soup, a Salisbury steak with green beans and mashed potatoes and the restaurant's signature rice pudding: a real three-course meal.

She took a few tentative steps away from her shopping cart, calculating how many boxes of Kraft Dinner that Murray's meal would buy and what she would have to give up in the next two weeks to pay for such an extravagance. Was it worth it? She clicked open her Woolworth's wallet and counted out its few crumpled bills. *No.* Sadie reclaimed her cart and stepped back into line.

27

Mac stood at the kitchen counter, his back to Bernie, tears streaming down his cheeks. He rinsed the teapot with boiling water from the kettle, spooned loose Royal Blend into the pot, filled it with water and covered it with a quilted tea cozy. It was crazy. How could he have a son? How could this boy be his son? Yet he knew it was true. Not because Bernie claimed it was but because deep in the heart Bernie had just broken with the news of Esther's death, a voice insisted that it was.

Mac trusted that voice. It was the same voice that told him, all those years ago at the Tate, that he was an artist. It was the same voice that told him what to paint and how to paint it. It was the same voice that told him to offer Esther his umbrella that day in Halifax and his heart soon after.

Now, that voice insisted, "It's true. This boy is your son, Esther's gift to you. She has come back for you in Bernie…in Bernard Marc."

Mac set the teapot on the table and sat down.

"Sarah said the first thing you would do would be to make tea," Bernie said, trying to make light of a moment that refused to be lightened.

"Sarah? Oh, you mean Esther's friend, your mother's friend, Sarah…Kaplan."

"Swartz now. She told me…everything, right after Mom died."

"Your mother never said anything about…?" He couldn't finish the question. He wondered why he'd bothered to ask it when he already knew the answer.

"Not even a hint."

Mac stared at the tea cozy with its faded cameo of Queen

Elizabeth flanked by the Union Jack on one side and the Royal Standard on the other. The legend underneath, barely decipherable after thirty-one years of continuous service, read "Coronation June 27, 1953." Emmeline had fished it out from the bottom of a bin at the Petticoat Lane Market and shipped it to him in Halifax. It was waiting for him when got back from Montreal in 1956…in August 1956…right after he and Esther…

Without moving his head, Mac raised his eyes to Bernie. Nothing had prepared him for this. Nothing had prepared him for fatherhood. Sure, when he was younger, when he and Esther first met, he fantasized about a family. Esther would stay with him. They would get married, or not. And there would be kids. Of course, there would be kids. But the bubble on that dream burst a long time ago. Nearly three decades ago.

"How old are you?" Mac asked. He tried to sound curious. It came out gruff.

"Twenty-seven," Bernie replied, wondering again whether he should have come at all.

"Your birthday?"

"May 11."

Mac said nothing.

"Nineteen fifty-seven," Bernie added. *Is he looking for proof? I should have brought my birth certificate.* "It was a Saturday, if that matters. A few minutes after ten in the morning."

Mac still said nothing.

"Don't bother doing the math," Bernie said. "I've already done it, a hundred times. If you go back nine months—"

"The Laurentian Hotel."

"The Laurentian Hotel."

Mac added a dash of milk to his mug than poured tea over it. Bernie picked up the creamer and did the same.

"No sugar?" Mac asked.

Bernie shook his head. "We take our tea the same way," he said, forcing a smile.

Mac nodded, almost imperceptibly.

Can this get any more awkward? "I should never have come like this," Bernie said after a strained silence. He stood. He would leave. "I should have—"

"No, Bernie," Mac interrupted. "Sit down. Please."

Bernie sat.

"I am the one who should be apologizing," he continued. "You came all this way, probably still in shock about your mother and about…and I—I— I'm acting like, like I don't know what. Like some sort of jerk." He reached across the table and took Bernie's hand. "I really am happy to see you, to find out about you…and me. But finding out about your mother's death and meeting you, all in the space of a few minutes…" He released Bernie's hand. "It may take some getting used to."

Bernie picked up his mug but didn't drink. He let the steam fog up his glasses so he didn't have to watch Mac's discomfort. "I didn't know how else to do this," he said into the tea. "I didn't have your address until a few days ago, so I couldn't write. I never found your phone number, so I couldn't call." He set his mug down and picked up a cookie. Instead of eating it he broke it in half, then in half again. "I think I would have been afraid to write or phone, in case…in case you…" He didn't dare finish the sentence.

"There was no good way to do this, Bernie. I know that. I'm just glad you did. It took a lot courage. Chutzpah, right?"

Bernie nodded. Maybe coming wasn't a mistake. Maybe it would be all right.

28

"Sarah!" Dominique Ryan let her tray clatter to the counter, wiped her hands on her apron and half-ran to the front door as Sarah shut it behind her. At a lithe six-foot-three, the owner of Café Bistro Chez Dominique towered over her favorite customer. She grasped Sarah's hands in both of hers then pulled her into a bear hug and toward an empty table by the window overlooking Sherbrooke Street, Sarah's regular spot. "Where have you been? I've been worried. I know it isn't any of my business, but after Esther…and then you not showing up every few days like clockwork, well—"

She pushed Sarah into the chair and dropped down across from her. "I'll be with you all in a few minutes," she called out to the scattering of mid-afternoon patrons. "But this is Sarah Swartz. She's been coming here for more decades than she would want me to say. Since before the war, and I don't mean Vietnam or Korea." She turned back to Sarah. "And she's been missing in action."

"I haven't been missing, Dominique." She pronounced the French name with the accent on the first syllable, the English way. "And there hasn't been much action. Not the kind you'd notice."

"I don't know about action, but you sure have been missing," Dominique insisted, "and missed. After I didn't see you here for a couple of weeks, I started asking my other regulars. I asked Mr. Levine. I asked Mrs. Fairweather. I asked the Reids and the Leblancs. I even asked Hugh Vickers, that old fart of a flirt." She counted them off on her fingers. "No one had seen you. Not even in the library. When you aren't here, you're in the library, you once told me. Or in the conservatory. So I asked the librarian. Miss Waugh. She knew you, of course, but she hadn't seen you, either. Not since you were in there with Bernie the day after Esther died, she said. Back in August. He's okay, isn't he? Bernie? You're okay, aren't you? You haven't been sick?"

"Oy!" Sarah exclaimed. She patted Dominique's hands. "I didn't know I was such a celebrity. I should be such a celebrity after I finish my book…if I finish it and if a publisher wants it and—"

"You've written a book?" Dominique called out to her customers: "Our Sarah has written a book!"

"Shh, already. Don't take out a billboard on St. Catherine Street. Not yet. I haven't finished it. Nowhere near. I'm writing it now. Well, not right now. At home. That's why I haven't been in here. I've been parked in front of my Smith-Corona typing and typing and typing. I hardly ever leave the apartment anymore, it feels like."

"You're eating, aren't you?"

"You're such a Jewish mother."

"Maybe in a past life. In this one, I'm a good French-Irish Catholic. Well, not so good as my maman would have liked. Now, there was a Jewish mother, even if she wasn't Jewish." She turned serious. "But you, you are eating, right? I know you don't cook."

"Look at me. I can afford not to eat for a few weeks. Maybe a few months." Sarah covered Dominique's mouth before she could protest. "I'm eating, Dominique. Mostly Chinese from that new Dragon place by the art store, because they deliver. I'm not eating here because this crazy book of mine won't let me leave the house, but I am eating."

"Good. That's all I needed to hear." Dominique pushed her chair back. "I'll bring you your tea with lemon and today's pie. It's apple-rhubarb. Is that okay?"

"Any pie of yours is more than okay."

"That's why I love you, Sarah." Dominique grinned. "And ice cream, of course."

"From St. Aubin?"

"Of course. Where else?"

Sarah watched Dominique disappear into the kitchen. Her old friend might never have become the ballerina she had once dreamed of becoming, but Dominique still moved with the easy grace of a dancer. It was almost as though she glided across a room. "Friend" might not be the exact word, considering that Sarah had never seen

Dominique outside her restaurant. But like Dominique announced to her customers, Sarah had been coming here since forever — she and Esther, together.

If marriage, the war and a move to Halifax forced them to suspend their regular visits, the ritual resumed when they returned to Montreal in 1947 — Sarah and Sammy Kaplan with their newborn, and a pregnant-but-soon-to-miscarry Esther Freed with her Morris. Stella's retirement in 1965 forced the women to move their regular rendezvous downtown, to the cavernous art deco restaurant atop the Eaton's department store. Only for five years. When Dominique rented and renovated her aunt's still-shuttered cafe, Esther and Sarah were the first in the door on opening day.

Sarah stared out the window to Sherbrooke Street. Traffic rumbled by like it always had. This was Westmount's main thoroughfare, after all, and at nearly twenty miles, one of the longest streets on the Island of Montreal. For an instant, though, it was not October 1984 she was seeing through the glass and she wasn't sitting here by herself. Esther was across from her and together they were moving through the years like in a flip book. Sherbrooke didn't change that much, not physically. The cars, trucks and buses were different. The people and their clothes, too. But the buildings looked pretty much the same, not like her and Esther. As Sarah's crude, movie-like animation propelled the street forward in time, both she and Esther aged, from nearly sixteen to just past sixty.

The main difference between the two friends through the years was that Esther was never not beautiful. Even in the months before she went into the Royal Victoria Hospital that last time, Esther was beautiful. Sarah? Sarah wasn't ugly, but she was plain. In the flip book of their lives together, Sarah went from young plain to old plain. *That's okay. Sometimes, being plain is easier than being pretty. That's a good line. I have to remember it. It could make it into the book. Or not. Who knows? With all the pages I have, lots and lots of pages, I still have no idea what this meshugena book is going to be.*

"I am going to write it simply," she recited in a whisper over the remembered clatter of the long-ago streetcar that had carried her and Esther to the Westmount Library nearly fifty years earlier, "and as Defoe did the autobiography of Robinson Crusoe. And she has and this is it."

How did I remember that after all this time? What else have I forgotten that I should be remembering for this book of mine?

"Were you saying something?" Dominique asked as she set a cup and saucer, a stainless-steel teapot, a plate of teabags, a bowl of lemon wedges and a dinner plate heaping with pie and vanilla ice cream onto the table.

"I was remembering," Sarah said. "So much to remember…"

"By Gertrude Stein?" Esther asked through chattering teeth. She shoved her hands deep into the pockets of her cloth coat and tried to stop herself from shivering. Montreal streetcars weren't heated and the day was gray, damp and cold — typical for November. So why were the windows open? That didn't make any more sense than Gertrude Stein writing someone else's autobiography. "That isn't how it works, Sarah. It can't be the *autobiography* of Alice B. Toklas. It has to be the *biography* of Alice B. Toklas. Otherwise…"

Sarah shut her latest notebook on the Gertrude Stein quote and returned it to the school satchel she insisted on carrying instead of a purse. "You'll see when we get to the library," she said.

Esther did see and she came to love the book as much as Sarah did. Not because Gertrude Stein was a successful Jewish writer, a *woman* Jewish writer, which was why the book would become Sarah's favorite. No, Esther loved *The Autobiography of Alice B. Toklas* because it introduced her to many of the artists she grew to admire. Maybe Marc Chagall wasn't part of the Stein-Toklas coterie, but Matisse, Rousseau and Braque were. And even if Manet, Cézanne, Renoir and Toulouse-Lautrec didn't frequent Gertrude and Alice's Paris salons, their paintings were mentioned frequently in the book.

"One day," she swore to Sarah, "my paintings will also be mentioned in a book. More than one book. Lots of books. One day everyone will know Esther Finkel, world-famous artist, and nothing Sadie can say or do will change that. Nothing."

Sarah sighed. If only… If only life was as simple as it seems when you're a teenager.

"Dominique," she called across the restaurant, now largely emptied.

"More hot water?" Dominique called back in reply. "Or pie?"

"Any more pie and I'll explode. No, I want to show you something if you've got a minute." Sarah opened *Canada: The Foundations of its Future* to page 224, to a color plate by Hal Ross Perrigard. It was a painting of the Parliament Buildings in Ottawa, with the sun's pastel rays illuminating both the Centre Block's iconic Peace Tower and, across the street, the National War Memorial.

"Sure." Dominique poured herself a mug of coffee and joined Sarah, straightening all the chairs she passed on the way. "Sylvie will be here in a bit. She can set up for dinner. What is it?"

Sarah rapped on the reproduction like she was knocking on a door. "Did you know this Hal Ross Perrigard?"

Dominique studied the picture. "Should I have?"

"He used to live up there." She pointed to the ceiling. "Apartment 52, right on top of us. He had a wife, Pauline. Maybe they ate here?"

"Perrigard..." Dominique looked up, imagining that she could see through the plaster and masonry into the apartment immediately above them. "How long ago?"

"It would have been in your aunt's time. He died in 1960, I think."

"I could have seen him, but I don't remember the name. Lots of people ate here and lots of famous people lived upstairs. Some royalty, even. Well, deposed royalty. But Perrigard..." Dominique peered at the artist's signature on the tissue overlay. She shook her head.

Sarah flipped back to page 195, another Perrigard: a black-and-white turn-of-the-century streetscape.

"Stella might remember," Dominique said, scanning the print. "It's crazy the details she remembers, when there's so much she doesn't remember."

"It doesn't matter," Sarah said, "not really. Not anymore. I just wondered." She thumbed back through the pages to the front of the book and read a sentence at random: "'The opportunities which lie open to Canadians inflame the imagination.' Hmm. I need to write that down." Sarah rummaged in her purse but found neither pen nor paper. *What kind of writer am I?* She turned to Dominique. "Do you—?"

"Of course." Dominique pulled a Bic from her apron pocket and dropped it on the table. "Let me find you some paper." She scurried into the back.

"I need to be carrying a copybook with me like I used to," Sarah muttered. *What happened to all those copybooks, I wonder? Sammy. Sammy must have happened to them, like he happened to so much else I cared about. Like Morty.* Her bastard of a husband had always been so mean to their son. He refused to understand that the Down Syndrome or whatever it was — they didn't have a name for it in those days — was not Morty's fault. He couldn't accept that no son of his could be so, well, defective. So, of course he couldn't accept that Morty was his son…as if Sarah would have had time to have an affair. As if any man would have noticed her. Only her Jack did, and by then both Morty and Sammy were long gone.

When did she stop writing in notebooks? It had to be when she was with Sammy, when there was too much to write and writing any of it seemed so pointless.

Maybe if I was still putting everything into notebooks and if I still had all those old ones, I would know what this book of mine is supposed to be about. Sarah sipped her tea, now cold, then absentmindedly pushed the final forkful of pie around the ice cream soup that had pooled on her plate.

Gertrude Stein had notebooks; hundreds of them, probably. Thousands. I bet they're in a museum or a college library somewhere. All of them. Because she never threw away any paper she'd written on. That's what she wrote in that autobiography book of hers. She was lucky. She had an Alice Toklas to make sure everything was saved. What did I have? I had a Sammy Kaplan.

Sarah swallowed the last piece of pie and spooned up the remaining ice cream slop. *I shouldn't say this, but it could be just as well that I had a Sammy Kaplan. If I had all those papers like Gertrude Stein, if Sammy hadn't gotten rid of them all, I would be spending all my time reading through them and I would never do any writing. Like I'm not doing right now.*

"Like I'm not doing right now." Sarah pushed herself to her feet. "I have to go home. I have to write."

What a difference ten weeks makes. Ten weeks ago I didn't want to start. Now, I can't stop!

"So?" Sarah asked, rolling a fresh sheet of twenty-four-pound bond into the typewriter and switching it on.

The green Smith-Corona portable hummed back at her.

"I'm supposed to be writing a book," she said. "Do you know how to write a book?"

The typewriter droned an unchanging monotone.

Not knowing what else to do, Sarah touched a key with her pudgy index finger. A capital E clacked onto the page. "I know there's gotta be at least one E in this book," she said to the keyboard. "I read somewhere that E is the most used letter in the alphabet, so how can I go wrong?" She paused. "I can't." She pressed the T, followed by the A. "Those are the next two most common letters, they say, but that's all I know."

She examined the three black letters on the otherwise pristine page. "Eta is a Greek letter," she muttered, "and ETA means estimated time of arrival. Not much of an opening for a book. I wonder what its estimated time of arrival is." Sarah pushed her chair away from the dining room table. It grated across the hardwood floor. "Not today," she announced and stood, smoothing her flowered housecoat.

"Yes, today," a voice countered.

Sarah raised her eyes to the ceiling. "Esther? Is that you, Esther? What do you want from me, Esther? I love you, but you aren't really here. You died on Tuesday. Besides, what did you ever know from writing books?"

She thrust clenched fists into her pockets, not eager to tame the tornado of boxes and papers strewn across every available surface in the living room behind her. It had to be better than starting this book she promised Bernie she would write. Or not. She fell back into her seat. The mess would have to wait. This book couldn't wait. She knew it couldn't.

"You win, Esther." Sarah reached across the mahogany table for the paper-clipped sheaf that was her *Good Jewish Girls Don't* story from all those years ago, the one that had caused her to ferret through all those boxes like a madwoman the day before. This was the piece of writing that had launched her short-lived journey as an author. She was fifteen then, with all the naive chutzpah of a teenager determined to mold her future to her will. It didn't take long, though, before marriage and motherhood got in the way — marriage to a man who thought writing was "dumb" and motherhood to a boy who was different, a boy who never really grew up, a boy who needed constant defending from his shvantz of a father.

"I should maybe go back to the cemetery? To Rosalie Friedman? Remember Rosalie Friedman, Esther? Maybe she would inspire me again." It was while they were in high school and during an illicit visit to the cemetery — Esther to sketch, Sarah to write — that *Good Jewish Girls Don't* was conceived. Using Rosalie Friedman's gravestone as support, Sarah had leaned back and, to her amazement, watched the story of six twelve-year-old girls determined to play street hockey in the boys' world of 1930s' Jewish Montreal play out in her mind's eye.

The sixty-one-year-old Sarah slipped off the paper clip and riffled through the pages of the story. Shaking her head, she let them flutter down to the table. "I would never find Rosalie. Not in a million years. Too many new people have died since then." Her eyes watered. "Like you, Esther. Like you."

Esther had been Sarah's closest friend for almost her whole life, since the moment they set eyes on each other in the confusion and cacophony that was their first day at Bancroft School all those births, deaths and husbands ago…all those loves, hates, joys and tragedies ago. They had been inseparable through those years, at least as inseparable as marriage and motherhood would allow. Now, they were separated for good. Sarah wiped the tears from her cheeks and shut her eyes.

If the air blowing on her from the air conditioner were warmer and moister, it could almost be the breeze in the cemetery that Sunday all those years ago. The fan? That could be the traffic on de la Savane, quieter but rougher-sounding than it would be today…than it had been just a few days earlier.

"Was it only Thursday that I was back at the cemetery, Esther? For your funeral? You die Tuesday night, you're buried Thursday morning and by Friday afternoon my whole world is topsy-turvy. Now, it's Saturday and I'm suddenly a writer again. Practically a whole lifetime has passed, and I don't mean since the last time I thought I was a writer. Two husbands and a son have passed since then. But since Thursday? Since yesterday, even, it's like I'm that teenager again, the one who not only wanted to write but had to write. And I did write. Thanks to Rosalie Friedman, who gave me a place to sit and maybe the idea, I wrote.

"That day it was like the world was exploding with plans and possibilities. Remember, Esther? Remember how excited we were? How absolutely certain we were? Then it was over. So soon, it was over. First war, then marriage, then Halifax and Morty, and my story's happy ending stayed on the page of the story. In real life, in my life and yours, Esther, good Jewish girls didn't. And now…"

"Now, you can have a second chance, Sara-without-an-h Schumacher. It isn't too late."

Sarah felt more tears roll down her cheeks. She let them fall to the table, then opened her eyes and wiped them with her sleeve.

"It's too late for you, Esther. Are you sure it isn't too late for me, too?"

Lucky Rosalie. All you have to do is sit there, wherever you are and let the years pass. Nothing touches you. Nothing, except the wind and the rain. You, too, Esther. The struggle is over. The doubts have passed. Who knows? After all this time, you could even have certainty again. A new kind of certainty, for sure. But more certainty than this.

She stared impotently at her ETA until it blurred. Then she yanked the page from the typewriter, crumpled it in a tight ball and hurled it over her shoulder into the chaos that was her living room.

"I have to do this," she declared, "for you as much as for me. For Bernie, too. Maybe even for Rosalie Friedman."

She rolled a fresh sheet of paper into the still-humming Smith-Corona and raised her two typing fingers above the keyboard. Unfortunately, the inspiration she expected her newfound determination to trigger continued to elude her.

"What would Mr. Littleton tell you to do?" Esther's voice again.

Sarah smiled. Frank Littleton had been their English teacher at Baron Byng. Sarah didn't know whether muses were supposed to be tall with wavy blond hair and look like Hollywood movie stars, but that was Frank Littleton. He immediately recognized Sarah's fledgling gifts and never stopped encouraging her, even when he was no longer her teacher. *I should have married him, not that son of a bitch Sammy Kaplan. If I had, I for sure would never have stopped writing. But without the son of a bitch, there would have been no Morty. Poor Morty.* After a moment's melancholy over her son, who died a few months before his twentieth birthday, Sarah returned her attention to Frank Littleton.

What would Mr. Littleton have said?

"Start anywhere, Sarah, with any word. It doesn't matter what the word is or where it takes you. If you believe in the story and trust it, it will take you where you need to go…where it needs you to go."

She pounded on the E, T and A keys again, this time with all her strength, daring them to defy her.

They didn't.

Two hours later, Sarah was still typing.

An hour after that, incredulous, she switched off the machine and straightened her stack of typewritten pages. "*Sara's Year* by Sara Schumacher," the title page read.

"See Esther? I got rid of the h in Sarah, like I said I would." She traced her name with her finger. "I knew it would look better this way. More exotic." She moved her finger up to the title. "But what is this *Sara's Year*? How can I have a title when I don't know what I'm writing?" When no answer came, she sighed and made her way through the paper-strewn living room to the fireplace, where she lit the logs and kindling she kept primed year-round even during the hottest days of a muggy Montreal summer. She then cranked up the air conditioning and settled into her favorite armchair.

"I did it, Mr. Littleton," Sarah whispered. "You always told me I could, and I didn't believe you." She watched the nascent flickerings in the fireplace explode into flame. "I know it's only a beginning," she said and turned to face her dining room table, her new writer's studio with its dozen double-spaced manuscript pages, "but, oy, what a beginning!"

29

Bernie watched the last of dusk's glimmer fade into night. Unlike Montreal, which experienced absolute darkness only during a rare power failure, Mac's patch of rural Nova Scotia lacked the permanent sky-glow of city life. No streetlamps illuminated Hubbard Mountain Road, no car headlights could reach Mac's end of the cul-de-sac, and a dense stand of sentinel spruce made certain that not even a wink of light made it through from neighboring houses. All Bernie could see in the new-moon blackness was his own silhouetted reflection in the window.

"There's more," Bernie said, not daring to turn around. This was almost as hard as telling Mac who he was. In some ways, it was harder.

"More?" Mac asked. "What more could there be?" *What more can there be?* Mac watched Bernie and waited.

Bernie opened his mouth. He closed it again without speaking. He continued to stare out the window, afraid to risk the tentative ease he and Mac had finally managed to achieve with each other.

It had not come easily. Tense silences more explosive than the most deafening of artillery blasts filled their first hour. Once the initial declarations had been made, neither knew what to say. How do two strangers erase twenty-seven years of mutual unawareness to become instant father and son? They don't. Instead, they avoid each other's gaze and nervously keep their mouths stuffed with shortbread cookies to avoid having to say anything.

Yet by the time afternoon tea dissolved into dinner, their initial awkwardness had begun to melt.

Now, they sat in Mac's den, polishing off a bottle of Saint-Émilion by the lambent glimmer from the fireplace. No, they weren't quite father and son. But they were discovering more shared tastes than the amount of milk they preferred in their tea. French Bordeaux was one, Irish stout another, french fries smothered in a goopy amalgam of ketchup and vinegar yet another. If each was reluctant to admit an uncool fondness for Nova Scotia's own Anne Murray, they easily confessed to their film addictions: the screwball comedies of the 1930s, the hardboiled films noir of the 1940s and extravagant musicals from any era. They also shared a penchant for Canadian literature, favoring many of the same books and authors — from Stephen Leacock, Robertson Davies and Mordecai Richler to Alice Munro, Margaret Laurence and Margaret Atwood.

They even found common elements in their personal histories. They were both only children, more uncommon in Mac's generation than in Bernie's, and came from surprisingly small families. For Mac, there was Aunt Emmeline, Aunt Agnes and a black-sheep uncle who disappeared into the Australian outback long before Mac was born. Bernie knew only his Auntie Sadie and Uncle Manny; his mother's other brother died in World War II and his father's brother and sister, twins, died in their teens.

"Your father. Morris, is it? Does he know about any of this?" Mac asked.

"Sarah doesn't think so," Bernie replied. "She's pretty sure Mom would never have told anyone. It doesn't matter. My dad died a long time ago. I was six. I hardly remember him. Not at all, really."

"I didn't know my father, either," Mac said. "Not my real father. He died before I was born. First World War, days before the Armistice. My mum was pregnant with me."

"You had no father?"

"A stepfather. I didn't know he wasn't my real father for a long time. Until the next war. After I was called up, my mum told me. In case anything happened, she said, she wanted me to know. I never thought of him as anything but my real father, only he wasn't."

"Like my dad, sort of."

"Sort of."

Through tea, dinner, dessert and wine, the one subject Bernie skirted was art — both Mac's and his own. He had come to Nova Scotia to find Mac for two reasons. He had successfully negotiated the first. Now, it was time for the second.

"There's more," Bernie repeated. He slipped his shoes on and stood. "I'll be right back."

Mac heard the front door close and squinted out the window to follow Bernie's shadowy form to the Corolla. A light flicked on when Bernie opened the door. It stayed lit long enough for Bernie to retrieve a canvas messenger bag from the back seat, then snapped shut. When Bernie returned, he switched on the floor lamp next to Mac's armchair, pulled out a sketch pad, opened it to the first page and wordlessly placed it on Mac's lap.

"What is this?" Mac glanced down at the rough pastel of two teenage girls sitting at an old-fashioned lunch counter; from the thirties, he guessed. "It's good." He scrutinized the sketch more closely and noticed a cramped signature in the bottom right corner: "B. Freed '84."

Bernie stepped away from the focused halo of the lamp and sat in the dark, his arms crossed over his chest, trying to sink into the upholstery. He stared into the fire. "I didn't want you to think that I chased after you because you're Marc-Allan Cameron, famous artist. That's the last thing I wanted."

"I wouldn't have thought that," Mac said softly.

"I needed to find you, to meet you. I had to get to know you, at least a bit, before…"

Mac flipped through the pad. Most of the sketches were closeup studies — flowers, small animals, architectural and automotive details. There was a series of the Montreal skyline, innovative in its use of line and form; a second series, of portraits, most of the same high-cheekboned young man who looked strangely familiar; and a third series, the largest and most distinctive in the nearly full pad, made up of images that were not entirely Impressionist and not entirely abstract, but some inventive blend of the two. While rough, all the sketches showed extraordinary promise.

"How long have you been doing this, Bernie?"

"Ten weeks. Since the day after Mom's funeral, the day after I found out about you." He uncrossed his arms and studied his hands. "Sarah kept saying I had artist's hands, like my mother's. I kept saying I couldn't draw worth shit. Even my high school art teacher told me I had no talent. He said I drew like I was in kindergarten." He laid his hands on his lap.

Mac flipped back to the opening sketch. "This was your first?"

Bernie nodded.

"And the rest in ten weeks?"

"Uh-huh."

"You're wasted at Revenue Canada. You're nearly good enough to be doing this full-time."

Bernie finally met Mac's gaze. "You really think so? You aren't saying that to be polite or because I'm my mother's son?"

"Not even because you're my son. I am not known as an idle flatterer. Ask any of my students. They will all tell you I can be a hard-ass critic. That's on a good day."

Bernie didn't know what to say. It was one thing for Sarah to maintain that he was gifted, but even she would admit that she knew "nothing from art." Sylvie Ryan? Well, she knew art…as an art historian not as an art-maker. And Erik? Erik was his biggest booster, but he was also his boyfriend. Bernie had done his best to believe them all, although part of him remained skeptical. Still, this was Marc-Allan Cameron telling him he was good, better than good. This was Canada's greatest contemporary artist talking, not his father. Maybe he really was good. Maybe he could be an artist, already was an artist.

"I didn't tell you the whole truth about Revenue Canada," Bernie mumbled.

"You aren't a tax accountant? Here I was counting on gaining not only a son but someone to do my taxes in April."

Bernie's lip started to tremble.

"I was joking, Bernie," Mac said gently. "I already have an accountant. I don't have a son. I mean I didn't have a son. I didn't know I wanted a son before today, but I do and it's you." He paused. "What's this about Revenue Canada?"

Bernie turned slowly back toward Mac. "I went to Revenue Canada straight from Concordia. I didn't know what else I wanted to do, and it was easy for me. Accounting, I mean. I stayed there pushing paper and crunching numbers until nine weeks ago, when I quit." He then told Mac about how, in the thirty-six hours after his mother's funeral, Sarah had nagged him into acknowledging a passion he never knew he had. He told him about the pact he and Sarah had made. He told him about Erik. Then he burst into tears.

30

Erik and Bernie stroll along the Wolfville dike, holding hands. Above, cottony powder puffs scud across an electric blue sky on a light summer breeze whispering in from the Bay of Fundy. Below, the mudflats are a gloppily rippled, milk-chocolate brown. This is one of Erik's favorite places to walk, especially at dawn when the light is perfect to paint by and few other people are around. It's even better now, with Bernie. Erik's joy is so clichéd he can almost hear angels singing overhead and he is sure that they are being followed by a ghostly trio of gypsy violinists.

A church bell chimes the midday hour. That's not right. The sun's barely up and Wolfville is not yet awake. The bell stops for a few beats then starts up again.

One. Two. Three…

Ten. Eleven Twelve…

It continues tolling — thirteen, fourteen, fifteen — then picks up volume, speed and intensity.

Seventeen.

Eighteen.

Nineteen.

It's angry, almost apocalyptic.

Frightened, Erik turns to Bernie, but it's no longer Bernie whose hand he's holding. It's Calvin, a zombie-like Calvin with a spectral face, black, empty eye sockets and a clammy, vice-like grip.

"C-Calvin?" Erik stammers, but he can't hear himself over the hammering of the church bell.

Twenty.

Twenty-One.

Twenty-Two.

Twenty-thr—

Calvin rips his hand free and in a single fluid gesture, lifts Erik up and pitches him down toward the mudflats, now quicksand-like deadly.

Erik squeezes his eyes shut and screams. Yet the bells' crashing is even louder than his shrieks…though not anywhere near as loud as Calvin's maniacal laughter, which grows increasingly piercing and hysterical.

Erik's throat is raw. His arms and legs flail against the inevitable.

The bells ring and ring and ring.

They're jangly now, almost like a telephone.

They are a telephone.

Erik's eyes open.

To nothingness.

Erik reached blindly for the phone, knocking it off the night table. "Hello?" he shouted into the blackness of the bedroom.

"Erik?" a tinny voice shouted back from somewhere on the floor. "What happened? Are you okay? Did I wake you up?"

"What?" Erik fumbled for the phone and pressed the receiver's mouthpiece to his ear. "Is that you, Bernie?"

The reply was muffled, indecipherable.

"Bernie?" Erik righted the receiver.

"I'm here. What's going on?"

"I must have fallen asleep." Erik groped for his watch then recalled that he'd lost it a few weeks before. He had probably left it at Bernie's. "What time is it?" Then he remembered: He had waited again until after one for Bernie's call. At one-thirty, trying hard to convince himself that Bernie was not another Calvin after all, he had let himself fall asleep.

"It's nearly three here. I'm sorry to be so late, and about last night. The phone at the B&B was out-of-order and there are no pay phones anywhere near here. I tried you this morning from the drugstore, but you'd already left. I—"

"It's okay." Erik switched on the bedside lamp and squinted against the glare. "I miss you."

"Me, too. Listen—"

"Wait a sec." Erik dropped the phone onto the bed and padded to the kitchen, where the coffeemaker was always switched on against the possibility of a middle-of-the-night creative brainstorm. He filled a mug, spooned in too much sugar, slopped in some milk, then noisily slurped down enough to make sure he wouldn't spill any on the way back.

"Okay," he said into the phone. "I'm caffeinated."

"You'll never get back to sleep."

"I don't intend to. I plan to have phone sex with you for the rest of the night."

"If you can keep it in your pants for another couple of days, you can have the real thing."

"You're coming home?" Erik sputtered. "What about Mac?"

"I just got back from his house and—"

"You found Mac?" Erik jerked up, spilling coffee all over the bed. "Shit." He dropped the phone and sprinted to the bathroom for a towel. "I'll be right back," he shouted from across the room. "Don't go away."

"Now, what happened?" Bernie asked into an empty bedroom.

"You found Mac?" Erik mopped up the spilled coffee with the phone propped between his shoulder and ear.

"Yup."

"Holy shit! Where the hell is he? Where the hell are you?"

"Wolfville, still. I have so much to tell you. God, I miss you. But I'm leaving tomorrow afternoon, so I'll see you in a couple of days. I'll tell you everything then."

"Now," Erik insisted. "I've had coffee and I'm awake. Tell me everything now. Was Mac okay with you showing up like that? Was he okay with what you told him, about your mom and about him being your father? Did you a—"

"Stop! If I tell you everything now, we'll be on the phone all night and I won't be able to leave tomorrow and who knows when I'll get to see you."

"But—"

"I'll make a deal with you. I'll tell you a bit tonight and I'll call you from the road every night on the way home to tell you more, even if I have to hike ten miles to find a pay phone. Okay?"

"Make it twenty miles, cowboy, and you've got a deal."

31

"Stay the night," Mac urged. "Stay as long as you want."

It was after two in the morning, and Bernie had already started for the door a half-dozen times, only to find himself caught up in Mac's obsessive zeal and unable to leave. His fears about how Mac would respond to his artistic aspirations had proven to be unfounded. Quite the reverse: Any residual awkwardness between them dissolved the minute they started talking about art.

In truth, Mac did most of the talking. It was like being in the classroom all over again for him. He switched on all the lights and danced from room to room and painting to painting, waving his arms wildly to illustrate one concept after another about art. Then he pulled stacks of books off the shelf, opening each to the relevant color plate and thrusting it at Bernie as he jabbed his finger at a particular texture, brushstroke, technique or color. Finally, he propelled Bernie through a whirlwind tour of his studio, explaining the purpose behind every brush, tube, paint pot, palette, rag, easel, canvas and sheet of paper in the room. At least that's how it felt to Bernie, who was sure his head would explode were Mac to hurl one more piece of information at it.

Now, they were back in the den. The lights had been re-dimmed, the fire rekindled and a fresh pot of tea had returned them to a more intimate version of where they had begun that afternoon.

"You're sure you won't stay?" Mac asked.

"I'm sure." Bernie's world had changed nearly as much over the previous eight hours as it had the day of his mother's funeral. He needed some time to himself. Mac must, too. Plus, he needed to talk to Erik. "This time I really have to go," he said. He stood and pulled his car keys from his pocket. "But I'll be back tomorrow like we talked about — for lunch instead of breakfast, if that's okay."

They had agreed that Bernie would check out of his B&B in the morning then return to Mac's to reconfirm their plans. From there he would make his way through Kentville to Highway 101, Digby and the Princess of Acadia ferry back toward Montreal to carry those plans out: putting his things in storage, subletting his apartment and hitting the road back to Mac's as quickly as arrangements would allow.

Erik wormed the whole story out of Bernie — from the stolen apple to the studio tour and Bernie's planned return to Nova Scotia. It wasn't hard. Once Erik got Bernie going, there was no stopping him, any more than Bernie had been able to stop Mac. When he finished nearly an hour later, Erik was uncharacteristically quiet.

"Erik?"

"I'm here."

"I thought you'd fallen asleep."

"I had coffee, remember?"

"I didn't mean to dump all this on you tonight. It's a lot to take in, especially the part about me coming back here." He waited a moment before continuing. "What do you think? Are you okay with it?"

"I—" Erik stopped. He was not okay with it, not really. But he would have to be. For Bernie. "I—," he began again. Again, he stopped. Whatever he said, Bernie would see right through it. Bernie could always read him. They could always read each other. That's part of what made them so right together.

"Erik?"

"Yeah."

"Tell me what's going on."

"I need another cup of coffee. I'll be right back."

Erik closed his eyes and inhaled deeply. As he did, he realized that he was okay with it. He was, because he now had a plan. He slowly made his way to the kitchen as he let the details crystallize in his mind.

"You aren't okay with it, are you," Bernie said when Erik got back on the phone with a fresh cup of coffee.

"I am. I swear I am."

"Look, this has to work for both us. We're a team, you and me, a forever team. So you have to tell me the truth."

"Are you crazy? Of course, I'm okay with it. I needed a couple of minutes to work things out. That's all."

"You're sure?"

"You just got yourself a father and world-famous art teacher all in one package. There are up-and-coming artists who would kill for less. I would kill for less."

"But you and me. It's only been a couple of months and—"

"I am madly in love with you, Bernie Freed, and that is not going to change because I don't get to see you for a couple of months."

"It could be more than a couple of months. I don't know how long I'll be here."

"I don't care if it's a couple of years. My thesis defense is in eight weeks. As soon as it's behind me, I'll be right behind you. If you'll have me."

"Are you crazy? What about Dawson?"

"Screw Dawson. I'd rather make art than teach it, and I'd rather be with you while I'm making it."

"You're really sure?"

"I'll stay with my mum until I figure stuff out. Besides, I would be an idiot to give up the chance to have Marc-Allan Cameron as my father-in-law." He giggled. "Now, how about that phone sex?"

32

Mac watched Bernie pull out of the drive. He waited until the Toyota Corolla had disappeared from view, and when he could no longer hear the crunch of tires on Hubbard Mountain Road, he turned into the house and crossed back to his studio.

Bernie had said little that morning. Mac knew that it was more than a lack of sleep. His son's life was about to change, again, in ways he couldn't imagine. Both their lives were. It had to be overwhelming.

Before he left, Bernie had asked to see Mac's studio again. As Mac stood by the door, Bernie moved through the room, on his own this time, his fingers brushing against a canvas here, a drawer of sketches there, taking in the professional studio of a celebrity artist who just happened to be his father, who just happened to have offered to share all Bernie was seeing with his son. Mac smiled. He would be counting the hours until Bernie's return.

Mac straightened a few palettes and trays, flicked a stray rooster feather onto the floor and pushed a chair against the wall. As he turned to leave, his eyes lit on the stubbornly blank canvas. He had said nothing about it to Bernie. There would be time enough for that. Maybe now it would not stay blank for too much longer.

He lifted the cloth cover. "Thank you for sending him to me, Queen Esther," he whispered to the elusive painting hiding within the canvas. "Thank you for sending our son home to me."

1988

33

"Can I get you something else? More coffee? Something to eat?"

Sadie saw Sylvie reflected in the cafe window, just beyond her own face. The petite server stood by the table, smiling tentatively. A real smile, not like those pasted-on smirks you saw so much in stores and restaurants these days. Everything was so plastic now, even people. Maybe especially people.

"That would be nice, dear," Sadie heard herself say as she turned away from the window to face Sylvie. *Dear? I never call anyone dear. Why did I call her dear?*

"It could be that you aren't such an obnoxious sourpuss of a witch after all," she heard from behind her, back in the window. "That's witch with a b."

Sadie eyed Sylvie. Had the girl heard? Or was Sadie the only crazy person here. Because she was crazy, talking to this mirror version of herself that wasn't there at all, that wasn't her at all, like in the Metro. *There isn't anyone there. There isn't. There can't be. Can there?*

"We don't do a lot of food here," Sylvie was saying, "mostly croissants in the morning, pastries in the afternoon and bar snacks later on. French fries and pizza-type things. I don't suppose you want anything like that?"

Sadie shook her head.

Sylvie pondered the possibilities. "I could make you a sandwich, if you want. Would that work? Would you like a sandwich?"

Until Sylvie asked, Sadie had not realized how hungry she was. Famished. *Maybe it's because I haven't eaten all day that I'm having all these hallucinations? Maybe if I eat something, they'll go away?* Sadie sighed. *Probably not.*

When was the last time she had eaten? It must have been that piece of dry toast she nibbled on before leaving for the cemetery. She didn't finish it, not that she could afford to waste food, but she was already so late getting up that she didn't want to take the time. Not even for a whole piece of toast. *Was that today? It must have been yesterday or last week or last year. It can't have been today.*

"A sandwich," Sadie said in a tone that was almost kindly. "That's exactly what I want. How did you know?"

How did this girl know that she needed food? Sadie had worked hard all her life to make sure no one ever knew what she was thinking, not since Ruth. Well, not since Jimmy. *Damn you, Jimmy, wherever you are.* Now, this girl, this stranger, could read her mind? That couldn't be a good thing. No one should know what went on in there. For sure, not today.

"Like I said, we don't have much in the fridge that could go into a sandwich. I could do ham and cheese—" Sylvie interrupted herself. "If you do ham, that is. If not—"

"Ham is fine. Cheese, too."

"On a croissant? Would that be okay? We don't keep regular bread here most of the time."

"A croissant is also fine." Sadie nearly added "thank you" but didn't. "And more coffee, too, if it isn't too much trouble." She sort of smiled.

"Sure." Sylvie grinned and disappeared into the kitchen.

"See? That wasn't so hard, was it?"

"Go to hell," Sadie muttered, turning back to face her nemesis, "and stop putting words in my mouth."

"Someone's got to do it. You can't say thank you, like a real human being? Like a mensch?"

"I can speak for myself."

"And where's that got you, Hadassah?"

"My name is Sadie," she blurted then jerked her head around to make sure no one had noticed her outburst. No one had. Was anyone else really here with her? Was this all some sort of dream? *A dream, yes. More like a nightmare.*

"Whatever you say, Hadassah."

Sadie twisted her chair so she couldn't see the window, even from the corner of her eye, and glared into her coffee dregs. After a few minutes she picked up *Sara's Year*, scowled at the cover and let it drop back onto the chair with a thud. This time the McGill professor glanced up, averting his gaze when Sadie glowered at him.

If she couldn't look out the window and wouldn't look at that *farkakte* book that she should never have bought, she had to look at something. She inspected her fingernails, but they were chewed up and ugly. What she wouldn't give for a manicure, for a real lady's hands not some pimply teenager's. She clenched her fists to hide her nails.

"This was not how my life was supposed to turn out," she whispered. She shut her eyes and for a moment it was 1934, the last time she had been inside this restaurant. The Berkeley was still a hotel then, almost new, and this was the Berkeley Cafe not a fancy schmancy Café des Artistes. It wasn't this silly art deco phoniness, either. It was an ordinary hotel coffeeshop with rows of square tables jammed together. Haimish, like it could have been on the Main instead of on Sherbrooke Street. What could be homier than checkered tablecloths and motherly waitresses with white aprons and caps? Everything was red, white and blue — plain and simple. Not this hard, shiny, black-and-chrome drek that was trying much too hard to be something it could never be. And no perky leprechauns trying to pretend like they were flappers. *I remember flappers, and this girl's no flapper. She's fake, fake, fake. Like everything else in this place. In every place these days.*

Sylvie set the sandwich and a mug of fresh coffee in front of Sadie, smiled at her, then moved on to see to the professor.

It isn't the girl's fault. I bet he makes her dress like that, the owner — probably some shlubby twenty-nine-year-old who wouldn't know authentic if it dropped on his head.

Curious that she should remember all that about the Berkeley, but not why she was here or who she was with. It can't have been a date. She didn't go on dates, except with— She shook her head to clear the thought. *Those weren't dates, anyhow. Not in the end.*

Sadie nibbled on her sandwich. Sylvie had made it on a fresh, flaky croissant with a kind of cheese that Sadie didn't recognize. Spicy. Sadie didn't usually eat spicy, but this was good. She didn't usually eat ham, either. Not because she kept kosher. Who should she keep kosher for? Besides, kosher was more expensive, and who could afford to pay extra to keep some rabbi in a job? *When did a rabbi ever do anything extra for me?* Ruth had kept kosher, of course. In those days everyone did. Yet because she didn't grow up with ham and pork and bacon, she never thought to buy it. She would, though, if the price was right. *I'll look next time I'm in Steinberg's. You won't mind, Mama, will you?*

"Mama won't mind," the voice in the window replied. "Not about that, she won't. About the way you turned out? That she would mind."

"Don't you dare talk about my mama," Sadie hissed. "Don't you dare."

"*Your* mama? Since when is she only your mama? You think you have some kind of monopoly?"

"Nate and Manny hardly knew her. Not Esther, either."

"That isn't what I meant, Hadassah. You know that isn't what I meant."

"Enough!" Eyes stinging, Sadie jerked her chair back. It scraped grindingly against the floor. The professor peered over his reading glasses at her. He frowned disapprovingly before returning to his essays. As Sadie pushed herself up, she knocked against the table, so hard that her mug toppled, sloshing coffee all over her sandwich. She leapt back before it could spill onto her then stood in place, staring impotently as the hot, milky liquid dribbled from table to chair to floor.

"Your book!" Sylvie cried, appearing from nowhere, it seemed. She scooped up *Sara's Year* from the other chair before any coffee could touch it. As she pushed the book toward Sadie, she noticed the cover. "It's—" She stopped to examine it more closely. "It can't be." She flipped it over and skimmed the blurb on the back. "Sarah?" She turned to Sadie. "I know her. It's Sarah. Sarah Swartz."

34

I can't escape. I can't escape from Sarah. I can't escape from Bernie. I can't escape from Esther. Esther? Are you haunting me, Esther? Are you trying to get back at me for— For what? You want injured party? Me, I'm the injured party. I'm the one who lost her mother. You never even knew her. I'm the one who had no childhood. I had to be your mother so you could have a childhood. Your father, too, practically. I'm the one who had no husband. You took all the men. All the boys, then all the men. You didn't only get to have a childhood. You got to have a child. I'm the one who had no ch—

Sadie stopped. She could not continue.

A full mug of steaming coffee, twin creamers of whole and skim milk and a freshly made sandwich sat in front of her on the still-damp table. *Sara's Year* rested on a triple-folded paper towel behind them. The floor glistened where it hadn't fully dried.

The professor had left in the midst of the catastrophe, and the tourist couple was also gone. It was just Sadie now. Sadie and this girl who used to work at the restaurant that was once Stella's, this girl who knew Sarah. For all Sadie knew, this girl had known Esther, too.

If Sylvie knew Esther, Sadie didn't want to hear about it. She had let Sylvie go on and on about Sarah and *Sara's Year*, about how she was Dominique's daughter, about how she not only knew Sarah from Dominique's but knew that Sarah was writing a book. "This book!" she had exclaimed.

Sadie had lied. Well, she didn't lie, but she didn't tell the whole truth. "I saw the book next door and thought it looked interesting," she said. It was sort of true, although "interesting" could not begin to cover it.

Then, just when Sadie thought Sylvie was done with the subject, there was more. How could there be any more? Well, there was. A kid from the back had finished clearing away Sadie's disaster and Sylvie had finally returned the book. She was on her way to the kitchen to replace the coffee and sandwich when she spun around and stepped back toward Sadie. Did Sadie know anything about the artist who was showing next door at the Klinkhoff? That was his painting in the gallery window. She was asking, she said, because she had met him at Dominique's, too. She would be going to the opening when she got off work.

"You should go, too," Sylvie said. "His work's really great. Different. Unusual, in a good way. They say he might be the next Marc-Allan Cameron."

He could be the next Leonardo da Vinci, for all Sadie cared. And who was this chaim yankel? She was supposed to have heard of this Cameron person? Well, she hadn't and she didn't want to. Not caring if she appeared rude, she turned away from Sylvie. It was then she noticed that one of the postcards she had snatched from Esther's grave was poking out of her purse. She pulled the bag onto her lap and clapped her hand over it, in case the postcard should choose this minute to jump out and give her away.

Sylvie took another step closer. "His name's Bernard Marc Freed," she continued, oblivious to Sadie's discomfort. "Bernie. He's a friend of Sarah's, from your book. You think he's in the book?"

Of course, he is. Why wouldn't he be? Esther can't torment me anymore so she sends Bernie. That hoity-toity Sarah, too, with or without her h.

Sadie stared at the sandwich, her appetite gone. *Bernie. Esther had Bernie. Me? I had no one.*

"That isn't exactly true, is it, Hadassah?"

Sadie couldn't lift her eyes from the plate to face her reflection. "That isn't fair," she whispered. "You know that isn't fair."

"You're talking to me about fair? How old would he be today, Hadassah? How old?"

"I couldn't. You know I couldn't."

"No, this time you're right. You couldn't."

"It would have been his birthday last month. Maybe this month."

"Maybe even today."

"Given my luck, probably today."

Sadie shut her eyes. Her hands dropped to her abdomen. Fifty years later, she could almost feel the pain. And the shame. It was hard to know which was worse.

No, it wasn't. The shame was worse. The pain went away after a time. The shame never did.

35

Sarah shut the menu and laid it on the linen tablecloth next to the champagne-filled crystal flute. She had picked up bits and pieces of French over the years. How could you not, living in Montreal? Especially these days. She had never picked up French-cooking French, though. That was beyond her. French cooking, too. Most cooking, if she was honest. French cooking even more. Too many fancy dishes with fancy names she couldn't understand and was sure she wouldn't like.

Sarah loved the idea of being at the Ritz for lunch. But the reality? She would never tell Bernie, but Dominique's was more her cup of tea. Simple food: soups, sandwiches, salads and spaghettis. What else do you need? Pie, of course. But no one could beat Dominique's pies, not even a famous French pastry chef. Of that she was certain.

Still, she was happy to be here. Who wouldn't be? The Ritz-Carlton was Montreal's swankiest hotel, and being here was special. More special for Bernie than for her. For Erik, too, of course. But mostly for Bernie. What a long way he had come in those four years since Esther's funeral. *Me, too, I suppose.* She stole a glance at the two copies of *Sara's Year* on the table, Bernie's and Mac's. She had signed them both, not sure what to write above her scribbled signature. The book was so new that she had not been asked to sign a copy before now. In the end, all she could think of to say was "thank you" to Mac and "with love" to Bernie. *I will have to do better at the book launch next week.*

Bernie was opening his copy and reading something aloud. Mac and Erik were laughing. All three turned to her and she nodded her acknowledgment, but she wasn't paying attention. It was as if it had taken until this moment for her to recognize the magnitude of her accomplishment, and she suddenly couldn't believe it. Had she really written a whole book? Had McClelland & Stewart really been eager to publish it? Were reviewers really raving about it? The book's early buzz had already prompted M&S to move her book launch from the Westmount Library's modest meeting room to the more spacious Victoria Hall next door. None of this could be possible. Yet it was. Thanks to Esther, it was. And to Bernie.

What a sweet couple they made, Bernie and Erik. Like Esther and Mac might have but couldn't. What would she have done had a Mac come into her life while she was married to that no-good Sammy? Would she have had more courage than Esther? Sure, she had urged Esther to run off with Mac. Would she have in the same situation? Could she have? She did not honestly know. *I am such a hypocrite, Esther. I'm sorry.*

Sarah watched Mac waving his arms as he told another story about his Aunt Emmeline. Now Emmeline would have run off had a Mac come into her life. Or maybe for Emmeline it would have been a Mabel, or both. Not that it mattered. Sarah was glad for Bernie that Mac was in his life. She was happy for Mac, too. The last time she had seen him, thirty-something years ago at Anne Savage's art opening, he looked so sad, like he had lost his best friend. He had. Esther. Now, he looked good, even more handsome than all those magazine pictures. He looked happy, too, also thanks to Bernie.

"Madame?" Sarah had not noticed the waiter approach.

"Oh, dear." She opened the menu. "Go ahead, boys. You order first."

Erik chose the bouillabaisse à la marseillaise; Mac, the feuilleté de saumon à la Ritz-Carlton; and Bernie, the mignonettes de boeuf, sauce marchand de vin. Why couldn't they call it what it was, Sarah muttered: fish soup, deboned salmon and steak.

"This duck," she tapped confit de canard du Lac Brome pommes sautées à la sarladaise, pronouncing it conn-fitt. "It isn't related to any of them, is it?" She gestured toward the white ducklings swimming in the Ritz Garden pond outside. The ducks flapped their wings noisily as if they knew they were being discussed. "I've never eaten a duck," she continued, "but I couldn't try it if it was."

"Non, Madame, these ducks, they are special."

"Do they mind?"

"Madame?"

"The ducks. The ones in the pond."

"Madame?"

"Never mind. I'll have the liver."

"The foie de veau poêlé à l'avocat. Of course."

"You wouldn't chop it for me, would you?"

"Chop it, madame?"

Bernie burst out laughing. "Stop it, Sarah. This is the Ritz, not the Brown Derby."

"Ah, I understand," the waiter said. "Chopped liver. I can ask the chef, if Madame would like me to."

"No, Mister Smarty Pants is right. This is Sherbrooke Street, not the Van Horne Shopping Centre. I'll take it as it comes."

"Oui, Madame. Merci, Madame." The waiter hurried off as quickly as was seemly in a Ritz dining room.

"A toast," Erik said. He stood and raised his glass.

"To my lack of class?" Sarah asked, wrapping her fist around the crystal stem. She winked.

"We can make that the second toast," Bernie quipped.

"To the best author and artists in Montreal, Canada and the world," Erik declared. "Here's to you three and more success—"

"No," Bernie interrupted. "That's not right." He touched Erik's arm then stood to join him. "Here's to the four of us: the world's best author and its three best artists. Skål!"

Eric clinked his glass against Bernie's. "L'chaim!"

36

Sadie opened her eyes. Closing them against the memory and the shame didn't help. It never helped. God knows she had tried. She had tried everything she could think of to erase that piece of her past, including doing her best to avoid the downtown Medical Arts Building. That building always brought it back to the surface. Always.

Thank God old Dr. Callendar had moved his offices out of there soon after the— Sadie still refused to put words to it.

The good news, if there was such a thing, was that once her doctor left the building forever, so did she. Sadie never set foot inside it again. The bad news was that building had not been torn down. Every time she walked by it, she remembered what she longed so desperately to forget.

Of course, she would have to pass it today, of all days. Why did she do it? If she was coming here to the Berkeley, she could have stayed on de Maisonneuve Boulevard all the way to Drummond or turned up any of the other four side streets to Sherbrooke. Better yet, she could have taken the Metro all the way to the Peel station. Instead, she had exited the subway on Guy Street and marched straight up to Sherbrooke, right up to the Medical Arts Building. Why had she come this way?

Because I didn't know I was coming to the Berkeley. Because I didn't know where the hell I was going. She paused. *Because God is a sadist.*

Sadie climbed down from the examining table as quickly as dignity would allow and installed herself on the adjacent metal chair. It felt like she was on exhibit up there, like she was in some sort of carnival freak show. She crossed her arms and legs against both the sterile room's perpetual chill and the violation that every doctor's visit seemed to her to represent. She tilted her head up toward Frederick Callendar and waited. The white-haired, ruddy-faced physician who had looked after her since she was born said nothing.

"There's something wrong with me. I know there is." Sadie shivered. "What is it? Tell me what's wrong with me."

"You're cold, Sadie. Get dressed and come back into my office. We'll talk in there." Dr. Callendar nodded at his Amazon of a nurse, who stood motionless and ramrod-erect by the window that overlooked Guy Street. "Miss Doucette will stay here with you in case you need anything."

"I don't need anything. What would I need?" Sadie reached for her dress, glaring at the nurse. Claire Doucette ignored her.

"So what is it?" Sadie asked again a few minutes later from another hard chair, this one in front of the doctor's massive oak desk. A miniature Christmas tree blinked distractingly at her from the corner. "What's wrong with me, doctor? Why am I not…you know… regular? I've never not been regular before. Not ever."

Dr. Callendar leaned back into the worn leather chair that was as old as his medical practice. It squeaked screechingly like it did every time he moved in it.

Sadie winced. *The man's a doctor, for God's sake. He can't afford a new chair? Or a can of oil, maybe?*

"Tell me, Sadie," Dr. Callendar began, tenting his fingers and leaning the tip of his nose into them. "Do you have a regular boyfriend these days? Someone you're seeing? Someone special? A fiancé, perhaps?"

"A boyfriend? A fiancé? What are you asking?" Sadie stared at the doctor as though he was jabbering on in some foreign language. "I don't understand. Why should you—" She stopped and gaped at him in horror. "You don't mean…" She shook her head. "No," she said firmly. "I am not. You must be wrong. It can't be. I can't be." She slumped back in her chair and kneaded the left sleeve of her dress with her right thumb and forefinger. "That's why…? You have to help me," she gasped after a few minutes' silence.

"That is for the father to do," Dr. Callendar offered.

Sadie clenched her fists until her knuckles were white. "You don't understand. It wasn't like that."

"I have been a doctor a long time, Sadie. I understand more than you think." He pressed a buzzer on his desk. Nurse Doucette appeared almost immediately. "Will you bring Miss Finkel a cup of tea, please?"

Only a single raised eyebrow disturbed the nurse's otherwise expressionless face.

"No," Dr. Callendar responded to the familiar signal. "Nothing for me."

Claire Doucette strode out of the room.

"He will have to marry you, of course," he said to Sadie after the door clicked shut. "The father." He hesitated. "He isn't married, is he?"

Sadie unclenched her fists and gnawed on her left thumbnail. A moment later, she dropped her left hand to her lap and clutched it in her right. "It doesn't matter," she said dully.

"Of course, it matters," the doctor replied with as much patience as he could muster this late in the afternoon and this late in his career.

"You don't understand," Sadie repeated. "He can't. I wouldn't."

Nurse Doucette reentered bearing a small metal tray. It looked like something that usually held medical instruments. She set the tray on Sadie's side of the desk, lifted out a bone-china cup of weak tea, a matching sugar bowl and creamer and a tiny, slightly tarnished silver spoon. She left as silently as she had come in, the tray under her arm.

"I understand that you are going to have a baby, Sadie Finkel," Dr. Callendar continued, a slight edge to his voice. "You are going to have to understand that, too. So is the father, whoever he is, whatever his situation."

"You aren't listening to me," Sadie shrilled. "The father won't do anything. Even if I could tell him, I wouldn't. Even if I did, he wouldn't do anything. He-he..." She dropped her voice. "I didn't want it," she whispered. "I didn't want to. He made me." She shuddered. "He r—" Sadie clamped her mouth shut. She could not say the words.

It was a Wednesday evening an hour after closing. Mrs. Reitman had asked Sadie to stay behind with her to sort through some stock.

The store was too busy for them to manage it during opening hours. Sadie readily agreed. She could use the extra cash, and she was grateful to have an excuse to avoid going straight home, where all she would do would be to cook another dinner for Nate, Manny, Esther and her father.

Sadie was stacking blouses into neat piles when she heard the phone ring out front. A few minutes later, Sarah Reitman bustled into the storeroom.

"I have to leave, Sadie. That was Mr. Reitman. Our boy is throwing up everywhere and Mr. Reitman doesn't know what to do. I told him what to do. I told him to call the doctor. He wants me to see first for myself, in case it's not so serious. He hates doctors." She rolled her eyes at the weakness of husbands. "We'll have to finish this another night. Maybe tomorrow? Could you stay late tomorrow?"

Sadie shrugged. She had hoped for more hours, but even adding a single hour to her paycheck would make a difference. As for tomorrow, Mrs. Reitman was known to forget things like that. It would either happen or it wouldn't. "I'm sorry about your son, Mrs. Reitman," she said. "I hope it isn't anything serious."

"Of course, it isn't. A mother knows." She pushed Sadie's coat at her and draped her own over her shoulders. "Men. Feh."

Sarah Reitman hustled Sadie out the front door and was locking up when she smacked the side of her head. "Oy! Harry Isaacs is supposed to be here with those samples for the holidays." She tilted her watch to catch the glow of the streetlight. "I can't call him. He'll be in his car by now." She squinted up the street as though it could be possible to see Harry's gray Hudson from across town in the dark. "I could tape a note to the door," she said half to herself, "but we have to see those samples right away and he goes to Ottawa first thing tomorrow. If he doesn't come tonight…" She thrust the store key at Sadie. "Do you think you could stay by yourself until Harry gets here? It'll be a half an hour, thirty-five or forty minutes at the most. You can lock up after he's gone and give the key back to me when you come in tomorrow. I'll bring my spare to open up in the morning."

Sadie didn't like Harry Isaacs. She didn't trust Harry Isaacs. She didn't want to be alone with Harry Isaacs. He was always looking at her funny.

Mrs. Reitman sensed Sadie's doubt. "This is important, so I'll tell you what I'll do. I'll pay you double what I was going to pay you to help me tonight and like I said, I'll still need you again after closing tomorrow. Would you? I know it's a big favor to ask, but…"

Double? That would mean that Sadie could finally buy herself new shoes. Her cheap pairs wore out so fast when she was on her feet all day. For new shoes, she could stand Harry Isaacs for a few minutes. Just. "Sure, Mrs. Reitman." She took the key and unlocked the door.

When Harry Isaacs arrived an hour later and found Sadie alone in the store, he did more than look at her funny. He did more than look at her. She tried to fight him off, but he said he would tell the Reitmans that it was all her idea. "I've known Herman and Sarah for years. Who are they going to believe, me or a nothing of a shopgirl? An ugly one at that." He shoved a fleshy hand into her blouse. "Be a good girl," he wheedled. She wriggled away. His voice grew steely, and he jerked her toward him. "Or I will get you fired. You know I can. I've done it before. I can do it again. Like that." He snapped his fingers as he pushed his mouth into her face.

And now she was going to have this mamzer's baby? Not if she could help it. "Can't you…you know…do something…for me?" Sadie pleaded.

"Don't be foolish," Dr. Callendar snapped.

"I can't have this baby. I just can't."

"I cannot help you that way," the doctor said. His voice softened. "I wish there was something I could do, Sadie, but there isn't. I could lose my license for what you're asking. Worse, we could both go to jail."

"I'd rather go to jail than have this baby."

"You don't mean that, Sadie."

"I do. I won't have his— this baby. I won't."

"Of course, you will. There's nothing else to be done." He reached into his drawer for a black, leather-bound address book, flipping through it until he found what he was searching for. "It's not all bad. I know a place you can go away to." He tapped the entry. "Outside the city. In Shawbridge. No one here needs to know anything about it, except your father. They're good people up there. When the baby is born, they will find it a home, you can come back to the city and it will be all over. How does that sound?"

Sadie got up to leave, her fists again clenched. She would not carry Harry Isaacs's baby. She would not let Harry Isaacs ruin her life. She would not. "If you won't help me," she declared angrily, "I will have to find another way. I will find another way. I'll do it myself, if I have to."

"Sit down, Sadie."

Sadie sat.

"You will kill yourself as well as the baby."

"If I have this baby," she retorted, "I might as well be dead. If I have this baby, I won't be able to stay here, and if I have to go away… No," she stated and stood again, more resolute than ever. "If you won't help me and if I can't find someone who will, I will do it myself. I hear the other girls in the store sometimes talk about things like this. I'll ask them what to do. I don't like it that they'll have to know, but I have to do something." Sadie pulled her coat off the coatrack and draped it over her arm. "I will not have this baby," she announced and turned to the door.

"Wait."

Sadie stopped, her back to the doctor.

Sighing, Frederick Callendar scribbled a name and an address on a slip of paper. "Take this," he said. "She can't help you herself, but she may know someone who can. Come back to see me when it's over, and I will do what I can to make sure you're all right. Will you do that?"

Sadie snatched the paper from the doctor's hand, scanned it to make sure she could read what he had written, stuffed it into her purse and left.

37

"You were one of the lucky ones, Hadassah."

"Maybe."

"What do you mean?"

"You know what I mean."

Sadie clutched the icy iron railing on the corkscrew staircase, trying not to lose her balance on the snowy steps. Manny had been in and out with the shovel all morning, but no one could keep up with the relentlessness of those fat, sloppy flakes. They had been swirling down from the wintry sky since the previous afternoon, and the man on the radio said it wasn't supposed to let up for another week at least. *So, what did I expect? It's January in Montreal. This is as good as it gets.*

Gingerly, her booted toe hunted for the next step. Another. Another. Her foot slipped and skidded. Sadie inhaled sharply, gripping the railing more tightly to steady herself. *I should just let myself fall. That would fix things. Maybe. No. That kind of brave I'm not. I'm not this kind of brave, either, but what choice do I have?*

When she reached the sidewalk, even worse because it didn't have a Manny to clear it and no city crews had yet found their way to Clark Street, Sadie turned north toward St. Joseph Boulevard. If she was lucky, she would find a taxi on St. Joseph. If she wasn't so lucky, she would have to tramp west through another four blocks of snow to busier Park Avenue. If the bad luck that had gotten her into this mess was determined to continue, she would have to take a streetcar. A couple of streetcars, or more. It was New Year's Day, so who knew whether there would be taxis around or what the streetcar service would be like.

What kind of narishkeit was it to shlep all the way almost to the end of the island — a dozen miles, probably — on January 1? But the doctor, if he was a doctor, was adamant. It had to be today. Today or no day.

A taxi would be expensive. But this horror was already going to cost her forty-five dollars she didn't have. She might as well spend the few cents more it would take to get her there and back, especially back, without having to deal with streetcars. And people. She could not deal with people today. She didn't know how she would deal with Manny, Nate, Esther and Papa when it was all over. Or Harry Isaacs, for that matter. She would have to, like she did every day. Only more so.

Sadie's coffee was cold; her sandwich, untouched. She had waved Sylvie away when she stopped by to see if everything was okay. Of course, nothing was okay. Had anything ever been okay? Maybe before Ruth died. But after? After had been one nightmare after another. And now...now, she was being forced to remember the worst of them.

She caught a glimpse of *Sara's Year* reflected in the window, its lettering mirror-backwards and its image distorted. *Just like me, everything an upside-down mess; Moishe Kapoyer, Mama would have said. Why couldn't the coffee have spilled all over the damn book, covering up that smug, stupid smirk on Sarah's fat, stupid face?*

A Veteran's taxi pulled up to the curb in front of Maison Alcan, its dome light off and its engine idling. After a few minutes, a woman in a dark business suit and stiletto heels and carrying a leather briefcase emerged from the building, crossed the pavement and entered the cab.

It should have been so easy to get a cab that day. It should have been. It wasn't.

Of course, there were no taxis on St. Joseph Boulevard. None on Park Avenue, either. In the end she caught a number 80 streetcar south to the Craig Street terminus. It took long waits in the cold for two more streetcars to get her all the way east to a shabby second-floor flat on Tellier Street.

The next hour was a blur. Sadie remembered a short man with greasy black hair and dirty, broken fingernails who wore mud-encrusted shoes and doctor's scrubs that must once have been white but were now gray and streaked with dried blood. He spoke broken English with a thick French-Canadian accent. He gave her no name and did not want to know hers, not that she would have told the truth had he asked. After he let her in, he glanced warily out the door then slammed it behind her. He pushed her down a dark hallway and into an unheated room at the back of the house that was not much brighter and was furnished with nothing but a hatrack and two wooden tables: a long one, slightly angled to the floor and partly covered with a towel, and a small one next to it that was empty but for a dented surgical bowl filled with metal instruments soaking in an awful-smelling solution that she prayed was disinfectant.

After she took four tens and five ones from her purse and handed it to him, Sadie hung up her coat and lay on the table with her dress pulled up above her waist, her panties down at her ankles and her eyes closed. She must have passed out almost right away, or she could have blocked it all out, because the next thing she remembered was a sharp pain down there and opening her eyes to an older woman covering her with a sheet. She looked a bit like the man, but at least she was clean. At least the sheet was clean.

"Rest," the woman said to Sadie in a tone that fell somewhere between brusque and kindly. More brusque than kindly. Her accent was not as strong as her son's, if it was her son. She set a glass of water on the side table. The surgical bowl was gone. "Go when you're ready. Don't be too long." The woman turned to leave but stopped at the door. "Don't you ever come back here again," she added sternly.

"Wait," Sadie croaked. "A taxi. Can you call me a taxi?"

The woman considered Sadie's question. "You leave now?" she asked.

Sadie nodded weakly.

"Can you walk to the end of the street?"

"I think so. I'll try."

"You will have to. The taxi will pick you up there."

"Like I said, you were lucky, Hadassah. You didn't die."

Sadie raised her hands from her abdomen, held them in the air for a few seconds, then returned them to the table, palms down. She gazed out the window, past her reflection, past Sherbrooke Street and out to some distant world beyond this one, to a place where, if she squinted just right and didn't blink, she could see Ruth, her mother, dressed in flowing, gauzy white. "I don't know," she whispered. "Maybe not so lucky.

38

Sarah sipped from her champagne flute and felt the bubbles burst in her mouth. They tickled. Not like seltzer tickled, or ginger ale. That was more like tiny needles poking. Champagne was subtler than a tickle…more like a pleasant tingling. Sarah was not any kind of wine connoisseur. The contents of her dusty liquor shelf proved it. But she knew what she liked. This, she liked. *I could get used to this.*

Sarah smiled sadly, closed her eyes and remembered. *"I could get used to this." That's what you said, Esther. You told me you said it to Mac at the hotel in Halifax that day, the day in 1946 when that first baby of yours was conceived, the one that miscarried. You said, "I could get used to this." But you couldn't, Esther. Not really. If you had, everything would have been different. You and Mac would never have lost each other, Bernie would have had an older brother or sister and maybe the cancer wouldn't have killed you. Maybe you would have been so happy that the cancer would never have had a chance.*

Esther cradled a cup of weak coffee in her hands and stared blankly into the tasteless liquid. The war had been over for more than a year but wartime rationing had not been lifted.

"No sugar again today," Sarah said. "Sorry."

"It doesn't matter." Esther added a few drops of milk and took a sip. It still tasted like dirty dishwater. She drank it anyway. "Oh, Sarah," she said, "I wish you had come with me to the picture yesterday."

"You know I couldn't." Sarah sat across from her at the rickety kitchen table, trying to ignore the glass of milk staring accusingly at her. She hated milk. Unfortunately, until the baby came, she was allowed only one cup of tea or coffee a day. On those rare mornings when she didn't throw up, she had her tea with lemon first thing. Today had been one of those days.

"If I could see my ankles," she continued, "I would know for sure how swollen they are. But I know how they feel. I can barely make it across the hall to the bathroom most days, let alone downtown. I'm sure I will love this baby when it comes. For right now, I'm not so sure." She raised her glass but didn't drink. "Listen," she said.

"What?"

"Nothing. That's just it. The radio stopped again. Would you go into the living room and give it a smack? I would get up but…"

"Hopefully, you'll be able to get a new radio soon," Esther called from the gloomy Kaplan living room, where the prewar tabletop Philco sat in a dark corner on the floor. She thumped it with the flat of her hand. It stuttered into a staticky hiss.

"Don't be gentle," Sarah shouted. "Wallop it. That's the only thing it understands."

Esther booted it lightly.

"Kick harder. You can't break it any more than it's already broken."

The instant Esther's heel connected with the side of the unit, the static sputtered into "The Gypsy," the summer's number one hit by The Ink Spots.

In a quaint caravan
There's a lady they call the gypsy
She can look in the future
And drive away all your fears
Everything will come right
If you only believe the gypsy

"Not my fears, she can't," Esther muttered on her way back to the kitchen.

"What's that?"

"Nothing." Esther added coffee to her cup from the aluminum percolator on the stove and sat down.

"The picture yesterday, it was that good?" Sarah asked. "You liked it? Was it good like the book? Irene Dunne made a good Anna?"

Esther didn't answer. She finished her coffee in silence, and Sarah watched her with mounting concern.

Nothing about Esther's appearance would have revealed her distress to a stranger. Her chocolate eyes were clear, with not a hint of red to suggest tears. Each wave and curl of her dark, Lauren Bacall hair lay precisely as Esther had brushed it into place before she left the house. And her rayon crepe dress in a flattering shade of deep cranberry was perfectly pressed without a speck of lint. It wasn't a put-together look. Somehow, everything about Esther always seemed casual, natural and effortless, at least to a stranger. Sarah was no stranger.

"Something's wrong, Esther. What is it?"

Esther lifted her coffee cup to take another sip but it was empty. She held it in front of her mouth for a few minutes before returning it to the table. "I did something bad," she said. "Something very bad. Very, very bad. It wouldn't have happened if you had come with me. It couldn't have. That's why I wish you were there. But you weren't. It isn't your fault. I know you couldn't come. What happened is my fault."

"You went to the movies. You went downtown to see *Anna* at the Capitol. What could be so bad? I know it wasn't taking a taxi that was bad. You told me Morris said it was okay to start taking taxis again, now the war's been over for a while."

"It wasn't the taxi. A hundred taxis would be less bad than this. A thousand."

"So, okay. What was it? You're a nicer person than me. What could you do that was so bad?"

"You wouldn't have done this."

"What? What is it that I wouldn't do that you did?"

Esther returned to the stove and poured the last of the coffee into her cup. She switched off the burner, put the pot in the sink and sat back down. "I kissed a man," she said. "A stranger. On the lips."

"On the lips?"

"On the lips. I met him outside the theater. I let him hold my hand during the picture. We went walking in the Public Gardens after. Then I let him kiss me. I'm a married women, Sarah, and I let a strange man kiss me. In public. On the lips."

"You'll tell me about him?"

"I don't know much, but I can tell you what I know."

Sarah watched Esther closely. There was something different about her today. Not the worry. She had seen that before. This was something else. Could it be…? It was. She was certain of it. "Before you tell me what you know," Sarah said, reaching for Esther's hand, "I'll tell you what I know about what happened."

"What? What can you know about it?"

"I know that whoever he is, you're in love with him."

"Narishkeit, you're talking. How can I be in love with him? I just met him. It's impossible. I'm married."

"How long have I known you, Esther?"

"All my life, practically. Why?"

"Your eyes shine when you talk about him. Your face gets flushed. Your voice changes. It's like you're talking from here." She touched Esther's chest. "Not here." She tapped her head.

Esther said nothing. Frank Sinatra's voice crackled on the Philco.

Give me five minutes more, only five minutes more

Let me stay, let me stay in your arms

"I know you, Esther. I know you like I know myself. Better. Like you know me. You're never like this when you talk about Morris. You've never been like this, ever, when you've talked about Morris."

"I love him. Morris, I mean."

"I know you do. But you've never been in love with him. Not really. Am I right? Not like you are with this stranger. What's his name?"

"Marc-Allan Cameron," Esther whispered, as if even speaking his name was a betrayal. "Everyone calls him Mac. It's his initials: M.A.C. He's Scottish, I think. He has a bit of an accent." She stopped. "This is embarrassing."

"In front of me you're embarrassed?"

"No, not that. It's just that I don't really know anything else about him." She looked away. "He calls me Queen Esther." She blushed.

"Will you see him again, this Mac?" Sarah asked.

"He wants me to."

"But will you?"

"I'm going to try not to."

"Will that work?"

"No, I don't think so."

"Sarah." Bernie shook her shoulder gently.

Sarah opened her eyes. "I was somewhere else, with your mother. A long time ago. Remembering." She took another sip of champagne and hiccuped. She clutched her chest and returned the glass to the table. "I like this," she said, hiccuping again. "I'm not so sure it likes me."

Erik topped up her glass. "Give it a chance to get to know you. I bet it'll change its mind."

"You're on, mister." Sarah picked up the champagne flute and wiggled her pinky. "That's so it knows I'm serious," she said, and hiccuped. She looked questioningly at Erik.

"Do it," he insisted. "Show it who's boss."

She sipped again, more slowly this time, and rolled the champagne around in her mouth before swallowing. No hiccup. She did it again. Again, no hiccup.

"Who's the boss now?" Erik asked, grinning.

"Sarah's always been the boss," Bernie replied. "Isn't that right?" he asked Sarah.

Sarah set her glass down. "I'm the boss?" she asked, turning to Mac.

"If Bernie says so." He winked at Bernie.

"Then I have a question for you."

"Fire away."

"So you couldn't paint Esther all those years," she said.

Mac nodded.

"That isn't a question," Bernie teased.

"Quiet, you. I'm getting there."

Erik clamped his hand over Bernie's mouth. "Go ahead."

"Ignore the kibitzers," Mac said. "That's the right word, isn't it?"

"More like nudniks," Sarah replied. "But never mind. Here's what I want to know: You painted so many other beautiful pictures in that time, famous pictures. Missing only one, would that have been so bad?"

Mac was not sure how to respond, what to say to explain his obsession.

Bernie touched his arm. "Let me," he said. He up picked his copy of *Sara's Year* and placed it on the table in front of Sarah. "When you knew you had to write this but you didn't think you could, how did that feel? I know it isn't exactly the same, but it's close."

Sarah dropped her eyes to the book, the book that had seemed so impossible once upon a time, then up at Mac. She remembered the struggle, the sense of impotence and paralysis, of unworthiness, of knowing she had to do this thing but didn't know how. How many times had she been convinced that she was letting Esther down, letting Bernie down, letting herself down? She felt all that that first day, until her memory of Mr. Littleton got her started. She felt it other days, too. Plenty others.

"It was worse for you, maybe," she acknowledged at last. "You already had so many great paintings. To then get stuck like that must have been… I can't imagine. As for me…" She shrugged.

Mac picked up his copy of the book. "Esther would have been proud of you. I'm sure of it. I understand how you had to write this for you, but it's also for Esther. I know it is. I know that wherever she is, she knows it, too, and thanks you for it. Let me thank you, too." He leaned over and kissed her on the cheek.

Sarah looked up at the ceiling. "He didn't mean anything by it, Esther. I swear it. He's still yours."

"I think Esther let me go a long time ago," Mac said. "I'm the one who could never let go, would never let go." He paused. "That brings me back to your question, about the portrait." He refilled his champagne flute and held it up to the light, watching the bubbles dance through the glass, dance him all the way back to prewar London.

"I remember my first picture," he continued. "It was a few days after seeing Anne Savage and all those other Canadians at the Tate. I was still in London at Aunt Emmeline's. She was so sure that her plan for me was going to work that she had already bought paints and a canvas, even before I got there." He laughed. "I stared at the canvas all day that first day, afraid to throw my first daub of color at it. I was afraid of getting it wrong, you see." He turned to Erik. "I know I taught you that there's no wrong in art. I couldn't know that yet. Emmeline taught me that. It's one of the many things she taught me. After watching me be paralyzed for most of the day, she picked up my hand, which was clutching my brush like my life depended on it, smooshed it into the yellow paint on my palette and shoved it onto the canvas.

"'There,' she declared. 'You have begun. Now, get on with it.' Years later I asked her why she had picked the yellow. 'Because you were acting like such a coward,' she said. Aunt Emmeline never minced words. She told it like it was."

Mac took a few sips of champagne, then set the glass down. "I thought about her and that first painting every time I uncovered one of my blank Esther canvases. I even reached for the yellow paint a bunch of times. It made no difference. I couldn't do it. I could do everything else but that. I would be lying if I said I haven't enjoyed the fame and celebrity, especially early on. But every time I stood staring at another Esther canvas, all that stopped mattering and I was sure that I was the world's worst failure. The one thing that mattered to me in those moments was that I could paint that one painting. It didn't have to be good. I just had to be able to start it. But I couldn't." He looked across the table at Bernie. "Not until this guy showed up. Even then, not right away. Bernie was worse than ten Aunt Emmelines. What a nag!" He reached over to give Erik a playful punch on the shoulder. "This one, too. Once he got back to Nova Scotia, he was determined to get back at me for all the hard times I gave him at NSCAD."

"That scorecard ain't balanced yet, professor," Erik said with mock seriousness.

Mac chuckled. "We'll see about that." He turned back to Sarah. "More than anything, it was Bernie. Not so much the nagging, although that helped. It's that he resembles his mother so much. It was like Esther was looking over my shoulder every day, pushing me to do it, telling me I could do it, cheering me on."

Sarah picked up *Sara's Year* and stroked the cover. "I felt that, too," she said softly, her eyes watering, "every day. It could be I'm not such a crazy person after all."

"Of course you are," Bernie said. "We all are, or we wouldn't be sitting here getting drunk."

For a few minutes no one said anything.

"She really loved you, Mac," Sarah said, breaking the silence. She squeezed his hand. "She loved you more than anything or anyone in the world except for Bernie. You may think she let you go. She didn't. Not ever."

Mac squeezed back. "I know that now. I didn't for the longest time. Not until Bernie showed up. Not until I was able to paint that portrait. I don't think I ever saw the love in Esther's eyes until I finished the painting. It was only then that I saw the depth of her love for me, staring back at me from the canvas. Only then."

39

"It wasn't my fault," Sadie murmured into the window. Outside, afternoon shoppers wandered past the Berkeley against a backdrop of the buses and cars crawling into rush hour. Above the roofline of the trio of repurposed Golden Square Mile mansions across the street rose the Mountain, its wooded slopes offering the promise of cooling shade on this muggy August afternoon. Sadie was oblivious to it all, just as she heard nothing of the bilingual chatter that now buzzed in typical Montreal fashion around her. All she saw were the hard, chiseled features of her own face and a voice that sounded like hers even if its words and tone were unfamiliar.

"Nothing is ever your fault, is it Hadassah? It's always someone else. Always."

"That isn't fair. I didn't take Mama away so young. I didn't make Papa the way he was after Mama died. Or Nate or Manny or Esther. I didn't deserve to be called a nafkeh at school. I never stole from Reitman's or anyone." She paused. "I didn't make Harry Isaacs do what he did to me," she whispered

The face in the window, her face, stared back without compassion. "When you're right, you're right, Hadassah. None of that was your fault. None of it."

"So why are you talking to me like it was? Why are you making me feel like a such bad person? All day long, you have been attacking me for things that were never my fault. Why? Why won't you go away? Why can't you leave me alone?" Sadie tried to see past the face in the window. Maybe if she could, it would go away. When it didn't, she tried to turn her head. But her reflection's eyes were locked onto hers so overpoweringly that she could not move.

"Something was your fault, Hadassah. The biggest something of all."

"What?" Sadie asked angrily. "I already told you I didn't do any of those things. I didn't do anything. Nothing."

"Yes, you did. You let all those bad things that happened to you turn you into the sour witch you are today. That isn't anyone else's fault. That's your fault. Only your fault. All your fault."

40

Sylvie leaned against her serving station at the back of the cafe and watched the strange woman by the window. She had been sitting at that table of hers for hours, barely moving. Except for her lips. They appeared to still be moving. Was she talking to herself? Maybe she was praying. Or maybe she thought someone really was sitting there with her. The odd thing was that she hardly seemed aware that she was sitting in a public place. At the beginning, yes, when she made a face at those Goth kids and stared down Professor Samuels. Later, too, when she knocked the table and spilled her coffee. Since then it was like she was lost in her own world, a not very happy world.

A couple of times she reached for her copy of *Sara's Year*, but each time she pulled her hand back as though the book might burn her. Mostly, she scowled at it like it made her angry for even existing.

Was she one of the crazies who sometimes wandered in, probably into every downtown store and restaurant? Sylvie didn't think so. More sad than crazy, if she had to guess, and less sad than when she first came in. The change was subtle. No one else would likely notice. But between observing people in her mother's restaurant for so many years and studying centuries' worth of paintings, frescoes and sculpture for her MFA, Sylvie had developed a keen eye. She could discern what most people missed.

When the woman first walked in, her lips were pressed so tightly together that the lines around her mouth were almost like trenches. Then, her shoulders were hunched, practically up by her ears, the veins in her neck and temples were throbbing and her eyes were impenetrable dark slits. Now, she didn't look calm or relaxed but her shoulders had dropped a bit, her jaw was a touch looser and her eyes had opened just enough to reveal their color, a deep sapphire. Yet if the strange woman was not as sad as she had been, she sure wasn't happy.

Sylvie loved to make up stories about her customers, like she did with the long-dead models of the centuries-old artworks she studied at Concordia University. What was this customer's story? It had to be tragic. For anyone to look this unhappy, she must have lost someone she loved, someone she loved a lot. The death of a child? Not much could be worse than that. Or maybe her fiancé went off to fight in World War II and never came back. Or maybe she was in Europe during the war and went through the Holocaust. If everyone she knew had been killed, that could make her bitter. That could make anyone bitter. Or maybe her husband left her for a younger woman, for his secretary. Her friend Carmela's father had walked out on his wife, only to marry someone barely older than Carmela herself. Stuff like that was always happening these days.

Sylvie watched the woman reach for *Sara's Year*. Her hand hovered over it uncertainly. Would she pick it up this time or push it away again?

41

Sadie's hand hovered uncertainly over her copy of *Sara's Year*. Should she pick it up and read it? Better she should give it to Sylvie and be done with it. What she really wanted to do was smack the self-satisfied grin off Sarah Swartz's face. Instead, she opened the book in the middle and began to read.

"I never saw the fist coming that first time, that day I stood up for Morty. I wish I could say it was the last time. It wasn't. There were others. Plenty others. It was as though that first punch of Sammy's gave him the permission he had been waiting for, and he kept hitting me. Not every day, not even every week, but often enough, right up to the morning of the day he died. Never again over Morty. Poor Morty. I wish Sammy would have died first so my Morty could have lived without all that hate, even for a few months. It wasn't to be.

"Never again over Morty and never in the face again. Nothing that might show. He wasn't smart, my Sammy. He wasn't stupid, either.

"You know, it never occurred to me that Sammy would hit me. For all his temper, I couldn't imagine it. Jewish men didn't beat their wives. Only goyim did that. That's what everyone said. That's what everyone believed. Everyone was wrong. Everyone was wrong about Sammy, and everyone was wrong about Esther's Harold.

"I didn't know, of course. Esther was too ashamed to tell me, like I was too ashamed to tell her. Best friends, and this was the one secret we ever kept from each other. I wouldn't have known if Bernie hadn't told me. And Bernie wouldn't have known if—"

Sadie slammed the book shut. It couldn't be true. About Sammy, yes. He was always too good-looking for his own good. He was sure too good-looking for Sarah, who was born a wallflower and would die a wallflower. A fancy book cover and fancy cemetery clothes didn't change anything. But Harold? Harold was a good man, a mensch. It couldn't be true. It couldn't. Could it?

"She threw you out? Out of your own house?" Sadie stared at Harold in disbelief.

Harold nodded. He stuffed a handful of ketchup-soaked Suzie Q curly fries into his mouth and washed them down with a half a mug of root beer. He then chomped on his steerburger, wiping the juices dribbling down his chin with a thick paper napkin. On another man it would have been crass and sloppy. But Sadie had never seen Harold Coopersmith come across as anything but elegant. Well into his sixty-first year, he could easily pass as fifty, with a full head of hair still sprinkled with more pepper than salt, a YMCA-enabled physique that would have been the envy of many thirty-year-olds and just enough wrinkles to give him a certain gravitas, though not enough to make him look old. And smart? Not that many Jews made it into McGill University back in the days of the Jewish quota. Harold was one of the chosen few. He got a PhD in English and was immediately snapped up by Sir George Williams College for its teaching faculty, growing with the institution as it expanded from Sir George Williams College to Sir George Williams University to Concordia University. Then for reasons he would never discuss, he unexpectedly took early retirement. Sadie had heard rumors about a pair of pregnant graduate students; she believed none of it. Harold was a gentleman. He should have been teaching at McGill, not at that second-rate Concordia. And he should have married her, not that ungrateful sister of hers.

"To throw you out after seven years of marriage, a good marriage." She tsk'd. "It isn't right."

Harold leaned back into the red-vinyl banquette and stared up at the lantern-like fixture suspended over their booth at the Mister Steer diagonally across from Morgan's. They had started meeting here when Sadie was forced to transfer to the main downtown store. Before that, they would meet at the Murray's near Esther's. Near Harold's.

"She'll come crawling back," Sadie insisted. "I know she will. She would be an idiot not to." Sadie took a deep breath to collect her courage and pushed forward to the edge of her seat, her elbows on the table. "You deserve better." She looked straight at him, but only for an instant before dropping her eyes to the half-eaten burger on her plate.

Harold leaned toward her. His eyes blazed with a malevolence so virulent that Sadie shrank back in shock. It was over so quickly that Sadie was sure that she had imagined it. Hadn't she?

Rattled, she grabbed the check and half ran to the front of the restaurant to pay. A hurried goodbye later she left, keeping to the south side of St. Catherine Street to avoid crossing at Aylmer. She would walk all the way to Union Avenue and around the block to get to the Morgan's employees' entrance rather than pass in front of Cinema 539. It was fine when it was the System. It was sort of fine during the years it showed those arty movies and attracted all those crazy hippy kids. But dirty movies and dirty old men? And right across the street from a big department store like Morgan's? Sadie shuddered. *No, thank you.*

"Yes, *please.*" Harold Coopersmith watched Sadie disappear from view then crossed St. Catherine Street at Aylmer. He leered at the trio of nubile, scantily clad nymphettes flaunting themselves in the street-front poster case, then slunk into Cinema 539 for his regular post-Sadie escapades.

Sadie started to open *Sara's Year* again but couldn't bring herself to face Harold, to face what her memory told her was true, even if her mind continued to resist. Instead, she squeezed her eyes shut. When she was little, long before Ruth died, she believed that if she closed her eyes, the rest of the world would vanish. If she couldn't see anyone or anything, how could they be there? Today of all days, she wished that were true.

Faygie Greenblatt at the seniors' center never stops going on about meditation, like it's somehow a better cure than chicken soup for everything bad. What narishkeit. You close your eyes, she said, and you breathe. More narishkeit. How can you not breathe? If you don't breathe, you're dead. Sadie lifted the last bite of sandwich to her mouth. Maybe crazy Faygie has something there. Maybe that's the best cure of all for me: not breathing. She snorted. With my luck, that wouldn't kill me, either.

Sadie dropped what was left of her sandwich onto her plate without taking a bite. *There's something else that meshugena said. What was it? Oh, yeah. Something like "meditating is about not thinking." Again, narishkeit. How can you not think?*

Shutting her eyes again, Sadie slowed her breath. *I could stand not thinking anymore today.* To her surprise, she began to relax. A little. *Maybe goofy Greenblatt isn't so goofy after all.* As her mind cleared, she became more and more attuned to the sounds around her. The traffic on Sherbrooke humming through the window, itself vibrating lightly. The faint clanking of dishes in the kitchen. The distant sound of water running. The unintelligible sound of a faraway conversation. And the music.

Sadie had barely noticed the music playing in the cafe before. Now with her mind emptying, she heard it clearly and it was faintly familiar. It sounded like some kind of overture. To a show she had seen? What show? Sadie had not been to any kind of show in years, not even to a second-run movie at Cinema V or the Seville. That was something else she could not afford on her pension.

She listened more attentively. No one was singing. It was instruments only — a bunch of violins, trumpets and clarinets, all playing 1920s kinds of sounds. *Fake, probably, like everything else in this farkakte cafe.*

Then the overture segued into another track. Sadie's eyes shot open. She didn't know whether to clap her hands over her ears and flee out to the street or, as she couldn't stop herself from doing, listen in gape-mouthed paralysis as Julie Andrews mooned over James Fox in the silliest movie she wished she had never seen...

His glance has fireworks in it
We kiss, my heart does a
Whiz-bang, flip-flop
Heaven for a minute
So coax me, implore me
I promise you won't bore me
Oh, Jimmy I might say yes

"No," she whispered. "Not Jimmy.

42

Jimmy Harcourt had never coaxed or implored Sadie Finkel. And despite what the song from *Thoroughly Modern Millie* said, they had never kissed.

If only he had asked… If he had, Sadie would have said yes, just like that Millie did.

Even after, she might have said yes.

But Jimmy wouldn't.

Jimmy didn't.

Jimmy couldn't.

43

"'It'll be like when we were kids,' she said," Sadie muttered when the overture ended and the curtains opened on phony flappers in phony flapper outfits prancing down a phony 1920s street in *Thoroughly Modern Millie*. She glared at Bertha Stein, but her friend was smirking like an idiot at Julie Andrews, Mary Tyler Moore and Beatrice Lillie and all their foolishness.

What do they know about the twenties? They weren't born yet. Well, Beatrice Lillie was. So she at least should know better. Maybe if she ever took anything serious, she would. I never thought she was funny when I saw her before, and I don't think she's funny now.

A dollar twenty-five down the drain. I should get up and leave. Bertha would never notice. Some friend. If I thought they would give me my money back, I'd do just that. They'd laugh at me, those babies out front, if I said that this wasn't how it was. They'd laugh at me and say, "Of course, it isn't, lady. It's a friggin' movie."

Like Beatrice Lillie, I should also have known better. I should have stayed home and watched Ed Sullivan on the television. At least Ed Sullivan doesn't cost me a dollar and a quarter. With Ed Sullivan, I can turn him off if I don't like his guests. But this? This is phony baloney, and I'm stuck with it for two hours. More, probably.

"So you stayed."

"If I could turn the clock back," Sadie replied. "I never would have gone in the first place."

"If you could turn the clock back, Hadassah, what else would be different?"

No clock could go back that far.

44

One of the few English boys in a neighborhood teeming with Old World immigrants, James Anthony Harcourt IV was a rare specimen: slight, fair and soft-spoken in a school bursting with dark, brash Jewish teenagers. His father had been transferred to Montreal earlier that year to take over as manager of the Bank of Toronto at St. Lawrence Boulevard and Prince Arthur Street; his wife, son and daughter followed a month later. As he had done when he managed the bank's Kensington Market branch in downtown Toronto, Harcourt chose to live as near as practical to his immigrant depositors. So he moved his family into a comfortable flat on tree-lined Esplanade Avenue, across from Fletcher's Field and Mount Royal Park and a block from St. Urbain Street and Baron Byng High School.

Coming from Harbord Street Collegiate in an equivalent Toronto neighborhood, Jimmy ought easily to have adapted to his new school. In a way he did: Jimmy never fit in at Harbord and he was no less an outsider at Baron Byng. It's not surprising that he would be drawn to the school's other outcast, Sadie Finkel.

At first Sadie resisted Jimmy's attentions. She was still struggling with Ruth's death and with her new role as mother-surrogate to two younger brothers and a sister. On top of that, she knew that the boys and more and more of the girls were calling her "slutty Sadie" in school, only barely behind her back — all because she had said no to Danny Marcus and punched him in the face when he wouldn't stop. What would a goyishe blond boy from Toronto want with her if it wasn't that?

It wasn't that.

When Mr. Carmichael paired them up in history class to work on a project about the Fathers of Confederation — they were assigned Sir Alexander Tilloch Galt — Sadie soon discovered a quiet, sensitive teenager who was even more shunned and lonely than she was. By the time they submitted their joint essay two weeks later (getting extra credit for identifying Baron Byng art teacher Anne Savage as Galt's great-niece), they were inseparable. They studied together in the library, gossiped together in the cafeteria at lunchtime and took long walks up the Mountain on the weekend. Sadie told Jimmy about her mother, about the burden of having to care for her family, about her tree in the alley behind the house and about Isadora Duncan and her once-upon-a-time dream of becoming a dancer. Jimmy talked about his uncommunicative father, his distracted mother, his lonely life in Toronto and the career plans that had already been mapped out for his future. The two of them shared everything. Almost.

As far as Sadie was concerned, she had a boyfriend, her first. So what if Jimmy never touched her? He was just trying to make sure her reputation around the school didn't get any worse. She loved him even more for that. So what if he wasn't Jewish? This was 1928, for God's sake.

Sadie and Jimmy continued to see each other after graduation, if not as often. By that time Jimmy was studying business at McGill's still-new School of Commerce. Harcourts had been bankers for as long as there had been banks, and Jimmy was expected to continue the tradition. There would be no college for Sadie, not even night classes at Sir George Williams. She was working brutal hours at two jobs to help keep the family clothed and fed. Every day since Ruth's death, her papa had grown more and more spectral. He ate little and said less, and his single suit — the one he had worn to Ruth's funeral and now wore nearly every day — hung loosely and awkwardly on him, making him look more like a bag of bones than a person. If he had not yet been laid off from the schmatta factory where had worked since before Sadie was born, his hours had been slashed because of poor performance, first by a third, then by half.

Someone had to take up the slack. That someone was Sadie.

It happened on a Sunday afternoon in 1939. Sadie and Jimmy were strolling along one of the broad gravel roads that wound up to the Mount Royal summit. It was one of those days Montrealers wait impatiently for throughout March, April and most of May: Winter's chill had finally fled, the temperature was warm enough for shirt-sleeves and the first brilliant green buds of spring had begun to dress the park's naked maples, birches, oaks and elms.

Sadie and Jimmy could meet on only occasional Sundays now; it was Sadie's sole day off from Reitman's and Jimmy, too, had work responsibilities that occupied most of his week. After finishing at McGill he had been hired by the Bank of Toronto and, because of his father's influence and position, now not only worked at the West-mount branch but was on track to become the company's youngest branch manager outside Ontario. If he was seeing other women, he never said. Sadie wasn't seeing other men and never had, unless you counted what happened with Harry Isaacs, and you couldn't count that. Sadie had never said anything to Jimmy about it. He would have to know one day, of course. When he asked her to marry him, she would tell him. Not before.

Sadie gazed up at the Mountain, aware of it for the first time that day as she recalled that other day, in 1939. *What were we talking about, just before…?* Maybe if she could remember what it was they were saying to each other, she and Jimmy, she could reach back in time and somehow prevent what happened next from ever taking place.

"Morris," her reflection in the window answered. "Jimmy was asking about Morris."

Jimmy Harcourt had met Morris Freed at a McGill Graduates' Society function and both were astounded to learn that each knew one of the Finkel sisters.

"The last thing you wanted to know that day, Hadassah, was that a young man was starting to get serious about Esther. After all, you had been walking out with Jimmy Harcourt for, what, ten years? Eleven? And here was your baby sister, already half-engaged to his lawyer friend. So what did you do?"

"Nothing," Sadie mumbled. "I did nothing. What could I do?"

"You could stop lying. You didn't do nothing, did you?"

Sadie turned away. She raised her coffee cup to her lips. It was cold. She drank it all the way down anyway.

"You can't hide from me, Hadassah. You know you can't."

"I am not Hadassah," she whimpered.

"That afternoon, at least, you were Sadie. So what did Sadie do?"

Sadie slowly set down her cup. Her shoulders shook but she swallowed back the tears, as she had done every time in her adult life, except for earlier that day at the cemetery over that elm tree from when she was fifteen. How stupid was that? What kind of baby was she that a tree could make her cry, and from so long ago? Sadie closed her eyes and tried to forget the past, to forget her reflection, to do Faygie Greenblatt's meditation mishigas so she could clear her mind of every thought, of everything. Instead, her mind jerked her back to that Sunday afternoon in May 1939 and she saw it all over again, felt it all over again, wanted to die all over again.

Maybe he's shy? Maybe that's why he's never tried to kiss me or put his arm around me? Or hold my hand? Maybe it's up to me. I'm nearly a year older than he is, after all.

She sidled a few inches closer to Jimmy.

He didn't respond.

A few inches more.

Nothing.

She let her hand brush against his.

Jimmy acted like he didn't notice.

She inserted her hand in his and waited for him to take it.

He didn't. Instead, he stopped, took three steps away, his face flushed.

"I-I—"

"What is it?" Sadie edged back toward him.

"N-no," Jimmy stammered. His eyes darted up and down the road, even into the underbrush that bordered it. No one was there. "We— Can we sit down?" He scrambled the few yards to the nearest bench, pulled out his handkerchief to wipe it clean for Sadie. "Please?"

Terrified, Sadie followed him to the bench. Had Esther said something bad to Morris about her? Had Morris then said something bad to Jimmy? Had Jimmy heard about Harry Isaacs? About the— She couldn't think the word, let alone speak it. She smoothed her skirt and sat down. Jimmy joined her, at the far end of the bench.

He wouldn't look at her. Instead, Jimmy studied the trio of pigeons waddling toward them in search of a handout. Then he watched a squirrel scampering across the gravel. It stopped at the side of the road, its nose quivering and tail erect. When it vanished up a maple tree, he shifted his focus to a pair of lovers. In a different reality, it could easily have been him and Sadie holding hands, aware of nothing and no one but each other. In another reality, not in this one.

"Jimmy," Sadie began. "I'm sorry, I—"

"No," Jimmy interrupted. "Let me. I have to." He swallowed hard. "I wish I wasn't such a coward." He hesitated. "I should have said something a long time ago. I should have. I was scared."

"You're no coward."

"You don't know, Sadie." He dropped his head into his hands. "You don't know."

Sadie longed to reach toward him, to touch his arm or his shoulder, to put her arms around him. She did none of that. She waited, almost afraid to breathe.

After what seemed forever, Jimmy sat up.

"Is it because I'm Jewish?" Sadie asked tentatively, afraid he would say yes.

Jimmy shook his head.

"Is it because of your family? Is it because of my family? I know we aren't rich like you are, and my father isn't important like yours is. I know I can't go to college like you did. I know I'm not as pretty as—"

"You are pretty. You're more than pretty. You're beautiful." He turned away, embarrassed. "I wish…" He tried to imagine a different life, a different Jimmy. "It doesn't matter what I wish," he said softly. "It never has." He said nothing for a moment, wiping his mind clean of all the wishes he would never see granted. "It isn't you. It isn't your family. It has nothing to do with any of that. It's me." He searched within himself for a way to put the unspeakable into words, wishing nothing more than to be struck dead before those words had a chance to leave his mouth. "I can't be with any woman, Sadie," he said, longing to look at her but terrified that he would be forced to witness the love on her face dissolve into repugnance. "If I could, I would want it to be you. I can't. It's not what I am. I'm—" He left the sentence hanging. He stared at his shoes.

"I don't understand," Sadie said. She didn't. Then she did.

"No," she whispered. "No." She pushed herself up and inched

away. "No," she repeated again and again as she turned her back on Jimmy and returned the way they had come, forcing herself to not break into a run and refusing to cry.

Sadie and Jimmy met twice more that summer. Both encounters were accidental, awkward and brief. Each time they silently wished that they could go back in time. Each time neither knew what to say.

Within days of Canada's declaration of war that September, Jimmy enlisted, or so Esther told her. Morris had learned about it at a Graduates' Society meeting at McGill.

That was the last Sadie ever heard about Jimmy. Had he been shipped overseas? Had he been taken prisoner at Dieppe, like so many other Canadians? Had he been killed there, like her brother Nate? Or had he made it through the war and found his way back home? If he had, where was he?

In the weeks after the first overseas troops began returning to Canada in mid-1945, Sadie walked by the Harcourt's Esplanade Avenue home often, hoping to catch a glimpse of him. In August, a week after V-J Day, she learned that Jimmy's family had left the neighborhood two years earlier. No one could tell her where they had gone or why.

Twenty-two years later when Julie Andrews as that thoroughly modern Millie sang about her love for Jimmy at the Alouette Theatre on St. Catherine Street, Sadie wanted to cry. The tears would not come.

Twenty years after that in the Café des Artistes on Sherbrooke Street, the tears still refused to flow, still refused to free Sadie from her past.

Jimmy, oh Jimmy, oh what joy
He makes your troubles fly
So coax me, implore me
I promise you won't bore me
Oh, Jimmy I might say yes

45

"Not bad for goyishe liver," Sarah said, stuffing the final morsel into her mouth. She chewed it slowly, savoring it before swallowing. "Not as good as Moishe's, of course, but not bad." She patted the corners of her mouth with the linen napkin with exaggerated daintiness.

Bernie rolled his eyes. "Sarah…"

"I'm making a joke, Bernie. Don't take everything so serious." She set her napkin down. "What I'm going to say now, though, is serious, and I shouldn't say it because generations of Jewish mothers will turn cartwheels in their graves when I do."

"What?" Bernie asked.

"This was the best liver I ever tasted, and I've eaten lots of liver." She raised her eyes heavenward. "I'm sorry, Gertie. Really, I am." She grinned at Erik, sitting across from her. "My mother, may she rest in peace but probably isn't resting so peacefully after what I just said, was a great cook, but never like this."

"You're lucky," Erik said. "My mother can barely boil water. It's a miracle I made it through my childhood. It was Campbell's soup, canned vegetables and Spam almost every day until I left to go to college."

"That's for sure worse than me," Sarah said.

"And that's saying a lot," Bernie noted. "You haven't tasted Sarah's cooking."

"I sometimes think my father checked out early so he wouldn't have to swallow another mouthful of Spam."

"Spam, Spam, Spam, Spam. Spam, Spam, Spam, Spam," Bernie sang.

"Don't laugh. That Monty Python sketch was my life."

"There's egg and Spam," Bernie quoted in a squeaky voice, "egg bacon and Spam, egg bacon sausage and Spam, Spam bacon sausage and Spam, Spam egg Spam Spam bacon and Spam, Spam sausage Spam Spam—"

"Enough with the Spam," Sarah cried.

"No, no," Erik exclaimed. "You're supposed to say, 'Have you got anything without Spam?'"

"You boys!" She turned to Mac. "I bet you're as bad as they are."

"I bet you're right. I hadn't laughed much in a long time, too long, until these guys showed up."

"Would madame et messieurs care for dessert?" the waiter asked. He had glided soundlessly to their table, as if by magic. "Today, we have tiramisu Martini aux noisettes; terrine de chocolat blanc, de mûre et de pistache; parfait praliné, meringue fondante et citron confit and a selection of glaces et sorbets."

Fancy cakes, puddings and ice creams. He can't just say that? Sarah eyed him doubtfully. "No pie?" she asked.

"You and your pies." Bernie laughed.

"Me and your mother and our pies."

"Madame is in luck," the waiter said. "I may have something for you. It is normally for the dinner menu only, but for a charming lady like yourself, I know le chef de dessert would make an exception."

"Ha, Mister Know-It-All Bernie!"

"It is a sort of pie, madame, but perhaps different from what you are accustomed to. It is a tarte Tatin aux pêches blanches, a sort of white-peach pie with Courvoisier and crème fraiches."

"Perfect, and a cup of tea, please, with lemon."

"Oui, madame." The waiter bowed slightly and turned to the men. "Would messieurs also like the tarte Tatin? Perhaps I can talk chef into making three more exceptions."

"Please," said Mac. "It's a special occasion, so we should all have the special dessert. If your chef will allow it, that is."

"I will do my best, monsieur. Cafés?"

"Three cappuccinos, I think."

Erik picked up *Sara's Year*, opened it to the first page and read silently for a few minutes. "This is so good," he said. "I can't wait for the movie."

Sarah chuckled. "You're crazy."

He read a few more lines. "Are you going to write another one?"

"What? Like an 'after' *Sara's Year*?"

"Something like that."

"Let's see if some kind of 'after' happens to me after *Sara's Year*. Then we can talk about it, along with that movie of yours."

"I think we should talk about it now," Bernie said.

"Me, too," Erik added. "From the little I've read, I know I'm going to want more."

"Read slow. It will last longer." Sarah let her eyes wander out through the french doors to the garden. She couldn't imagine doing it all over again. With some things, once was enough. This had got to be one of them. No. No more books.

"Remember how you didn't think you could write this one?"

Esther?

"Who else?"

So, what would I write about?

"Did you know what you were going to write with this one?"

You know I didn't.

"Well?"

Well, nothing. You're crazy like Erik's crazy. And I'm crazy to be hearing your voice in the middle of the Ritz-Carlton Hotel.

"Maybe, yes. Maybe, no."

More like yes.

"Maybe it isn't just about you, this new book."

Like who? Anyhow, I never said I would to do it.

"You never said you wouldn't."

I'm saying it now—

"Earth calling Sarah. Earth calling Sarah."

"Yes, Bernie," Sarah said distractedly, still staring out to the garden. "I'm here, more or less."

"More less than more, if you ask me."

"Yes, maybe. It's been a big day. I'm a little tired."

Could I? I'm already sixty-six.

"Two words: Grandma Moses."

You're going to stop throwing that at me when?

"When you're a hundred and one, like she was when she died."

If you see her up there, tell her she has a lot to answer for.

"I'll do that."

See that you do.

"I have three more words for you, Sara-with-no-h Schumacher."

You're gonna throw another Methuselah name at me?

"Maybe later."

And for now?

"Talk to Erik."

About what I should talk to Erik?

But Esther was gone, if she had ever really been there. Sarah watched Erik. He was gesturing like a crazy person to describe something about his mother and Sven. Something about roller skating? Sarah wasn't listening.

What am I supposed to talk to this boy about? The least you could have done, Esther, would have been to tell me. Suddenly, she knew. She pushed her chair back. "Come," she said, pulling Erik to his feet, "you and me have to have a talk with the ducks." She pushed him out into the Ritz Garden.

"Now, you're in trouble," Bernie called after them.

"Not as much trouble as you'll be in if you touch my dessert," Erik called back.

Erik took Sarah's arm and helped her down the three stone steps to the flagstone path.

"You're a good boy, Erik." She propelled him toward the wooden bridge that crossed over the pond.

"What's this about?" Erik asked. "I hope you haven't called me out here to ask if my intentions to Bernie are honorable. Cuz if you are, it's way too late. They aren't."

"I figured. Anyhow, some things are none of my business. Not many, but some." She stopped in the middle of the bridge. Four white ducklings fluttered their wings at the entrance to their tiny blue-and-white house at the water's edge then tottered down the ramp into the tiled pool. "It's good these aren't the ones on the menu," she said.

"The brochure in the room says that these aren't eating ducks. They're barnyard ducks, from farms in the Eastern Townships. They come here for three weeks and are then replaced by new ones. It's sort of like a duckman's holiday."

Sarah groaned. "You're as bad as Bernie with the puns."

"Worse. At least that's what he says."

Sarah watched the ducks glide across the water. "You know, for a three-week holiday at the Ritz, I would swim around in that pond all day, too."

"Did you know that when the garden was built in the fifties, they were going to fill the pond with beavers? That was also in the brochure."

"Beavers?"

"In the end, they realized it was a dam bad idea. That would be d-a-m."

"Oy, more puns."

"We drive Mac crazy."

"He can use some crazy in his life. Good crazy." Sarah started across the bridge. "Come, let's sit down." She settled onto a bench by the water. "It's pretty here, isn't it? Who knew they had ducks and a garden hidden away from all the noise and traffic on Sherbrooke Street. Thank you for bringing me here."

Erik sat next to her. "I'm glad you and Bernie finally got together," he said.

"Me, too."

Erik watched Sarah contemplate the ducks swimming slow circles around the pond.

"Why do I get the feeling that this is about more than ducks?"

"Because you're a smart boy, like I said." She looked up, as if expecting another communication from Esther. None came.

"So, you think I should write another book?"

"Is that what this is about? I was teasing, you know. Well, partly. It's a good book. I can tell. Why not write more? Grandma Moses—"

"No more Grandma Moses. I've heard enough about that alteh machashaifeh for one day." She paused, gathering her thoughts. "What were we talking about?"

"Your book. The new one."

"We'll come back to that. I want to talk about something else first." She turned to Erik. "Weren't you supposed to have a show at Galérie Cinq Arts?" She pronounced it sink arts. "Not just one picture hanging so you can pick up good Jewish boys like Bernie. A real show. Your own show. With lots of pictures."

"No one knows about that," Erik said, startled. He looked away. "Not even Bernie. How did you find out?"

"I know things. I hear things. I see things. It's a small town, Westmount, at least compared to the rest of the city. Dominique's makes it smaller. I couldn't find out anything about Bernie all those years, but I made friends with the Cinq Arts boys and they told me about this promising artist they were going to show who dropped everything to run back to Nova Scotia. I thought maybe the two of you didn't make it and you left town. Who knew that Bernie was in Nova Scotia and that you were going home and chasing after him all at the same time?"

"No one. Bernie didn't want the world to know that Mac was his father. He said he wanted to make it on his own name first. And Mac had become such a hermit, even more than when he was my professor. We wanted to respect that."

"Of course. So about this show…"

"I had to give it up. I couldn't risk losing Bernie."

"Like Mac lost Esther."

Erik nodded. "I never told him about the show. If I had, he would never have let me come. You won't tell him, will you?"

"Are you painting?"

"Yeah…"

"Like you were before Bernie?"

"Uh…no."

"How come?"

Erik shrugged. "It's been so intense, the Bernie and Mac thing. Then he got the Klinkhoff show. I didn't want to get in the way of all that." He began to cry. "I love him so much. More than anything in the world."

Sarah patted his knee. "It's like Esther and Mac all over again, in a good way. The right way, I hope. That would be a good thing."

Erik wiped his face with the back of his hand. "I know. It's crazy, isn't it."

"Listen, boychik. I don't know if I have another book in me, an 'after' *Sara's Year* like you want me to write. You? You have lots of paintings left in you. Good paintings, if the boys at your art gallery know anything. I know you want to support Bernie, and that's important. It's important to support the person you love. I should know. I had one husband who didn't and one who did, and it still took me too long to live my dream, until it was almost too late."

"Will you write another book?"

"I'm coming to that." Sarah watched two twin girls in frilly white dresses toss bits of bread into the water for the ducks, who fought each other off with noisy quacks and flapping wings.

"I like you, Erik," she continued when the melee ended. "A lot. I've just met you and I like you and I think you're good for Bernie. God knows he deserves some real happiness. I like you, but what I am about to say I'm not doing for you. It's for Bernie I'm doing it.

"I don't want you should both grow old together— Well, I do want you should both grow old together. What I don't want is that you should grow old and resent Bernie because he lived his dream and you didn't get a chance to live yours. I want you to be a success in your own right because only that will keep you two together and happy. That's why I'm doing it.

"Of course, I'm happy if you're happy. Like I said, I like you. But I owe it to Esther to do what I can to make sure he's happy. So, I think you and me should have a pact, like me and Bernie did. Only maybe not one that lasts four years."

"What do you mean?"

"You get back to your painting, really get back to it, and I promise to try to write another book."

Erik watched the ducks waddle onto the path foraging for more food. He waited until they had returned to the water. "I think I can do that," he said. "Once we're back home."

"There's more."

"More?"

"You have to promise to call the Cinq Arts boys tomorrow and set a date for when you will be ready for your show. I know they still want you. They said as much to me."

"They do? I was afraid to go in, in case…"

"I know you're going back to Nova Scotia with Bernie and Mac, so I can't make you meet me here again next year…although another liver lunch like that I wouldn't turn down. So, I want you to call me. Every month I want you to call me. Reverse the charges if you have to. You'll tell me how your painting's going and I'll tell you if my writing is going—"

"*How* you're writing is going. Not if."

"Didn't I say you were a smart boy? Too smart for me to fool you. You're right, of course. How my writing is going. You'll paint and I'll write. I don't know that I can bring a published book to your art opening, but I'll be there with whatever I have written, even if I have to carry it in a Steinberg's shopping bag like I did that first year at the cemetery, when there was no Bernie." She thrust her hand out at Erik. "Is it a deal, mister?"

He grinned and took her hand. "Deal."

"Good." She pulled Erik up and started back toward the restaurant. "I have to go back in. There's a piece of pie in there with my name on it."

46

"It's time, Hadassah."

Sadie opened *Sara's Year* to the title page. "I know."

"You might not like what she says about you."

"I know that, too."

Sadie signaled to Sylvie, who was serving another customer at the far end of the cafe. The young woman waved. "Be right there," she mouthed.

"I'd like more coffee, if that's okay," Sadie said when Sylvie stopped by her table a few minutes later.

"Of course. Can I get you anything else? Would you like some dessert to go with that?"

Sadie was about to say no then changed her mind. "Do you have any pie? I all of a sudden remembered my mother's pie. I don't know why. It's crazy." She gazed past Sylvie...into the past. "It was so good," she said half to herself, remembering. She returned her focus to Sylvie. "I haven't treated myself to a slice of pie in so long."

"Let me tell you a secret," Sylvie said. "My mother also makes fantastic pies, maybe not as good as your mom's. But I think it's the best on the planet, and I'm pretty fussy."

"My mama hasn't been making pies for more than sixty years now. I think after all this time she'd be okay conceding the title to yours."

Sylvie laughed. "I'll tell her."

"Psst." It came from the window. "You made a joke, Hadassah. An actual joke. Not a super-hilarious joke, but still a joke. When was the last time that happened? When was the last time you made anyone laugh? Smile, even? Maybe around the last time you had a slice of Mama's pie?"

Sadie ignored the voice.

"Remember I mentioned Dominique's?" Sylvie asked. "My mother's restaurant in Westmount?"

"In The Richelieu." Sadie pronounced it rishaloo.

"You have to go there and try the pie," Sylvie insisted. "It's worth the trip, I promise. If my mom's there, tell her I sent you." She tapped her name tag. "It's Sylvie. Sylvie Ryan. Don't forget. But here, there's no pie. I'm sorry. We have pastries and fruit tarts, tiny fruit tarts. They're sort of like pies. Well, not really."

"No pie?" Sadie's face fell, and Sylvie's heart broke. This was the first time all afternoon that the woman had started to look even halfway happy.

"I'll tell you another secret," Sylvie said. "My mom's pies? I have one with me. In the back. Peach pie. Fresh out of the oven this morning. One of her first batches of the season. I stayed over at her place last night and she gave it to me before I left for work. It's here, in the back."

"*Peach* pie?"

Sadie was nine years old and still letting herself be called Hadassah the afternoon Max burst into the house cradling a basket of ripe peaches. "Fresh from the tree," he announced.

"Whose tree, Maxie?" Ruth asked, wiping her hands on her apron. The new baby would be arriving any day and she was off work until after it was born. Without pay, of course.

"Mendelssohn. Well, not his tree. He got them from Schwartz who got them from Silverstein who got them from I don't know who. I thought maybe…"

"You thought maybe I could make you a peach pie?"

Max grinned sheepishly. "Not for me. For us. We haven't had fresh peaches since I don't know when."

"Since before we were married."

"That long. And you haven't had the time to make a pie since—"

"Longer."

Sadie jumped up and down clapping her hands. "Peach pie peach pie peach pie," she chanted.

Ruth rubbed her belly. "I'll make it tomorrow, zeeskyte, if there's no baby."

Sadie replaced Ruth's hand with her own. "The baby will want peach pie, too, Mama."

Ruth laughed as Max scooped Sadie up into his arms. "Babies don't eat peach pie," he said.

"Why not?" she asked. She let her head drop to see an upside-down Ruth behind her. "Does that mean you won't make the pie, Mama?"

"Of course, I'll make the pie, even if the baby can't have any."

Sadie straightened up and pressed her nose to Max's glasses. "I don't understand, Papa."

"What, Princess? What don't you understand?"

"Is it just peach pie or all pie? That babies won't eat, I mean."

"All pie, Princess."

Sadie frowned. "That can't be good."

"It's not so bad." Max twirled Sadie around then set her back on the floor. "In fact, babies not eating peach pie is a good thing."

"A good thing? How can babies not eating peach pie be a good thing?"

"It means more pie for you and more pie for me."

Sadie giggled. "I think I'm going to like this baby."

"Do you like peach pie?" Sylvie asked.

"It used to be my favorite," Sadie replied.

"Used to be?"

"It has been so long since I've eaten any kind of pie that I don't know that I have a favorite anymore."

"But you think you like it?"

"Sure, I guess. Why?"

"Here's what I'm going to do." Sylvie leaned in toward Sadie, glancing around to make sure that no one was within earshot. "I'm going to bring you your coffee like you asked." She peered into the twin creamers. They were nearly empty. "I'll bring you more milk, too. As soon as the boss leaves, I'll bring you a coffee refill, along with a big slice of my mom's peach pie. One thing, though. Could you kind of hide it while you're eating it? I don't want anyone else to see and ask for a piece."

"That's generous, dear, and sweet. But you shouldn't. It's your pie, from your mother."

"That's right. My pie. If I want to share it with you, I can. And I want to, so I will." Sylvie thrust her hand out at Sadie. "Do we have a deal?"

Sadie smiled. She actually smiled. She could feel muscles in her face that she had not felt in decades, that she forgot she had. "We have a deal," she said and shook the girl's hand.

Thirty minutes later, Sylvie emerged from the kitchen carrying a napkin-covered desert plate in one hand and a fresh mug of coffee in the other. Sadie was so engrossed in *Sara's Year* that Sylvie didn't want to disturb her. She slid them onto Sadie's table as quietly as she could and slipped away.

47

Sarah scraped the final crumbs of her tarte Tatin onto her fork. "That was almost the best peach pie I ever had," she said.

"Almost?" Bernie asked.

"Nothing beats Dominique's, not even a fancy French name and a fancy French pastry chef. Peach pie is peach pie, and Dominique's is still the best." She licked her fork.

"Don't tell the waiter," Bernie said, grinning. "I think he has a crush on you."

"You're meshugena." She pressed her index finger onto the few remaining specks on her plate.

"He gave you the biggest piece, didn't he?"

Sarah sucked on her finger. "You're jealous."

"You bet I am."

"Next time we come to the Ritz, you can have the bigger piece."

"You mean for the launch of *After Sara's Year*?"

"Yeah," Sarah replied, "for that." She winked at Erik.

"Okay, kids," Mac said, glancing at his watch. "We need to go in a few minutes."

"Are you excited?" Erik asked.

"I'm terrified," Bernie replied. "It's going to feel like I'm running down St. Catherine Street naked at noon."

"I'd like to see that," Erik quipped.

"I bet you would."

"Seriously," Erik continued, "that's how I felt when Jeffrey and Pierre first hung my painting in their gallery. I would hide in the back and peek out front to watch people's expressions when they looked at it. Sometimes, I could hear what they were saying. A lot of the time, I wished I couldn't." He batted his eyes at Bernie. "When I wasn't picking up cute guys, that is."

Bernie laughed. "How many cute guys were there?"

"Just the one." Erik let out an exaggerated sigh. "It turns out that having an abstract painting hanging in a Westmount art gallery is not the best way to meet men." He leaned over to kiss Bernie. "Lucky for me, it only took one."

"For me, too."

"What about you, Mac?" Sarah asked. "Do you still get scared?" She picked up *Sara's Year*. "I know that when I got my first copy and held it in my hands, I was excited and panicky and relieved and I don't know what-all else — all at the same time. I couldn't even open the package for twenty-four hours. But me, I don't have to sit on shpilkes next to people while they read my book and worry about what they're thinking."

"It isn't ever easy," Mac said. "I don't know that it gets any easier. You would think it would." He turned to Bernie. "The best news for you right now is that your work is good. It's better than good. I've told you before: Walter Klinkhoff is unbelievably fussy about what he will let hang in his gallery."

Bernie opened his mouth to argue. Mac wouldn't let him.

"I know what you're going to say," Mac continued, "but Walter did not get his reputation in the art world by doing favors for old friends. Trust me: If he didn't think your work was world-class, he would not be showing it." He paused. "That brings me to something we need to talk about, before we go next door. I was going to wait until after today to tell you, but...but I think I should do it now."

"Do you need some father-and-son time?" Erik asked, half-standing. "Sarah and I can go back outside to chat up the ducks again. Right, Sarah?"

"Please stay," Mac said. "Some of this is for you, too, Erik."

"Now, for sure, I want to go talk to the ducks." Erik dropped back into his seat. "What's the bad news?"

"It isn't bad news," Mac said. "Not really, although it might sound that way. Only at first."

Erik grabbed Bernie's hand.

"I have given this a lot of thought, especially since Walter decided he wanted to show your work." Mac fidgeted with his napkin. This was not going to be easy, but he knew it was the right thing. "The only way to say this is to say it."

Bernie gripped Erik's hand. "What is it?" he wanted to ask. The words wouldn't come.

"I don't want you coming back with me to Nova Scotia."

"What? What do you mean?" Bernie and Erik asked together.

"It's time you moved out of the nest, Bernie. You're an artist in your own right, a major artist, on your way to becoming a big-time artist. Like I said, only world-class artists show at the Klinkhoff. World-class artists don't need to be living with their old dads."

"Even if their old dad is Canada's greatest living artist?"

"Especially if he's Canada's greatest living artist."

"For now," Erik piped in. "Bernie's right behind you, old man."

"I know he is, and that's what this is all about. Come back, both of you, to make your plans and get your stuff. After that move back to Montreal, if that's what you want to do. Or Toronto. Or go to New York for a year. Or LA. Or Florence. Or Venice. Or Paris. Or London. Go where the art is. It isn't on Hubbard Mountain Road. It isn't in Nova Scotia. Not for you. You need to be out in the world. Seeing. Experiencing. Experimenting. Painting.

"Remember what I told you last month at the house? You don't need me as an art teacher anymore. You don't need any art teacher anymore. It's time to let the world teach you. You are that good. Both of you."

"I still need you as a father," Bernie said softly.

"Good," Mac said, taking Bernie's other hand, "because I still need you as a son. I spent too many years not knowing you existed to let you go now. What I need to know now is that I have an adult, independent son who is making his own way in the world." He grinned. "And who will be there for me when I need someone to fetch my walker, shawl and ear trumpet."

Bernie smiled, but sadly. The past four years had been the best of his life, the most exciting and rewarding of his life. The only thing missing had been his mother, yet it was because of her that he had experienced them. Mac was right. He knew it, even as he felt the way Sarah described holding her book that first time: excited and panicky and relieved and God knows what-all else. He already had lots of anxiety about what was waiting for him across the street at the Klinkhoff Gallery. Now, he was more anxious still about what was going to happen afterward.

"Go live your life," Mac continued. "Do it for me, do it for your mother and, most important of all, do it for yourself and for Erik. Come back and visit. Send for me and I'll come visit you, wherever you are. I'll even bring Sarah, if she'll let me. If she isn't too busy writing all her books."

No one said anything for a few minutes. Finally, Erik broke the uneasy silence. He pulled Bernie to his feet and pushed him toward the door. "Let's get over there and knock 'em dead!"

48

"It's time, Hadassah. Again."

Sadie shut *Sara's Year*. "I know."

"Ask the girl. You know what to ask?"

For the first time that day, Sadie viewed her reflection voluntarily. The face that gazed back at her was the same one she had seen in the mirror that morning before leaving for the cemetery. Yet at the same time it wasn't. It was no longer stiff, no longer stern, no longer hard. The lines around her eyes and mouth had softened, her lips no longer drooped into a perpetual frown and there was a touch of both humor and grief in her eyes instead of the impenetrable veil that had cloaked them for decades. She touched her face in disbelief. "I know what to ask," she whispered.

When Sylvie brought the check a few minutes later, Sadie pushed it away. Instead, she slapped a twenty and a five onto the tray. "Keep the change," she said.

Sylvie blushed. "It's too much."

"No," Sadie declared in a tone that brooked no argument. Her voice softened. "It isn't enough for what you have done for me today," she added. She glanced around the cafe. It was empty. "I know it isn't a normal thing," she said, "but could you sit for a minute, maybe? For a minute, only. There is something I want to tell you."

"I shouldn't," Sylvie said. But then she saw the mix of sadness and hope in Sadie's face and sat down across from her, where she could keep an eye on both the front door and the kitchen. "For a minute," she said.

"You told me your secret, about your mother's pie," Sadie said slowly, forcing herself to continue. "I have a secret to tell you, too."

Sylvie wanted to stop her from continuing. Sure, she had grown to sort of like this woman, but did she want to get involved? "No, really, Ms.—"

"My name is Sadie. Sadie Finkel."

"Mine wasn't much of a secret, Ms. Finkel."

"No Ms. Just call me Sadie." She picked up *Sara's Year* and continued before Sylvie could interrupt. "This Sara Schumacher? That was her maiden name. She was my sister's best friend, almost their whole lives, until my sister died four years ago."

"You mean Mrs. Coopersmith? Esther?"

Sadie nodded. "You know her from your mother's restaurant, right?"

This wasn't such a big secret. "Of course," Sylvie said. "Your sister and Sarah came in all the time. For my mother's pie." She stopped, confused. "But you— I never saw you there— I didn't know…"

"No, you wouldn't have. We didn't get along."

"You and Sarah?"

"Me and my sister. Me and everyone."

Even that wasn't such a big secret. "There's lots of people I don't get along with," Sylvie said. "Lots, including my mother, sometimes."

"There's more." Sadie opened the book. "I'm in here. A lot."

"That's terrific." *I can deal with secrets like this.* "You didn't get the last copy, did you? Now for sure I have to get the book."

"If you know Sarah and Bernie and knew my sister, you should. It's a good book, from what I've read so far." She didn't want to continue, but she knew she had to. "There's something else you should know."

"What's that?"

Sadie ran her finger down the page. "What Sarah says about me?" She hesitated. "It isn't so nice."

"That can't be right. You seem like a good person. Sad, if you don't mind me saying so, although I know it isn't any of my business. Why would she do that? It's so mean. I thought she was such a nice woman."

"Sarah is a nice woman, Sylvie. I was the not-nice one. For the longest time, I was the not-nice one. Maybe until today. Maybe I'm still not so nice. What you have to know is that everything she says about me in her book is true, at least as far as I got."

"I don't believe—"

"Believe, shaineh maidel. Believe. I wish I could tell you not to." She shut the book. "So if you do read it, when you read it, promise me that you won't be mad at Sarah. Maybe you could try not to be mad at me, either. Can you promise me that?"

Sylvie touched Sadie's arm. "I promise."

Sadie pulled the crumpled postcard for Bernie's exhibition from her purse. "There's one more thing, if you can stay another minute."

No customers had come in.

"Sure."

"You said you were going to this art show next door. Bernie's art show." She studied the postcard. "My nephew's art show." It sounded strange to say it. Strange, but right.

"When I get off work." Sylvie checked the time. "In about an hour. I'll be getting off for good. This is my last day here."

"You're leaving for something better, I hope." She gestured at all the fakery. "You're better than this."

"Oh, it isn't so bad. It helped get me through school. Now I get to do what I really love. I'm going up to Kleinburg, north of Toronto, to be an assistant curator at the McMichael Collection."

Sadie stared at her blankly.

"You know, Tom Thomson and the Group of Seven. Arthur Lismer and A.Y. Jackson and that gang."

Sadie remembered the names, vaguely. Anne Savage must have talked about them. That was a long time ago and she was done with the past. Well, almost.

"That art show next door," Sadie said. "You said before that I should go."

Sylvie nodded.

"I'm thinking maybe I will. Maybe I should. Do you need a special invitation or can anyone just walk in?" She smoothed the postcard on the table. "Is this some sort of invitation?"

"No, but I'm sure it'll be fine. An art opening can be sort of private but not, all at the same time. I guarantee you that they will never notice one more person."

"You're sure?"

"If you want to wait, you can go in with me. Would that help?"

"You're a sweet girl, but I— I have to be somewhere before it gets dark. If I'm going to go, I should go now."

"Then go," Sylvie said. "If anyone asks, say you're a friend of the artist. Or that you're family."

"I don't think I want to say that. The family part."

"Flash Sarah's book and say you and Bernie are in it. He is in it, isn't he?"

"Everyone's in it, zeeskyte."

49

No one noticed the spindly, white-haired woman in dirt-smudged slacks, teal top and white-and-magenta Adidas slip into Galérie Walter Klinkhoff a few minutes after six that sultry August evening. They were all too absorbed in each other, in their wine and canapés and in the rare presentation of a debut artist on the walls of the venerable gallery. Of course, the unveiling of a new Marc-Allan Cameron, something unlike anything the internationally celebrated artist had ever shown, also contributed to their jammed-together presence in the renovated Sherbrooke Street graystone. This was Montreal, so even the casually dressed were stylishly elegant, designer jeans mingling easily with Armani suits and Oscar de la Renta cocktail dresses.

Sadie moved tentatively through the dense crowd, stopping briefly at each painting she was able get near enough to glimpse. These were not like any pictures she knew from magazine articles or from her long-ago high school art classes with Anne Savage, and she didn't understand anything of what she was seeing. Yet from the snatches of conversation she picked up as she passed from one room to the next, people who knew more about art than she ever would thought it was good, whatever it was. To Sadie's surprise, she discovered that she was pleased for Bernie.

She ignored the young woman in a tuxedo who pushed a wine tray at her, but managed to snatch an hors d'oeuvre off another tray borne by a young man in a hurry who was wearing an identical outfit. It was something dark on a cracker. Some kind of blackberry jam? She stuffed it in her mouth, expecting it to taste sweet. It was salty, like lox. Sadie was so startled by the incongruity that she raised her palm to her mouth to spit it out. She reconsidered when she recalled her surroundings. After rolling it around in her mouth for a few minutes, trying to decide whether she should swallow it or find some less obvious way to get rid of it, she decided that it wasn't so bad.

Several more Beluga caviar snacks later, Sadie caught sight of the one painting she knew, from the postcard she had taken from the cemetery and now held in her hand. Even from ten yards' distant, she could see how unlike they were. The difference was staggering. She could almost see the breeze from the fan riffling Esther's skirt, could almost smell the smells from the kitchen, could almost hear Esther's voice. Sarah's, too. And those red shoes? They glittered, not in a cheap sparkly sort of way. In a just-right way, like Judy Garland's ruby slippers did in *The Wizard of Oz.* You'd think shoes like that would be out of place on Esther's feet and at a plain old lunch counter. They weren't. They were perfect, like everything else about the painting. No printer could reproduce the texture and vibrance of what she was seeing in the original in front of her, let alone its emotional depth.

For an instant, Sadie was transported back to Baron Byng and to the murals that by now probably covered every wall in the old school building. Sadie had already graduated by the time Miss Savage launched her project to remove every trace of institutional green in the school and replace it with student paintings. Still, she remembered Esther's picture. She could almost see that flock of Canada geese in flight again if she shut her eyes. Not normal Canada geese, like Sadie would have painted, if she could paint. Something more fanciful. Mystical, even. Sadie flushed with shame as she recalled how dismissive she had been when Esther proudly showed off her masterpiece on the day of her high school graduation.

"I'm sorry, Esther," she murmured.

As awed as she was by *At Stella's,* the painting that Sadie saw next left her gasping. It had been obscured by a clutch of admirers and when they moved away, Sadie half-staggered a step closer. She did not need to read the card clipped to its easel to know what she was seeing but squinted at it anyhow. "*Queen Esther / La reine Esther.* Marc-Allan Cameron. 1988." She didn't have to see another artist's name on the card; she knew the portrait could not have been Bernie's. It was too intimate to be a son's depiction of his mother.

Cameron had painted Esther in three-quarter view, her face angled just enough to let both her eyes be seen. There was an almost Rembrandt-like quality to the portrait, with glowing skin tones that contrasted against a rich, dark background. When you looked at it, it was as if her sister's face wasn't lying flat against the canvas but was some kind of hologram hovering in front of it, its inner light revealing the essence of Esther's soul.

The old Sadie would have dismissed what she was seeing, especially the title. "That Esther," she would have sniffed, "always acting like she's better than everyone else. Queen Esther, indeed," she would have harrumphed. The new Sadie, one she herself barely recognized, felt tears welling in her eyes. Her sister was so, so…beautiful. So luminous. "She was a queen," Sadie breathed.

A moment later another cluster of people edged aside and there they were, a dozen steps to Sadie's right: Bernie, Sarah, that boy from the cemetery and the man from the bookstore, the one she had mistaken for a politician.

This was Sadie's last chance to turn back, to leave the gallery and pretend she had never been. It would be easy. The only people who knew her had not seen her, and most people would think she was some cleaning lady who had wandered in off the street, if they noticed her at all.

I can't do this. I don't need to do this. It's better if I leave before they see me. Much better. This is Bernie's day. I would just ruin it by shoving myself in his face.

Sadie pushed her way back through the crowd to the front door. But before she could open it, her reflection came into focus in its glass pane. She didn't wait to hear what it had to say.

50

Bernie didn't recognize her at first, the incongruously unstylish woman with the choppy white hair who was weaving through the crowd toward him.

Sarah did. "Sadie," she muttered derisively. "What chutzpah to show up here."

"You're right," Bernie noted, surprised. "My Auntie Sadie," he whispered to Erik and Mac. "I told you about her. Why would she come here?" Then he noticed the copy of *Sara's Year* she was clutching. "Unless…" He turned to Sarah. "You don't think…?"

"Even Sadie would never dare make a scene here," Sarah said. "At least I don't think so."

Warily, the four of them watched her approach.

"Mazel tov, Bernie," Sadie said softly. "You, too, Sarah. You both did good."

"Auntie Sadie," Bernie said coolly, doing his best to be gracious. "Thank you. Thank you for coming."

"You don't mean that, Bernie—"

"No, I—"

"Shush. I know you don't want me here."

"No, I mean yes. Of course, I do. I'm happy to see you."

"You aren't and that's okay. You don't have to lie to be polite. Not to me. Not after— Never mind that, for now." She tapped the exhibition postcard. "I had to come when I found this at…at— It doesn't matter where I found it. I saw it and I had to come."

I can't do this. I really can't do this. I can't breathe. She started to teeter. *I think I'm going to faint.* She groped blindly for something to grab onto. There wasn't anything. Erik took her arm.

"Thank you, young man," she managed to choke out. She closed her eyes and waited for the dizziness to pass and for her breath to steady. "You're a good boy. I can tell." She turned back to Bernie and Sarah. "It's been a long day. Longer than I expected. Longer than I'm used to."

"Can I get you a glass of water?" Erik asked, still holding on to Sadie's arm. "Or a chair or something?"

"No, no. I'm fine." Gently, she pulled her arm free and patted Erik's. "Thank you," she repeated. She then tried to focus all her weight into her feet, planting them as firmly as she could on the carpeted floor. "I had to come," she continued, "but I never thought I would come inside, that I would have the chutzpah to do it. Then I saw it in the window. I know it's like on the postcard, but it wasn't the same, seeing it in the window, so big for everyone else to see, too. Seeing Esther, your mother, again. Like she was.

"I thought it would make me mad, seeing her up there, like she was acting all important." *Tell the truth, Hadassah.* "If I'm truthful, I would have been mad if I saw it a few hours ago. I won't tell you what I would have said then because it wouldn't have been real polite. But all afternoon, I've been sitting in the restaurant next door thinking about things. All sorts of things." She touched Sarah's arm then pulled back when Sarah recoiled slightly. "Your book helped me think, Sarah. Helped me remember, too. I've been thinking and remembering and feeling bad, more bad than I have felt in a long time. Longer even than you've been alive, Bernie."

For a moment nothing and no one else existed for Sadie. Just her and Bernie. And Esther. "Maybe I haven't felt anything in that long," she continued, her voice gaining assurance. "Maybe the only thing I felt for that long was sorry for myself. It's a long time to feel sorry for yourself, Bernie. It's a long time to be sad. It's a long time to be mad. Too long. So I had to come in. I had to come in because I couldn't stay outside anymore. Because I couldn't stay mad anymore. Because I couldn't feel sorry for myself anymore."

Sadie took a deep breath. "I had to come in to say I'm sorry. I said it to the painting on the postcard, to that Esther I forgot that I loved. I have to say it to you, too. To you, also, Sarah Schumacher, and maybe to this boy, too, who I can see is so special to you all, even if I don't know who he is."

"He's—"

"After, if you want to introduce me, that's fine," she said to Bernie. "To this man, too, who I was rude to this afternoon."

"He's—"

"No, Bernie, let me finish, while I still have the mut, the courage to do it. When I came in, after I apologized to my little sister in your painting, Bernie, I saw that other painting." She pointed to Esther's portrait. "You did that?" she asked Mac.

"Yes," Mac said.

"It's a pleasure to meet you, Mr. Marc-Allan Cameron. I'm sorry about before, in the bookstore. I wasn't very gracious."

"It's all right. I—"

"I don't want to be rude again, but I have to keep going. If I stop to let you talk, I might not be able to."

Mac nodded.

"I'm Sadie, Mr. Cameron. Esther's sister. If you knew Esther, and I can tell from that picture that you more than knew her, then you've heard about me."

"I—"

"No, I'm still not finished. Whatever you heard, Mr. Cameron, from Bernie and maybe from Sarah, too, it's true. Whatever my sister told you about me, it's true. All of it. I wish it wasn't, but it was. I don't know who my Esther was to you, Mr. Cameron, and I don't need to know. I know from that picture that you loved her. Anyone who looks at it would know. Nobody could paint something like that who didn't love. I know that because I never loved anyone, I don't think." Sadie thought of her mother and remembered Jimmy. "Well, almost never. But that's my story and you don't need to hear it. That's not why I came in. I came in to say I'm sorry, for everything, for all the hurt I caused. I came in to say I'm sorry to all of you, but mostly to you, Bernie."

She stepped over to Mac's portrait of Esther. "No, mostly to you, Esther. I'm so sorry, so very sorry. I'm sorry I wasn't the sister you needed. I'm sorry I didn't let you be the sister I needed. I'm sorry I never got to know you." She stared at the painting in silence for a few minutes longer before slowly turning to Bernie. "I'm also sorry for coming, Bernie, and I hope I didn't ruin your simcha, your celebration. You're a talented young man and you deserve lots more simchas and lots more success." She paused. "I'm proud of you. I know I have no right to say it and I know it means nothing, but it's true." It took all her strength to look Bernie in the eye. "I've said what I came to say. Now, I should go and leave you to your party."

Bernie reached for Sadie's arm. "Don't go, Auntie Sadie, please."

"No, no. This is your celebration and your life. I lost any right to be part of it a long time ago."

"Please stay. I want you to meet my friends. I want you to meet my father." He continued, his voice cracking. "I want you to be part of my family again. Will you? Will you stay?"

Sadie considered the offer then shook her head. "Right now, there's something I have to do. Something important, more important than anything else. I have to do it before it gets dark. But here—" She pulled a pen and a scrap of paper from her purse and scribbled down a phone number. "If you want, if it feels right, if you mean what you say — and it's okay if you don't. If you do, call me. We can have a cup of tea or a glass wine and we'll start over. Bring your friend, your friends. You, too, Sarah. Only if you want."

Sadie didn't wait for an answer. Before Bernie could say anything, she turned and walked out of the gallery.

51

Sadie stepped out of the de la Savane Metro station as the bells of St. Luc's tolled the half hour. It would be getting dark soon, so there wasn't much time. She didn't know when they locked the gates, but it wouldn't be long. Tired as she was, she quickened her pace. She crossed the street and made her way into the cemetery and along the gravel road to her mother's grave. As she had done only hours earlier but what seemed like lifetimes ago, she stroked the top of the granite marker.

"I know I was just here this morning, Mama, but so much has changed. Everything, maybe, has changed. I don't know why or how, really. But it has." She knelt in front of the marker as hot tears rolled down her cheeks and into the earth at her feet. "I haven't been a good person, Mama. It's worse than that. I've been a bad person. A witch." She half-smiled, wiping her eyes. "That's witch with a b. You're going to say that I should never use bad language, Mama, but there's no other word for it.

"I know you were proud of me once…a long time ago. So long ago I can hardly remember. I hope after today you can be proud of me again." She stood, brushing the dirt from her slacks. "I'm going to see Esther, now, Mama. I know I went this morning, but that was by accident. This time, I'm going on purpose. I'm going because I have to go. I'm going because I want to go. I'm going to give back what I took. I'm going because it's time."

She added another pebble to her collection. "I'll come back to visit in two weeks, Mama, like usual. But I didn't want to go see Esther without telling you. I knew you would want to know."

Sadie stood motionless at Esther's grave. She wanted to caress the top of this stone like she had done with their mother's, but she didn't have the right. How do you make up for a lifetime? How do you make it up to a life that has already been taken?

You can't. All you can do is what you can do.

Sadie traced the letters etched into the granite. "Esther Finkel Freed. 1923-1984. Beloved mother, wife and friend."

"You were right, Esther," she said, "to leave Harold out. I never knew about what he did, what he was like. Deep down I guess I did know, but I couldn't let myself see." Then she saw what she had failed to observe that morning, what she hadn't noticed at the stone's unveiling ceremony three years earlier, what she had never noticed. "You were right to leave me out, too, Esther." She touched the space where the word "sister" might have been then stepped back.

"I don't know what's next for me, Esther. I'm old and I don't know who I am anymore. But it isn't too late. I won't let it be. You've given me a second chance. I don't know what I'm going to do with it. Not yet, I don't. But I won't waste it. I promise. "

Sadie reached into her purse for the two postcards, the one advertising Bernie's art show and the one announcing *Sara's Year*. "I know I should have asked before borrowing these," she said, "but without them…" She touched each to her lips. Then, as Sarah had done that morning, she placed them against the foot of the granite marker.

"Thank you, Esther," she whispered. "Thank you.

Sadie & Sara's Yiddish Glossary

If this is not your first introduction to Sarah and her friends, you may recognize some of the same Yiddishisms in this book that you encountered in *Sara's Year*. This glossary, however, is more than a refresher course: It includes words and phrases unique to this book.

Alte kacker (*AL*-teh *KAH*-ker) — Old man, often derogatory
Alteh machashaifeh (*AL*-teh makha-*SHAY*-feh) — Old witch
Balagan (bah-lah-*GUN*) — Disorderly, chaotic, mess
Boychik (*BOY*-chick) — Term of endearment. Literally, young boy
Bubeleh (*BUB*-eh-leh) — Darling, sweetie
Chaim yankel (*KHAY*-im *YUNK*-el) — A condescending way to refer to someone whose name you don't know
Chaleria (kha-*LAIR*-eeyah) — Nasty, shrewish woman
Chaloshes (khah-*LOH*-shess) — Disgusting
Chazerai (khazer-*EYE*) — Junk, garbage
Chutzpah (*KHOOTZ*-pah) — Nerve, gall
Drek (*DRECK*) — Garbage, dirt, manure
Einhoreh (ain-*HOAR*-eh) — Evil eye
Farkakte (far-*KAK*-teh) — Lousy
Faygele (*FAY*-geh-leh). **Plural: Faygelech** — Gay, often derogatory. Literally, little bird
Gonif (*GOH*-niff) — Thief
Gott in himmel (gohtt een *HIMM*-el) — Exclamation of shock. Literally, God in heaven
Goyishe (*GOY*-ish-eh) — Non-Jewish, non-Jewish looking
Haimish (*HAYM*-ish) — Homey, homelike
Kibitz, kibitzer (*KIH*-bitz, *KIH*-bitz-er) — Joke around or meddle; jokester, meddler

Kvell (*KVELL*) — Burst with pride

L'chaim (le *KHA*-yim) — Traditional toast. Literally, to life

Mamzer (*MUM*-zer) — Bastard

Mazel tov (*MAH*-zel tov) — Literally, good luck. Used most often to convey congratulations

Megillah (m'*GILL*-ah) — The Old Testament's Book of Esther

Mensch (*MENCH*) — A good person

Meshugena, Mishigas (meh-*SHOO*-ghe-nah, mih-shih-*GUSS*) — Crazy or crazy person, craziness

Moishe Kapoyer (*MOY*-sheh ka-*POY*-er) — Someone who always does everything backwards or upside down

Mut (*MOOHT*) — Courage

Nafkeh (*NAHF*-keh) — Slut

Narishkeit (*NAHR*-ish-kite) — Foolish, foolishness

Nudnik (*NOOH*-dnik) — Pest, nuisance

Putz (*PUTZ*) — Derogatory. Literally, a prick

Shlep (*SHLEPP*) — Haul/carry something heavy or awkward; take a tedious or difficult journey

Shaineh maidel (*SHAY*-nuh *MAY*-d'l) — Term of endearment. Literally, pretty young girl

Shvantz (*SHVUNTZ*) — Vulgar insult. Literally, penis

Simcha (*SIM*-kha) — Joyous occasion, celebration

Shlubby (*SHLUB*-bee) — Ignorant, stupid, lazy

Schmatta (*SHMAH*-tah) — Literally, rag. Often refers to the clothing trade

Schmuck (*SHMUCK*) — Stupid or contemptible person. Literally, penis

Shiva (*SHIH*-vuh) — The traditional seven-day mourning period that follows a Jewish funeral

Shpilkes (*SHPILL*-kess) — Nervous energy, impatience. To sit on shpilkes is to fidget or be restless

Shtetl (*SHTET*-l) — A pre–World War II market village in Eastern Europe with a mostly Jewish population

Shtup (*SHTOOP*) — Have sexual intercourse

Tuches (*TOO*-khas) — Butt, backside

Zeeskyte (*ZEESS*-kite) — Sweetie

*** Yiddish pronunciations can vary widely and there is no universal standard for transliteration.*

How *Sara's Year* Got Its "After"

When the earliest readers of *Sara's Year* approached me in the days and weeks following the book's publication, they spoke with a single voice, and an unexpected one: "We want more," they cried.

Many wanted to know what was next for Marc-Allan Cameron (Mac), the celebrity artist in *Sara's Year* who turns out to be as unlucky in love as he is lucky with fame. Others demanded to know the fates both of Bernie Freed, the young man who walks out on his mother's funeral and spends the rest of *Sara's Year* discovering all that he never knew about her and about himself, and of his friend, Erik Donnekin. And what about the title character, still others asked: What's her after *Sara's Year* story?

As I wrote in the introduction to *Sara's Year*, that book was sparked by a series of health scares, in the midst of which I asked myself what I would want to make sure I accomplished should the worst occur. The answer was a new novel. *Sara's Year* was the result.

It was to be a one-off. When *Sara's Year* was finished, I planned to produce a new book for writers.

Sarah's fans had other ideas. (That's not a typo: There's a reason why Sarah the character has a different spelling than *Sara* the book.)

At first I insisted that there would be no *After Sara's Year*. I felt complete with the story and its characters and felt no call to continue the saga. But as readers continued to push and prod, I began to reconsider.

In fact, the more I thought about it, the more I had to confess that I, too, was curious about the fates of Mac, Sarah, Bernie and Erik. But the character who most intrigued me, the one that no one ever asked about, was Sadie Finkel.

If you've read *Sara's Year*, you'll remember Bernie's aunt as the quintessential alteh machashaifeh; that's Yiddish for old witch ("that's witch with a b"). Sadie was so utterly unpleasant in *Sara's Year* that the author in me wondered how she had become that way and whether there could be any hope for her.

It didn't take me long to realize that the only way I would find out what happens to Mac, Sarah, Bernie, Erik and, yes, Sadie would be to write them into another *Sara* story. So here it is!

Although *After Sara's Year* is officially tagged as the second book in what I am now calling *The Sara Stories*, you don't have to have read *Sara's Year* in order to be able to follow this new story. The two books are interconnected, but each telling stands on its own.

By the way, *The Sara Stories* will not end with *After Sara's Year*. I had barely begun a second draft of this book when an idea for a third installment in the series popped into my head. No, I won't be calling it *After After Sara's Year*, but it looks as though it will include all your favorite *Sara* characters.

For now, though, thank you for entering (or reentering) the world of Sarah and her friends in *After Sara's Year*, the book I could not have written without the encouragement of readers like you. May it have moved you to laughter and tears as often in the reading of it as it did for me in the writing of it. And now that you have journeyed through its pages, may it remind you that there is no heart that does not yearn to be remembered and no heart that does not long to open.

Mark David Gerson
August 10, 2016

Author's Note

Like every novel grounded in a real time and place and much like its *Sara's Year* predecessor, *After Sara's Year* is a collage of fact and fiction blended together to create what I hope is a compelling story. I have done my best to portray Montreal, Nova Scotia and London as accurately as possible during the time periods chronicled here. At the same time, I have never hesitated to borrow biography and massage history and geography to suit the overarching needs of the story and its characters.

Even as several of my story's people have historical equivalents — artists Anne Savage and Paul-Émile Borduas and Reitman's founders Herman and Sarah Reitman, for example — my versions of these people are entirely fictional.

The real Anne Savage, however, did teach at Baron Byng High School for many years and was responsible for the mural project there, a project my mother participated in when she was a Baron Byng student back in Esther's day. While Savage's *The Plough* was part of the landmark Tate exhibition in 1938 in London and is currently part of the Montreal Museum of Fine Arts' permanent collection, *Quebec Farm* has never seen the inside of the Westmount Public Library. Quebec's Paul-Émile Borduas was fired for the manifesto mentioned in these pages but to the best of my knowledge, he never lectured at the Nova Scotia College of Art, which was, indeed, founded by Anna Leonowens, the Anna of *Anna and the King of Siam* and *The King and I.*

Speaking of Anna's college, it was the Victoria School of Art and Design when Anna and three local women established it in 1887 in a Halifax that was then a cultural backwater. The school was renamed the Nova Scotia College of Art in 1925 and renamed again in 1969 as the Nova Scotia College of Art and Design, when it also adopted the NSCAD (pronounced *EN*-scad) acronym. Today it is known as NSCAD University.

The university's Anna Leonowens Gallery on Granville Street is no relation to my fictional Leonowens-Fyshe Gallery, which I located on Prince Street in what is now The Press Gang Restaurant and Oyster Bar, around the corner from the Carleton — then a hotel and now a popular live-music venue.

From what I have been able to discover, artist Hal Ross Perrigard did create a mural for the Laurentian Hotel and did live in Apartment 52 of The Richelieu, a building that was also home at one time to deposed royalty (I was never able to discover which ones) but that never housed either a Stella's Lunch or a Café Bistro Chez Dominique. Ironically, it did have a Murray's restaurant, which I removed for the purposes of this story.

The other Montreal and Halifax Murray's outlets mentioned in these pages did exist, although not always when I said they did. The final Murray's, the one for which Sadie nearly abandons her Provigo shopping cart and which was around the corner from where I grew up (*not* on Eden Road), closed in 2009. Mister Steer was luckier: The iconic local hamburger chain lives on, even if the outlet where Sadie meets Harold is no longer there.

Sadie might have revered Isadora Duncan, but she could never have seen the real-life Isadora on stage. I have found no record that the legendary dancer ever performed at the Monument National, or anywhere else in Montreal.

While there is a Jewish cemetery by the de la Savane Metro station in Montreal, it is not as old as the one where *After Sara*'s Rosalie Friedman and Ruth Finkel are buried, and it has no buttinsky of a basilica as its neighbor.

Sarah's preferred pie topping in both this book and its *Sara's Year* predecessor comes from St. Aubin in the Montreal suburb of St. Laurent. Unfortunately for Sarah and for many Montrealers, the dairy closed its doors in the mid-1980s after nearly six decades as a local favorite.

If you have been to Montreal recently, you may notice that today's Ritz-Carlton Hotel does not consistently match its description in these pages. That's because the Grande Dame of Sherbrooke Street marked its 2012 centenary with a mega-million-dollar facelift. But thanks to the engaging Ritz history mentioned in this book's acknowledgments, I was able to recreate something of the hotel's

1980s look and feel, including my description of former Prime Minister Pierre Elliott Trudeau's regular breakfast.

As for the Berkeley Hotel building, while it remains the centerpiece of an award-winning heritage development, it has never sported a street-level cafe, at least not since its hotel days. Nor has the former Atholstan mansion at the east end of the Alcan compound ever housed a bookstore, although Lord Atholstan did establish what was once Montreal's premier English-language daily paper, the now-defunct *Montreal Star*. In the second graystone to the west of the Berkeley is the Klinkhoff Gallery, which has been promoting the best in Canadian art for more than sixty-five years. It is currently owned by Eric Klinkhoff, Walter Klinkhoff's son, and still represents Anne Savage's work.

It was fun for me to situate Mac at the end of Hubbard Mountain Road in the farming foothills of Nova Scotia's Kings County. That's because I lived there myself while I was writing the second draft of my first novel, *The MoonQuest*. However, even though the area is known for its apple orchards, Mac's Hubbard Mountain Road bears little resemblance to the one I experienced in 1995, except for Rocky: We, too, had a rooster that, like Rocky, had his own unique concept of time.

Gratitude

If my first books of fiction were epic fantasies that required no research, these *Sara Stories* have served up a radically different experience, requiring an attention to cultural, geographic and biographic detail that I never had to bother with in my *Legend of Q'ntana* fantasy novels. As such, I am grateful to the many people, organizations and resources — too many to list here by name — that assisted me in getting *After Sara*'s times, places and people right. Much of this story's accuracy and richness is in large measure because of them.

For an inside look at the Ritz-Carlton as it was before its recent makeover, I am indebted to Adrian Waller's *No Ordinary Hotel: The Ritz-Carlton's First Seventy-Five Years*. I leaned more on Anne McDougall's *Anne Savage: The Story of a Canadian Painter* in *Sara's Year*, the first book in this *Sara* series, but I drew on it for this second story as well. *Canada: The Foundations of its Future*, commissioned by the House of Seagram in the 1940s to support the Canadian war effort, supplied me with images of Hal Ross Perrigard's work that I could find nowhere else.

Among the individuals who assisted me directly with my research were Justine Hickey of customer relations at Marine Atlantic; Danièle Archambault, archivist at the Montreal Museum of Fine Arts; Anthony Chiasson, Westmount's city archivist; and Jane Martin, archivist at the Westmount Historical Association. Members of two Facebook groups also contributed their time and energy, as they did with *Sara's Year*: "Montreal Then and Now" and "Vintage Postcards and Photos of Halifax and Nova Scotia." In particular, I would like to mention Conrad Payette and Alan Hustak with Montreal group and Tom Deyoung with the Nova Scotia group for replying promptly, personably and helpfully to my online research queries.

I am one of those writers you often see in restaurants and cofeeshops, huddled over their laptops with worried expressions on their faces. Worse, I'm the one who writes and revises his work by mumbling it aloud as he goes; to many, I must look as crazy as Sadie does when she's talking to her reflection in Café des Artistes. So, to the baristas and customers of the many cafes that have doubled as my writing studio, thank you for your patience and indulgence.

None of my writing in recent years could have come to pass without the encouragement and support of my friends — Kathleen Messmer, Sander Dov Freedman, Joan Cerio and Adam Bereki, first among them. For their unfailing belief in me and my work, especially when I couldn't believe in it or in myself, I have no words (not a good thing for a writer) to express my gratitude.

Finally, to all the fans of *Sara's Year* who pushed, prodded and cajoled me into continuing the story, insisting that they *had* to know what became of their favorite characters: Thank you. There would have been no *After Sara's Year* without you!

THE EMMELINE PAPERS

The Sara Stories

When Emmeline Mandeville spends the final months of her 93rd year reflecting on her eccentric, past, she can't know how profoundly her reminiscences will weave through Bernie, Erik, Sadie, Sara and Mac's lives 15 years later.